THE
STAINLESS
STEEL
RAT GOES
TO HELL

TOR BOOKS BY HARRY HARRISON

Galactic Dreams
The Jupiter Plague
Montezuma's Revenge
One Step from Earth
Planet of No Return
Planet of the Damned
The QE2 Is Missing
Queen Victoria's Revenge
A Rebel in Time
Skyfall
Stainless Steel Visions
Stonehenge
A Transatlantic Tunnel, Hurrah!

THE HAMMER AND THE CROSS TRILOGY
The Hammer and the Cross
One King's Way
King and Emperor

HARRY HARRISON

THE STAINLESS STEEL RAT GOES TO HELL

A TOM DOHERTY ASSOCIATES BOOK/NEW YORK

This is a work of fiction. All the characters and events por-
trayed in this novel are either fictitious or are used fictitiously.

THE STAINLESS STEEL RAT GOES TO HELL

Copyright © 1996 by Harry Harrison

A Tor Book
Published by Tom Doherty Associates, Inc.
175 Fifth Avenue
New York, NY 10010

Tor Books on the World Wide Web:
http://www.tor.com

Tor® is a registered trademark of Tom Doherty Associates, Inc.

Design by Lynn Newmark

Library of Congress Cataloging-in-Publication Data

Harrison, Harry.
    The Stainless Steel Rat goes to hell / Harry
Harrison.—1st ed.
        p. cm.
    "A Tom Doherty Associates book."
    ISBN 0-312-86063-3 (alk. paper)
    1. DiGriz, James Bolivar (Fictitious character)—
Fiction.
    I. Title.
    PS3558.A667S712   1996
    813´.54—dc20   96-19967
                                             CIP

First Edition: November 1996

Printed in the United States of America

0 9 8 7 6 5 4 3 2 1

THE
STAINLESS
STEEL
RAT GOES
TO HELL

I POURED A GOOD MEASURE of whiskey over the ice, scowled at it—then added a splash more. But, as I lifted the glass and drank it with glugging pleasure, my raised eyes drifted across the clock that was set into the wall above the bar.

It was just ten in the morning.

"My, my, Jim, you are hitting the sauce a little earlier each day," I growled wordlessly. So what? It was my liver wasn't it? I gurgled the glass empty just as the house computer spoke to me in rich, educated—and possibly sneering?—tones.

"Someone is approaching the front door, Sire."

"Great. Perhaps it is the booze shop delivery?" Venom dripped from my voice; but all computers are immune to sarcasm.

"Indeed not, Sire, for Garry's Grog and Groceries delivers by freight tube. I identify the person approaching as Rowena Vinicultura. She has stopped her popcar on the front lawn and is emerging from it."

My morale plummeted as the name slithered across my eardrums. Of all the beautiful bores on Lussuoso, Rowena was possibly the most beautiful—and certainly the most boring. I had to flee—or commit suicide—before she came in. I was already heading for the back of the house, to possibly drown myself in the swimming pool, when the housebot's computer voice stopped me in my tracks.

"Ms. Vinicultura appears to have fallen down onto the plastic mat outside the door that spells out WELCOME in six languages."

"What do you mean *fallen?*"

"I believe the description is an apt one. She closed her eyes and her body became limp. Then she descended slowly towards the ground and is now lying, unmoving, with her eyes still closed. Her pulse appears to be slow and irregular as detected by the pressure plate in the mat. Lacerations and bruises on her face . . ."

The thing's voice followed me as I ran back through the house.

"Open the door!" I shouted. It swung wide and I dived through.

Her cameo face was pale, her dark hair tousled gracefully, her ample bosom rising and falling slowly. There was blood on her cheeks and a darkening bruise on her forehead. Her lips moved and I leaned close.

"Gone . . ." she said, barely audible. "Angelina . . . gone . . ."

It felt as though my body temperature had dropped thirty degrees. This did not slow me in the slightest. While I was still reaching down for her I managed to tap the number 666 into my wrist communicator.

"Where is the home medical treatment center?" I shouted as I slipped my arms under warm thighs, soft back, and lifted her as carefully as I could.

"The settee in the library, Sire."

I ran, ignoring the cold knot of despair her words had punched into me. Since both Angelina and I were strenuously healthy we had never used the medical services in this house. I had glanced at the specs when I signed the rental agreement; with the price we were paying, the medical arrangements should equal that of a provincial hospital at least. By the time I had carried Rowena to the library the settee had vanished into the wall and an examining bed had risen in its place. Even as I laid her on the bed the detectors were snaking down from the med-bot that had popped out of the ceiling. An analyzer fastened onto the back of my neck and I slapped it away.

"Not me! Her, on the bed, you moronic machine."

I stepped back out of reach while it set to work with mechanical enthusiasm. A glistening row of readouts sprang to life on the screen. Everything from temperature and pulse to endocrine balance, liver function, hair-follicle growth and anything else that could be measured or assessed was there.

"Speak! Tell!" I commanded and there was a rustle of electronic activity as the various expert programs shuffled and sorted their input, compared and interacted and agreed on the results in a speedy microsecond.

"The patient is concussed and contused." The computer-generated voice was deep, male and reassuring. "The bruises are superficial and have been cleansed and sealed," there was a scurry of flashing apparatus, "and the appropriate antibiotics injected."

"Bring her to!" I snapped

"If you mean, sir, that you wish the patient restored to consciousness that is now being done." If a computer can sound miffed—this one was miffed.

"Whasha?" she muttered, blinking lovely purple eyes that were blurrily out of focus.

"You've got to do better than that with her," I said. "Stimulants, something. I must talk to her."

"The patient has been traumatized . . ."

"But not badly—you told me that. Now get her to talk, you overpriced collection of memory chips or I'll short-circuit your ROM, PROM and EPROM!"

This seemed to do the job. Her eyes blinked again and looked at me.

"Jim . . ."

"In the flesh, Rowena my sweet. You're going to be fine. Now tell me about Angelina."

"Gone . . ." she said. And fluttered her luxurious eyelashes.

I felt my teeth grating together and forced a smile.

"You said that before. Gone where? Gone why? Gone when—" I shut up since I was getting into a rut.

"The Temple of Eternal Truth . . ." was all that she said as her eyes closed again. It was enough.

I shouted to the housebot as I bolted out the door.

"Cure her. Guard her. Call an ambulance."

I did not mention the police since I didn't want their flat-footed presence interfering with my investigation.

"Switch on!" I shouted to the atomcycle as I jumped into the garage. "Door open!"

I landed in the saddle, hit full power and tore off the bottom half of the garage door, it wasn't opening fast enough, as we burst through it. I managed to miss a strolling couple on the pavement, shot between two vehicles and roared down the road. Shouting into the atomcycle's phone since it would be nice to know where I was going.

"AdInfo, emergency access. The Temple of Eternal Truth—coordinates."

A street map was projected onto the now-cracked windscreen and I screeched tires around the first corner. As I straightened out I saw that the com light was blinking. It could only be an answer to my emergency call since only Angelina, James or Bolivar could access this number after that call went out.

"Angelina is that you?!" I shouted.

"Bolivar here. What's up, Dad?"

I explained briefly and curtly, then repeated myself when James signed on. I had no idea where they were—I would find out later—but it was enough to know that they were informed and on the way. This was the first time we had used the 666 call. Major emergency. Drop everything and assemble. I had set it up when they had left home and both gone their individual ways. To help them in the future, I had imagined; now I was the one who was calling. They clicked off, not wasting my time or attention with needless comments. They were listening and would be here.

I blasted around the last corner and stood on the brakes. Oily smoke was billowing into the air—already dying down as white spray from a fire copter played over the wrecked building. The cold clutch on my chest was physical now. I took a moment to regain control, to breathe carefully. Then ran towards the ruins. Two men in blue uniforms were in my way and both sprawled and bounced. Then there was a bigger one before me with lots of gold braid; massed minions closed ranks behind him. I got control of my adrenaline-zapped reflexes and put my brain into gear.

"My name is diGriz. I've reason to believe that my wife is in there . . ."

"If you will step back and—"

"No." I spat the word like venom and he recoiled automatically. "I pay taxes. Lots of taxes. To pay you. I am more experienced in police operations than you are." I neglected to add on which side of the law I had gained that experience. "What do you know about this?"

"Nothing. Fire and police have just arrived. There was an automatic alarm call."

"I'll tell you what I know. This is—or was—the Temple of Eternal Truth. A survivor just came to my house. Rowena Vinicultura. She said that my wife was here."

I could hear the police computer buzzing in his earphone. "Admiral Sir James diGriz. We will do everything we can to find your wife . . . Angelina. I am Captain Collin and I note that your status permits you to accompany this investigation under your own cognizance and responsibility."

Purely by reflex I had established my forged bona fides as an Admiral of the Fleet when we had first come to Lussuoso. Basic precautions always pay off.

We followed a large and well-insulated firefightbot into the ruins. It plowed a careful path, occasionally spraying a smoking remnant, recording for later examination every movement that it made, every obstacle it put aside. A hanging door screeched and fell and we entered the smoking interior of what had been a good-sized meeting hall. Roblights suspended from whirring blades floated by above us and illuminated the smoke-filled interior.

Destruction on all sides—but no bodies to be seen. The cold knot was still in my midriff. The room had been seriously decorated with carved wood paneling and—now smoking—draperies. Rows of pews faced towards the destroyed side of the room where the smoke was thickest. Precipitators soon cleared the air and the floating lights glinted from wrecked and twisted machinery.

"We'll hold it here," Captain Collin said. "The disaster team takes over now."

The disaster team was embodied in a single metallic gray robot. It was undoubtedly packed full of expert programs produced in collaboration with fire and forensic investigators, along with detectors and probes of microscopic efficiency. Logically I knew it would do an infinitely better job than we fumbling humans: I still wanted to kick it aside and rush in.

"Do you see any . . . bodies?" I called out.

"No living creatures. No corpses of humans or animals detected. No—yes. Correction. Red liquid on the floor. Detection processing. It is human blood."

My throat was almost closed. My voice grated and I had trouble talking. "Primary test. Blood type?"

"Testing. O positive, Rh negative."

I didn't hear the rest—nor did it matter. Angelina was a sturdy type B—and Rh positive. I relaxed, but only so slightly.

In a very few minutes two important facts were made clear. Other than the drops of blood, there were no visible human remains or traces of anyone living or dead. There was the ruined hall and next to it the burnt and crushed room that had held large amounts of electronic equipment. All of it now apparently—and deliberately—destroyed beyond any possibility of recognition.

But where was Angelina?

I waited until the ruined building had been examined and re-examined. Nothing new was discovered and I was just wasting my time at the site. The police had vetted every spacer that had left the planet since the explosion and would keep on doing so. Neither Angelina—nor even anyone who resembled her in the slightest—had been recorded as being aboard any of them. There was nothing I could do here.

I drove slowly home, obeying all traffic regulations. Stopping for pedestrians and waving them on. I rolled through the remains of the garage door and parked the bike. Went straight to the bar where I threw out the flat drink sitting there and prepared a small but stiff replacement before I dug into the E-mail printouts. The twins were on the way. Both were off-planet so it would be a few days at least before they arrived. They did not go into details but I knew that they were now buying, cajoling, bribing—perhaps stealing—the fastest means of transportation in the known universe. They would be here. Our little clan may have rejected the outside worlds and their values—but this made our own cohesion that much stronger.

But now we had to wait for plodding technology to sift, examine and assess the ruins of the Temple of Eternal Truth—and present a coherent picture of what had happened there. There was nothing I could do until I got the police report. I tried to contact Rowena in the hospital but was given the brush-off. Querying her more would have to wait until she had recovered a bit. Lussuoso was rich and technically efficient and would do the search-and-analyze job as well as—or better than—any other planet we had visited. I hated this place but gave it all credit for technical competence. My mind kept trying to numerate all the terrible possibilities of Angelina's disappearance. . . .

Don't dwell on it, Jim, I told myself firmly. You have chosen to lead what others might consider a strange and possibly criminal life. I began to wish I had stayed with crookery and away from the Special Corps. I was always uneasy on the right side of the law. Even more I regretted coming here. Yet it had seemed like a good idea at the time.

This was a paradise planet and unbelievably expensive. To move here I had had to tap into bank accounts untouched for years. I even had to draw in some long-overdue debts and that had not been easy to do. I mean not easy in the sense of heavy weapons and a number of people in the hospital before the accounts were closed. A life of crime is not always profitable—particularly when I had some unwelcome assignments from the Special Corps. Certainly my saving the universe had been exciting, but not money-making in the slightest. The same thing happened when I ran for president of Paraiso Aqui. Good fun, but again no money involved. So between these kinds of legal jobs, Angelina and I had done a number of other jobs that filled our coffers while depleting those of others. Enough had been stored away for a rainy day that had proved to be a sunny one here. It had all been well worth it since Angelina was happier here than she had ever been before. I even forgot how much I hated the place when she smiled and kissed me. It had all started simply enough.

"Have you ever heard of Lussuoso?" she had asked.

"A new drink—or something you rub onto the skin?"

"Don't always play the fool, Jim diGriz. I mean every day there is something about it in the news—"

"Vicarious thrills and sheer jealousy. There isn't one person in a trillion who could even afford a day's visit there."

"We could. I'm sure."

"Of course—"

Of course. Famous Last Words. Springing to my lips engendered by relaxation and mental sloth. By hindsight it was obvious that every word of that simple conversation was planned and orchestrated by my dearest. She was a woman who, when she knew what she wanted done, got it done.

Lussuoso. Famous in myth and legend and galactic soap operas. A paradise planet. Populated only by the very, very rich and those who were richer. I had been intrigued by this phenomenon at first and had done a bit of research. I was in an exotic enough income bracket to quickly discover why it was so attractive.

It was the galactic center for rejuvenation treatments. These were so hideously expensive that you had to be a millionaire to even see their price list. The treatments were painless but time-consuming. Depending upon the degree of customer decay this could take years. Since a clinic would be a bore, and there was no shortage of money in the project, an entire planet had been terraformed into a holiday world. Luxury villas rivaled each other in exuberance. Operas, theaters and entertainments of all kinds abounded. All the sports from deep-sea diving and fishing to mountain climbing and hunting were there for the taking. But hidden away from all this consumptive capitalism were the clinics and surgeries where the rich got younger and, if possible, poorer. This was the taboo subject and never mentioned—but was the real reason why the planet existed in the first place.

I had discovered all this and had instantly forgotten it. Angelina had not. I knew that my fate was sealed, my goose well-cooked, served and carved, when she stopped in front of the hall mirror one day just before we left for dinner. She patted her immaculately groomed hair as women are wont to do—then leaned closer. Touching the corner of one eye with a delicate fingertip.

"Jim—is that a line, right here?"

"Of course not. Just the way the light is falling."

Even as I spoke these polite, truthful and simple words my thoughts were briskly whirring forwards. Years of happy marriage had taught me one important fact—if not a lot of important facts. Women speak with many levels of meaning. As simple a question as *Are you hungry?* can mean *I* am hungry. Or have *you* forgotten we have a dinner appointment? Or I'm not hungry but I'm sure you will be bothering me about lunch soon. Or any other of countless convoluted interpretations. So a possible line in the corner of an eye, following soon after a simple query about Lussuoso and the chance appearance of a gilt brochure on the end table could mean only thing. I smiled.

"I am beginning to feel that this world has worn out its welcome and is starting to bore more than a little. Have you ever thought of passing a spell on, I don't know, some grander and more exciting planet?"

She whirled about and kissed me enthusiastically. "Jim—

you must be a mind reader! What do you think about . . ."

I really didn't have much to think about. Other than remembering long-forgotten bank accounts.

But it had been well worth it. For awhile. Angelina absented herself from time to time—but we never discussed the rejuvenation treatments. I am forced to admit that, after noting my touches of gray hair, as well as a slight tendency to be short of breath after serious exercise, I was not that adverse to a medical session or two myself. After all I was paying for it. And Lussuoso was as jolly and entertaining as the brochures had said. Our house was lovely and our friends lovelier still. I don't know how beautiful these people had been before they had become beautiful people—but they were sure good to look at now. Neither age shall wither nor time detract. They used to say that money couldn't buy everything, but this cliché had long been extinct. On Lussuoso they were all young, handsome and rich. Or rather rich first—therefore young and handsome.

It did not take me long to discover that they were also boring beyond belief.

Making a lot of money seems to produce people who care only about making money.

Now I am not a snob—far from it. My circle of friends and acquaintances contains weird and wonderful examples from all walks of life. Conmen and connoisseurs. Forgers and foresters, police and politicians, scientists and psalm singers. All of them entertaining and good company in a variety of strange and interesting ways.

Yet after a month on Lussuoso I was ready for anything but more of Lussuoso. Suicide perhaps, or back into the army again, maybe swimming in a lake of sulfuric acid; any of these would be preferable.

But I bided my time and increased my drinking for two reasons. Firstly I had paid a satellite-sized bundle for the medical treatments and I was going to get my money's worth. Secondly, and more importantly, Angelina was having an incredibly good time. Our lifestyle had previously prevented her from having female acquaintances or close lady friends. Her early and murderous life, before the psych treatments that had turned her into a more civilized, though still criminal, person, was far in the past and hopefully forgotten. We never discussed those early years when I—for a rare change!—was on the side of law enforcement. And she was a criminal on the run. A very nasty criminal indeed and I could not understand how one so beautiful could be so devious and cruel. Until she trusted me, perhaps she loved me even then, and had opened the locket with the secret of her past. Her beauty had been the product of the surgeon's knife. That had changed her from what she had been to how she looked now. Only her criminal existence had enabled her to pay for the operations. Because of this, and our extra-legal standard of living, we might have had a lonely existence in many ways. We had not led a solitary life, but it had certainly been a different kind of life from the normal ones led by the other 99.99 percent of mankind.

Having the twins had been a novel experience for both of us. One that I had not looked forward to with a great deal of enthusiasm. But I had changed, for the better Angelina always said, and she should know. When the boys were growing up we had seen that they had received the best education. We had discussed it a lot and had finally agreed that they could choose the style of life that most appealed to them. In all fairness, when they were old enough, we had introduced them to some of the more interesting aspects of our lifestyle. I am happy to say that they took to it instantly. All of this kept us busy enough and, since Angelina had never had any close friends, she apparently had never missed the acquaintance of those of the fairer sex. Now she had them in abundance.

They went out together and did things together. Just what I was never quite sure. But she—and they—did enjoy themselves. She had even mentioned lightly, and oh how I wish I had listened more closely, the Temple of Eternal Truth. She hadn't seemed terribly interested but had gone there at a friend's insistence.

Now this. I sipped long and hard at my drink and resisted a refill.

"DiGriz here," I called out at the instant the communicator buzzed.

"It is Captain Collin, Admiral. We have some more—and very puzzling—information about the Temple of Eternal Truth. Do you think you could come to my office . . ."

I was out the door even while he was still speaking.

CHAPTER 2

"WHAT HAVE YOU FOUND OUT?" I asked brusquely as I stamped into Captain Collin's office. He was speaking on the phone and he raised his hand signing me to wait.

"Yes. Thank you. I understand." He hung up. "That was the hospital. It seems that Mrs. Vinicultura is suffering from post-traumatic amnesia—"

"She's forgotten everything that happened?"

"Precisely. There are techniques that could get access to those memories but their application must wait until she has recovered from the shock."

"That's not why you called me here?"

"No." He ran his finger around inside his collar and—if it were possible for an overmuscled police captain to look embarrassed—he looked embarrassed.

"Here on Lussuoso we pride ourselves on our security and the thoroughness of our records . . ."

"Which means," I interrupted, "your security has been penetrated and your records are doubtful?"

He opened his mouth to rebut me. Then closed it and slumped in his chair. "You're right. But it has never happened before."

"Once is once too often. Tell me about it."

"It is this Temple of Eternal Truth. It appears to have been duly registered as a qualified religion. They kept accurate records and reported regularly on their financial position, though of course like all religions they pay no taxes. Everything seemed quite aboveboard. The directors are on record and, most discreetly of course, we know about all of its members . . ."

"*Know* about? Would you like to explain that?"

He looked uncomfortable. "Well, like any civilized planet we practice the galactic constant of complete freedom of religion. You have heard of the Interstellar Freedom of Religion Act?"

"Vaguely, in school."

"The Act is not vague. The history of religion is a history of violence. Only too often religion kills, and we have had enough killing. Therefore no state or planet can have an official religion. Neither can a state or planet make any laws controlling religion. Freedom of worship and assembly is essential to civilization."

"What about nut cults?"

"I was coming to that. Galactic law requires us not to interfere with any religion and to adhere to that rule sternly. But since the weak and the juvenile require protection so that, always legally and with the utmost caution, we do investigate all religions thoroughly. We make ongoing investigations to assure that religious rights are not violated, that each religion has the freedom to practice in its own way, that minors' rights are not violated, that parishioners have complete freedom of choice—"

"What you are trying to say is that you keep tabs on who goes to what church and how often and you know what they are getting up to."

"Precisely," he growled defensively. "The records are secure and can only be accessed at the highest level in case of emergency."

"All right. We have an emergency and they have been accessed. Tell me."

"Rowena Vinicultura is one of the first members of the Temple. She attends regularly. She brought your wife to exactly four seances or sessions or whatever they call them."

"So?"

He was beginning to look uncomfortable again. "So, as I have explained, our records are detailed and complete. Except, that the leader of the Temple of Eternal Truth, one Master Fanyimadu, is, well . . ."

His voice ran down and he stared at his desktop. I finished the sentence for him.

"Master Fanyimadu does not appear in any entry in any of your records."

He nodded without looking up. "We know his place of residence and have documented his attendance at the temple. However to preserve religious freedom we have done no more than that."

"No investigations? No cross-reference with Immigration or Criminal Affairs?"

He shook his head in silence. I glowered.

"Let me guess. You don't know how he came to this planet, or if he is still here—or if he has left. Is that correct?"

"There has been . . . a certain failure of communication, an oversight."

"Oversight!" I exploded, jumping to my feet and stamping the length of the room and back. "Oversight! Fire and blood and an explosion, a woman in the hospital and my wife vanished—and you call that oversight!"

"There is no need to lose your temper—"

"Yes there is!"

"—we are proceeding with the investigation and have already made some progress." He ignored my sneer. "The blood found in the temple has been subjected to analysis down to the molecular and subatomic levels. These results have been compared to those of *everyone* on this planet. We keep complete health and hospital records as you might imagine. Computers are accessing this immense data base at the present moment. When I called you earlier the search had been narrowed to less than twenty possibilities. As we talked I have been following the progress on this readout." He tapped the screen on the desk. "The exacting comparison has now been reduced to five. No— four. Wait—there are only three now. And two of them are women! And that remaining man is . . ."

As he tore the slip from his printout we turned as one and raced for the door.

"Who?" I shouted as we ran. He read without breaking his stride.

"Professor Justin Slakey."

"Where?"

"Under sixty seconds' flight from here."

At least he was right about that. The copter was airborne even as we fell through its door. The military must have had the news the instant that the police did because a cover of military jets roared by above us. Even before we began our descent we could see that copcopters were already hitting the ground and unloading troops to surround the house. Rotors roaring we dropped down onto the stone-flagged patio. Collin had produced a large gun and was a fraction of a second ahead of me as we kicked open the doors.

The house was empty, the bird flown.

A suitcase was obviously missing, a gaping hole like a missing tooth from what had been a row of four in the bedroom closet. The garage door gaped open. A commofficer strode in, saluting as he pulled a printout from his chest pack.

"Gone, sir," he said. Collin snarled as he grabbed the sheet.

"Professor J. Slakey, passenger on the stellar liner *Star of Serendipity*. Departed . . ." He looked up and his face was grim. "A little over an hour ago."

"So they are already in warpdrive and cannot be contacted until they emerge." I considered the possibilities. "You will of course be in touch with the authorities at their scheduled destination. Which is an operation that might work normally—but this is not a normal situation. I have a strong suspicion that this suspect is ahead of us all of the way. Contacting the ship's destination will probably do no good at all because the spacer will arrive instead at some unscheduled chartpoint. If you ask me you've lost him, Captain. But you can at least tell me who—or what—he is supposed to be."

"That is the worst part. He really *is* Professor Slakey. I started a search as soon as his name appeared. I have just received a report directly from the medical authorities. He is a physicist of interstellar repute who was requested to come here by the Medical Commission, no expense was too great to acquire his services. Something to do with retarded entropy as applied to our hospital work."

"Sounds reasonable. Slow down entropy and you slow down aging. Which is what this planet is all about. Was he for real?"

"Undoubtedly. I had the privilege of meeting him at a function once. Everyone there, the scientists, physicists for the main part, were greatly in awe of his talents and the work that he did here. I am getting reports now," he touched his earphone, "that they all refuse to believe he had anything to do with the Fanyimadu personality."

"Do you?"

Before he could answer there was a shouted exchange outside, then the door was thrown open and a policeman ran in. Holding an insulated container.

"The search team found this when they were going through all the debris in the Temple of Eternal Truth, Captain—crushed under the machinery in the temple. We had no idea it was there until the wreckage was lifted. It's a . . . human hand."

He put it on the table and, in silence, we looked through the transparent side at the crushed and mangled hand inside. I had a long moment of panic before I could see by the size, the shape, that it was certainly male.

"Did anyone think to take the fingerprints of this?" I said.

"Yes, sir. They were sent for comparison . . ."

He was interrupted by the ring of the phone. Captain Collin put it to his ear, listened, replaced it slowly.

"Positive identification. This is—Professor Slakey's hand."

I pointed. "If you need proof, there it is. They were one and the same person. The blood tests, now this. Slakey was Fanyimadu. Keep me informed of everything. Understand?"

I did not wait around for an answer. Turned on my heel and left. Called back over my shoulder. "I assume that *all* details on Slakey will be in my commhopper when I get home."

So much for the police and the authorities. It was time to get to work. I radioed for a cab, told the driver to have my own car returned from the Central Police Station—one of the perks of the rich is letting the menials do as much as possible—and planned each step of the action that must be taken.

"Let me off here," I ordered while we were still a kilometer from my house. I was too jumpy to be driven around in luxury. I wanted to walk—and think. I had the strong feeling that the police were not going to come up with any answers for this one. They had been out-thought right down the line. But could I do any better?

The homes were luxurious, surrounded by brilliant gardens, the air rich with bird sound. I heard little, saw nothing. Though I was aware when I walked up the path to my home that the front door was slightly open. I had left it closed. Thieves? No way—at least they took care of the ordinary kind of crime on lovely Lussuoso. I was smiling as I banged my way in. James jumped to his feet and we embraced warmly. Or was it Bolivar?

"It's James, Dad," he said, knowing my weaknesses. "One day you better learn to tell us apart."

"I do. You usually wear blue shirts."

"This one is green—you have to do better than that."

He poured a drink for me, his already in hand, and I reported the progress or lack of it by the police. Then he spoke the words we had been both avoiding.

"I'm sure Mom is all right. Disappeared, yes. In trouble, undoubtedly. But she is the toughest one in the family."

"She is, of course, comes up aces always." I tried to keep the gloom from my voice, could not. He grabbed my shoulder, very hard.

"Something terrible has happened. But that Rowena

women said *gone*—not *dead.* So we get to work to find her and that is that."

"Right." I heard the roughness in my voice; a sentimental old gray rat. Enough. "We'll do it. If the diGriz clan can't do it—it can't be done."

"Damn right! I have a message from Bolivar. He should be here very soon. He was in a spacer doing a lunar geological survey. Dropped everything and should be in faster than light drive by now."

"Lunar geology? That's a change. I thought he had become a stockbroker?"

"He was—found it too boring. When he had stacked away his millions, more profits than those of his clients I am sure, he burnt his business suits and bought a spacer. What do we do next."

"Top up this drink, if you please." I dropped into a chair. "Fill it with one-hundred-proof Old Cogitation Juice. We have some work to do."

"Like what?"

"Like first forgetting about collaboration with the authorities. They have got this investigation completely wrong so far and can only get it worse."

"And we can do better." He said it as a fact—not a question.

"That's for sure. The bureaucrats are going to do an incredibly detailed and thorough search for this Slakey. We are not." I saw his eyebrows rise and I had to smile. "If their search is successful, which I doubt, we will hear about it quickly enough. Meanwhile we want to find out everything we can about the Temple of Eternal Truth. We go to the horse's mouth, so to speak. The church members will tell us what we want to know." I waved the membership list I had extracted from the police with not too much difficulty. "There are three of these ladies whom we are very closely acquainted with. Shall we begin?"

"As soon as I dipil my face and get a clean shirt. I'm a handsome devil and have a way with women."

I sighed happily. Some might have called this braggadocio, but I saw it as simply speaking the truth. In this family we do not condone false modesty. "You do that. Meanwhile I'll fire up the family car."

An expression empty of meaning since this healthy planet had what was probably the most rigidly enforced clean air act in the galaxy. You would probably get clapped in jail for even thinking about an infernal combustion engine. Vehicles were powered by atomic or electric batteries. Or, like our luxurious Spreadeagle, they ran on the energy stored in a flywheel. It plugged into the electricity supply at night and the motor was run up to speed. During the day the motor became a generator and the spinning wheel generated electricity for the driving wheels. All six of them. A heavy flywheel made for a big car— I had stinted on nothing. The robot driver tooled the thing out of the garage when I whistled, nodding his plastic head and smiling inanely. The gold plated door to the passenger compartment lifted heavenward while soft, welcoming music played.

I sat on the divan and the television came on. It was a news program with no news I wanted to hear. "Sports," I said and a high speed balloon race replaced it. The bar served me a glass of champagne just as James appeared.

"Wow!" he admired. "Real gold?"

"Of course. As well as diamond headlamps and a prescription windshield. No expense spared."

"Where to?" he asked, sipping his drink.

"Vivilia VonBrun is first on the list. On anyone's list I imagine. Incredibly rich, desirably attractive. I phoned and she awaits our pleasure."

She swept out to greet us, smiling compassionately. She had permitted a tiny rim of red to remain around her gorgeous eyes, to express her unhappiness at recent events. Which of course had been described in gruesome detail by the news programs. She was wearing something diaphanous and gray, which revealed enticing glimpses of tanned skin when she moved. She looked too good to be true, twenty-five years old, going on twenty-six maybe, and she was. Too good to be true, that is. I didn't dare think of her real age; the number was too large. She extended a delicate hand to me; I took it and kissed it lightly about the knuckles.

"Poor, dear Jim," she sighed. "Such a tragedy."

"It will all end well. May I present my son, James."

"What a *dear* man. How nice of you to come. My husband, Waldo, is away on one of those boring hunting things, blowing up wild animals. So if you need a place to stay . . ."

Vivilia wasted no time. While Waldo was destroying robot predators she was doing a little predation herself. And she was probably old enough to be James's great-great-grandmother. Which meant she certainly had some experience—I put the thought from me and got to work.

"Vivilia, you can help us find Angelina. You are going to tell us everything you know about the Temple of Eternal Truth."

"You are *so* forceful, Jimmy. I'm sure that your son takes after . . ."

"Facts first, lust later," I snapped.

"Coarse but to the point," she smiled, uninsultable. "I'll tell you *everything* that I know."

Enjoyable as that prospect was it would have taken far too long. I kept her memoirs to the point. A very interesting point as it turned out to be.

With boredom at Olympic intensity on Lussuoso, sports, escapism and cult religions were going concerns. Master Fanyimadu had begun to appear at various soirees and parties, his fascinating beliefs excelled only by the intensity of his gaze. Ladies of leisure looked in on the Temple of Eternal Truth and most went back a second time. It was easy to see why. Vivilia explained.

"It wasn't so much the consolation of his religion as the positive promise of eternal bliss. Not that he doesn't preach a good sermon, mind you, better than TV any day. It is what his sermons are all about. He tells you that if one attends often enough and prays with great intensity, as well as donating enthusiastically, one might get a little look-in on Heaven."

"Heaven?" I asked, trying to remember some rudimentary theology.

"Heaven, of course, you *must* have heard of it? Or perhaps in your religion . . ."

"Dad's an atheist," James said. "We all are."

Vivilia sniffed meaningfully. "Well, I suppose most people are in this age of realism and social equality. But there is a down side to that, to worshiping the nitty-gritty of society. It is boring to be so practical. Therefore you can understand why some of us with more sensitivity search for a higher meaning."

It was I who sniffed meaningfully this time but she graciously ignored me. "If you had studied more diligently in school and not ignored your Applied Theology class you would know all this already. Heaven is the place where we go after we die and if we have been good, there you will reside in happiness forever. Hell is where you go if you have been bad, to suffer intensely for eternity. I know it sounds very simplistic and illogical. I, as well as lot of the other girls, felt that way when we first heard of Heaven and Hell. But as I said, to add weight and gravitas to Heaven it is possible to visit the place, at least temporarily. So you see, having been there I have lost, shall we say, a certain amount of credulity."

"Hypnotic suggestion," I suggested.

"Jimmy, you sounded *just* like Angelina when you said that. She flared her nostrils and snorted lightly in exactly the same way. I told her that I had felt exactly the same way when other of my friends had told me about their Heavenly excursions. But I know hypnotism when I see it—and this was no trance. I can't begin to describe the process of going to Heaven. But I *was* there, with Master Fanyimadu holding one of my hands and that incredibly stupid Rosebudd holding the other. I don't think she has enough mind to hypnotize. Yet we saw each other in Heaven, experienced the same things. It was simply wonderful and too beautiful to explain in mere words. It was very . . . inspirational." She had the grace to blush when she spoke the word; inspiration not being her usual line of work.

"Had Angelina been to Heaven?" I asked. "She never mentioned anything about it to me."

"I know nothing about that. I would *never* think of snooping into another person's personal secrets."

She ignored my lifted eyebrow at this preposterous statement. Nor would she go into any more detail. Saying that if we had the faith we would see Heaven for ourselves. She was very determined and sure of that; a rock of belief. It was only after she had changed the subject and taken James by the arm to show him the house I knew that I at least had worn out my welcome. She was reluctant to let him leave, but a provident call from Bolivar from the spaceport supplied an inescapable reason to escape.

As we drove towards the spaceport I found myself scowling as I grew more and more angry.

"Rrrrr . . ." I finally said.

"That was a pretty fair growl, Dad. You wouldn't care to expand upon it?"

"I would—and I shall! I'm angry, James—and growing angrier by the minute. There are a lot mysteries here—but one thing is not mysterious at all. This con man and his fake church are raising the wrath in me."

"I thought you had a soft spot for cons and scams?"

"I do—but only when it comes to bilking the filthy rich. I don't con widows or orphans or those who can't afford it. And I work for money. Good old green, the folding and golden stuff . . ."

"I get you now," James said, his angry scowl matching mine. "You're for a good clean con, taking money from the rich and giving it to the slightly less rich. Namely you. But no one gets hurt in the process."

"Exactly! There is money involved in this con, sure, but there is also belief. This fake guru is trampling about where he doesn't belong. In people's beliefs, their most intimate feelings. In the matter of religion it is live and let live, I say. I tell no one what to believe. I even listen carefully to sincere beliefs, no matter how nutsy they sound. But Slakey-Fanyimadu is playing with fire. Preaching fakery, using machines to con the unsuspecting into believing in an afterlife that in this case can't possibly be true. If Heaven is the place you go after you die—well there is only one way of getting there. Guided tours for a quick inspection are just not in order. What is going on here is very dirty and could be very hurtful as well. If he were showing his unsuspecting marks a real Heaven they would go to, well fine. He would only be depriving them of their money, which is a wonderful and noble thing to do. But he is depriving them of their individuality and their trust. He is lying to them, preying upon their fear of death. When they discover what has been done to them they will be hurt, shattered, emotionally destroyed. Whatever else happens—he must be stopped."

We growled in unison as we pulled up at the arrivals terminal. Bolivar waved and opened the door. Tanned by UV and still wearing his spacer's gear, we brought him up to date during the drive home. Once in the house I felt a twinge of appetite. I glanced through the autocook menu with little enthusiasm, unadventurously punched up three of my usual aardvark steak and fries. Silently wishing that I had been ordering for four—a banquet of exotica had that been the case.

"Very well done, Dad, you're quite a cook," Bolivar said pushing away his plate and untouched glass of wine. "It has been dehydrated-rehydrated space rations for far too long. I have been thinking of eating their wrappings, which would probably taste better than their contents. So, time to get down to work . . ."

At this precise moment as the clock struck the hour, the central computer terminal buzzed, while its screen lit up with Angelina's image.

"I've left this recording for you, Jim," she said, and my heart, which had leaped up into my throat, settled slowly back to its usual position. "I'm off to church soon, for what promises to be an interesting experience. I don't believe any of the guff this meandering idiot Fanyimadu has been feeding us—but I do *know* that something most interesting is happening. Physical travel of some kind and, I suspect, it may be offplanet. I can't tell you more right now since I am going mostly on guesswork and, don't laugh, intuition. It will be dangerous, but I'm going prepared. So if you lose track of me for a bit—don't lose hope. Bye."

She blew a kiss in my direction and the recording clicked off.

"Did she say offplanet?" Bolivar asked. I nodded. "Let's play it again."

We did. And when it ended a second time my mind was made up. "She said offplanet—and she meant it. Any ideas?"

"Plenty," Bolivar said. "Let us forget Slakey, as you suggested, Dad. The police can search the police files without our help. But this recording tells us things they don't know. Offplanet covers a lot of space—and so will we. We must start searching the galactic records. We have to find this Temple of Eternal Truth when it surfaces again—under any other name or guise. We list the characteristics it must have and get our search agencies to digging into the records."

"Exactly so," I agreed. "We will be looking for the modus operandi."

"I'm not so great on the old dead languages, Dad," Bolivar said. "But if you mean we will track down this joker and that nutsy religion I am for it!"

"That's the idea. It may very well have a different name, and different ways of bringing in the suckers—but the operating basis will be the same."

"What is that?"

"I haven't the slightest idea. You'll have to work it out as you go along."

"And we search in the past as well as the future," James said. "There is no reason that this church should be confined to just this one planet, and every reason to believe that it isn't."

"Too right," Bolivar agreed. "That goes into the search plan."

I was proud of my boys. They were taking over, plowing ahead without a moment lost. As for me, I wasn't that rusty an old rat—not yet.

But it was nice to see a couple of shiny young ones sharpening their teeth.

They started at once, putting the search operation into effect. Dividing up the planets between them and working out in an ever-expanding sphere of communication and interrogation. I left them to it. Found a cold beer, took it to my study and whistled at my computer terminal to turn it on. I sipped the beer while I surfed through various data bases, zeroing in on Religion. I needed to know more about this Heaven and Hell business. I found what I needed under Eschatology. It was all about future life after death and was all very confusing. Down through the ages there have been a bewildering variety of beliefs held by an even more bewildering variety of social groups. Sometimes future life was seen as a continuation of present life, under more or less favorable conditions. Though at other times retribution for sins or evil deeds made this future life the very opposite of the one we know. I boned up on Heaven and Paradise, then went on to Hell, Hades, and Sheol. All very complex and very much at loggerheads, one religion with the other. Though not all of them. A lot of them were very derivative and borrowed bits and pieces from each other. My head was beginning to ache.

But out of all the confusing theorizing and philosophizing one thing was very clear. This was very heavy stuff. A matter of life—and then death. The earliest religions were obviously pre-science. They had to be because they made no attempts to consider reality, but were based purely on emotions. A desire to find some solutions to the problems of existence. When science finally appeared on the scene these religions should have been replaced by observation and reason. That they were not was sure proof of mankind's ability to believe two mutually exclusive things at the same time.

It had been a very long day and I found my eyes first glazing then closing as the multicolored aspects of future life passed before me. Enough! I yawned and headed for bed. A well-rested rat would be of far more use than an exhausted one with wilting whiskers.

I crashed and ten seconds—or ten hours—later I blinked up blearily at the figure shaking my shoulder.

"James . . . ?"

"It's Bolivar, Dad. We've found another Temple of Eternal Truth."

I was wide awake and standing next to the bed, almost in eyeball contact. "Not under the same name?"

"Nowhere close. This one is The Seekers of the Way. No names, books, or characters are the same as in the Temple of Eternal Truth. But they are identical if you do a semiotic comparison."

"Where?"

"Not that far. Planet named Vulkann. Mining and heavy industry for the most part. But it does have an attractive tropical archipelago that is devoted only to holiday making and retirement homes. Apparently so fascinating that it draws customers from all the nearby star systems."

"We leave—"

"As soon as you're packed. Tickets waiting at the shuttle flight. One hour to liftoff."

I checked my wallet and credit cards. "I'm packed. Let's grab some passports and go."

CHAPTER 3

EVER CAUTIOUS, WE TRAVELED UNDER new names with new passports; I had dozens of them, all genuine, locked away in the safe. The only equipment we took was a brace of electronic cameras—which I had improved far beyond their manufacturer's wildest dream. I of course had my diamond dress studs, as well as a few bits of jewelry and other innocuous items in a small sealed case.

Our arrival on Vulkann was most dramatic. As we stepped out of the space shuttle, along with a gaggle of brightly togged tourists, a brass band began to play lustily. Everyone cheered— and cheered even louder when the Corps of Guides marched up before us. Black-booted and high-heeled, skintight and most flimsy bright red uniforms graced their perfectly formed forms. At a barked command they stamped to a halt and broke ranks. Assignments had been made and a most attractive blonde with exquisite freckles on her nose marched up to us and gave a very nice salute.

"Sire Diplodocus and sons, I greet you. My name is Deveena De Zoftig, but my friends call me Dee."

"We're your friends!"

"Of course. I am your guide and at your service as long as you are on our wonderful world. May I be most informal and call you Jim, James and Bolivar?"

"You may," the twins chorused, their smiles echoing her white-toothed one.

"Wonderful! Be prepared for the holiday of a lifetime."

"We're prepared," they breathed, and the warm radiance of passion flamed from their skins.

"Then this way if you please. Kindly wave your health certificates in the direction of the doctor there, well done. And now to your luggage, which is awaiting you and being carried by that porterbot. Exit through this gate, thank you. The machine in the gate has X-rayed your wallets and verified your credit cards. You will have a lovely and expensive vacation on our planet."

Such honesty was most refreshing and I was beginning to like Vulkann almost as much as the boys liked Dee. I hated to spoil our fun with business—but that was why we were here.

"We need a luxurious hotel," I said.

"We have thousands."

"We would like one that is close to the Church of the Seekers of the Way where we are meeting some friends."

"You are indeed in luck for also located on Grotsky Square is the Rasumofsky Robotic Rest. A fully automated hostelry without a human employee, that is wide open and wonderful both day and night and never closes."

"Suits our needs," I said. "Lead the way."

"Your rooms are ready and waiting," she said as our taxi stopped in front of the hotel.

"Welcome! Welcome!" Irritatingly cheerful bellboybots chimed as they seized our bags.

"These are for you," Dee said, placing a jeweled flower on each of our shirts. "I will leave you now but I will never forget you. You have but to speak my name into your flower and I will return as quickly as I can. I bid you only to enjoy! Enjoy!"

"We will, we will!" we chorused in return and let ourselves be guided to our rooms. Before we went to work I checked for messages back on Lussuoso. Nothing discovered, no trace of Angelina. I had the gut feeling that we were right to take her advice and follow the trail offplanet.

"Nice," Bolivar said as he spun the cutter against the window and removed a neat disc of glass. The glass cutter clicked back and became a pocketknife as he fixed the camera, that was more than a camera, with its lens projecting through the opening. "Now we can not only photograph them as they come and go, but we can get their voices on the record as well."

"Very good," I said, peeking through the viewfinder. I set the controls and turned it on. "All automatic now."

"Memory?" James asked.

"About ten-thousand hours at a molecular level. More than we are going to need. Now let us get a drink and a meal and some sleep and see what morning will bring."

Morning brought more darkness instead of sunshine since Vulkann had a ten-hour-long day; daylight had come and gone while we slept. The sun was speedily rising again by the time we had finished our breakfast. We looked on unenthusiastically as the servbot cleared away the dishes while the beds made themselves. Since this was an all-robot hotel no notice was taken of our surveillance operations. Across the road the first parishioners were entering the church. None were familiar. By the time the church doors had closed I found myself nibbling my nails: I jumped to my feet.

"I'm going to work out in the gym and have a swim," I announced.

"Be there before you," Bolivar said, hurtling towards the door to his bedroom.

When we entered the pool room and threw aside our towels we were delighted to see that our guide Dee had entered through the other door and had thrown aside her towel as well. Since there is no nudity taboo on Vulkann this was a serious towel-throwing.

"I hope that you are enjoying your visit to our fair world," she said with a broad smile just as lovely as the rest of her.

The answer to that question was obvious. I dived into the

pool and swam a number of enthusiastic laps while the twins indulged in enthusiastic conversation with her, for such is the way of youth. I could see the attraction of this, particularly when I came up for breath and paused to admire the scenery.

We met in the gym and the boys worked up a good lather of sublimation since we were here for work, not dalliance. All this mindless exercise cheered us greatly—and kept our thoughts off of the Seekers of the Way. Refreshed, and with lunch holding breakfast down nicely, we trooped back to our rooms. I fast-reran the recording, then played back some of the conversations. Then amplified the images of the parishioners so I could make prints of their faces. Spread them out on the table so we could look at them.

With mutual feelings of glum depression. It was James who spoke for all of us.

"One thing certain—none of us is going to be able to join up and make any investigations inside that church."

"Not without some radical surgery," Bolivar said with a broad smile; we glowered back.

Everyone who had visited the church so far had been a woman.

"We need help," I said.

"Still in touch with the Special Corps?" James asked.

"There is no escaping them. Though I have not talked to our noble leader, Inskipp, for a long time. Which is all for the best." I glanced at my watch, then hit a few settings and smiled. "Very good news. It is now the middle of the night at Prime Base. I will be forced to wake that dear man up."

His secretary answered first but I knew the code that bypassed its tiny robotic mind. After a number of rings, growing steadily louder since Inskipp was a heavy sleeper, a familiar and angry voice rustled in my ear.

"*If this isn't a major emergency you are dead, whoever you are,*" Inskipp growled.

"Jim diGriz here, good friend. Did I awake you—"

"*I'm issuing an order now to seize all the assets in your bank accounts. Even the ones you think I don't know about!*"

"I need help. Angelina is missing."

"*Details,*" he said, voice calm, threats ended. I told him exactly what had happened. While I was doing this the boys were E-mailing copies of all the files—including Angelina's recorded message. He did not waste time in commiseration and was calling in the troops even as I talked. As head of the Special Corps, the most secret of secret forces that defended the peace and protected the galaxy, his powers were awesome. And he knew how to use them.

"*A cruiser is now on the way to Vulkann. Aboard it is a Special Agent who will be using the name Sybil. Up to this moment she has worked directly for me and for no one else. Now she is under your command. I will add that she is the best agent I have ever had.*"

"Better than me?"

"*Everyone is, diGriz, everyone. Report to me when you learn anything.*" He hung up, and knowing him, was probably already back to sleep.

At flank speed a Special Corps cruiser can outrun—or catch—anything else in space. Time still dragged. I kept busy for some hours as I hacked my way into the local police computer network, a terribly simple job. Once this was done we had no trouble discovering the identities of the church-goers that we had photographed. Nor, after cracking into their totally secret bank records, were we surprised to discover that all of them were filthy rich. The Seekers of the Way, like the followers of the Temple of Eternal Truth, were expected to part with a good few credits if they were to get the blessing of the church and peek in at the joys of the hereafter.

We took turns at the monitor screen and tried not to drink too much when we weren't watching it. I had just returned from doing forty laps in the pool when Bolivar jumped to his feet and shouted "Wow!"

James and I cracked our heads together as we jumped to look at the screen.

"Wow is indeed right," I said. "Even double-wow. Not only is he not of the female persuasion but he looks very familiar."

"Starkey-Fanyimadu?"

"None other."

"He has his right hand in his pocket," Bolivar said.

"So would you," James answered with cold lack of compassion, "if your arm ended at the wrist."

As if in reply the subject lifted his right arm to wave to a parishioner. "Pretty good prosthetic," I said.

"And done pretty fast as well," Bolivar added with more than a trace of suspicion in his voice. "First chance I have I would like to shake hands with that particular villain."

Something caught my attention, a movement of air—a sound perhaps. I looked over my shoulder and saw that the hall door, securely locked and bolted, was now standing open. A woman stepped through and closed it behind her.

"I am Sybil," she said in lush contralto. A tall, tanned redhead, poised and beautiful. Her dress was one of those spundiamond creations that were so popular, glinting and shining with an albedo like a searchlight. A woman had to have a perfect figure to wear something so outrageous and skintight. She had it.

The twins turned at the sound of her voice—looked at her in appreciative silence. I appreciated that as well, but appreciated her arrival even more.

"I'm Jim diGriz. These are my sons, Bolivar and James. Have you been briefed?"

"Completely."

"Good. What you don't know is that Slakey is here, in that church across the road."

"And he has a new right hand," Bolivar said. "We're glad you're here."

"I'll need to get inside the building as soon as possible. I am sure that you have already found out about the church members while I was on my way here. Which of them have you selected as the best possible contacts?"

"There are three strong possibilities," James said, taking the photos and identification from the stack and handing them to her. "All rich, young, or young-looking after rejuvenation, all very social, attending plenty of parties and receptions, so they will be easy to meet."

"I'll do that now. I'll contact you again after I have become one of the Seekers of the Way."

The door closed behind her and we were all silent for long moments.

"Pretty sure of herself," Bolivar finally said. It was a compliment and not a negative observation. "The best agent he ever had—isn't that what Inskipp said?"

I nodded. "May he be right—just this once."

Apparently he was, because three hours later we saw her walk through the carved marble entrance to the church, arm in arm with Maudi Lesplanes. The first name on the list that we had given her. Almost two hours passed before she emerged from the church. This time we were all staring at the door when it opened and she came in. She looked at us and smiled.

"Would one of you gentlemen mind getting me a drink? Tall, wet and alcoholic if you please."

I stepped aside as the twins rushed the bar. She went to the couch, sat, and signaled me to join her.

"I didn't mean to be brusque earlier, Jim. I was tired and I thought that you would appreciate action before conversation. I'm so sorry about Angelina. I listened to the message that she left for you and I believe, as you do, that she will be found. But not back on Lussuoso. We *will* find her. I promise."

From anyone else these would have been polite words. But Sybil spoke with an authority that rang true. I wanted very much to believe her.

"For you," my son said, holding out a glass.

She took the drink, drank, smiled—and sighed.

"Thank you, Bolivar. I needed that."

"I have another one—if that's not enough."

"Not quite yet, James."

"You're sure you're not mixing them up?" I blurted out.

"Impossible to do, as you well know, Jim. I imagine James has always had that tiny scar on his left earlobe."

I blinked. It was almost impossible to see.

"Since I was four years old. Bolivar bit me."

"Believe that and you'll believe anything."

She smiled at both of them. Then turned to me and was serious again; playtime over.

"The service of the Seekers of the Way seems to be a near replica of the one described in the briefing for the Temple of Eternal Truth. Uplifting organ music, a good bit of incense to mask the smell of tylinyne. As you undoubtedly know that is a mild tranquilizing drug. No lasting effects, but it does relax the subjects, makes suggestion much easier. Not that it was much needed since everyone there was very convinced to begin with. The sermon was most inspiring and very strange to hear from a physicist of Slakey's reputation. Heavily mystical, plenty of guff about the hereafter and the good life and good deeds that pave the road to Heaven. After some more music some of the women spoke with great warmth about their visit to Heaven, after which they donated impressive sums for the furthering of the good works. Sounded very much like the recorded statement of Vivilia VonBrun that Jim made."

"Different church, same scam?" I asked. She nodded.

"If scam is the right word. These people sound absolutely convinced. I'll know more after I've made the trip myself. Inskipp will scream when he sees how much of his funds I have invested to hurry that day."

"When?" Bolivar asked.

"As soon as possible without raising Slakey's suspicions. For the record, he is now called Father Marablis. There is another thing about him that I find particularly interesting. Before leaving I made a point of approaching him to gush over his sermon. He liked that. Nor did he mind when, in the heat of the moment, I seized him by the hand, the right hand, and squeezed it with heartfelt emotion."

I leaned forward intently. As did the twins. We did not have to ask the question. She nodded.

"A warm human hand—not a prosthetic."

"But—" I stammered. "I saw the severed hand. It was positively identified."

"I know. Interesting, isn't it? I look forward to coming events with great anticipation."

The boys stared at her, smitten. Their kind, our kind of person. If anyone could find Angelina she could; I was sure of that now.

Two days—and two very large donations—later she was told to prepare for her visit.

"Do I look all right?" she asked, turning slowly. Women only ask that when they know the answer. She was wearing something black, tight, expensive, with matching hat and even more expensive jewelry. "Are you sure that this can't be detected?" she asked, touching the tiny diamond brooch pinned at her throat.

"Only under a microscope—and you would have to know what to look for," I said. "The center diamond is the lens. I usually wear it as a shirt dress stud. I've added the jeweled setting to make it into a more exotic piece of jewelry so that you can wear it. The diamond lens focuses the image onto a series of nanoformed recording molecules that are carried beneath the lens by Brownian movement, which is energized by body heat so there is no detectable power source. Don't worry about the light level since, like the human eye, it can perceive as little as one photon of light energy. What you see, it will see—and record."

"I've never heard of anything like it before."

"Nor has your boss, Inskipp," James said proudly. "It's one of Dad's inventions."

"However all this turns out you can keep it," I said. "I'll give you the developing and printing module later."

"It's the only one in existence," Bolivar said.

"I—I don't quite know how to thank you." The emotion in her voice was not faked, that was certain. She left quickly.

Moments later we saw her stroll across the street and walk through the door of the church.

CHAPTER 4

A HEAVY TROPICAL RAIN WAS falling, lit by sudden flashes of lightning; thunder rumbled. The Church of the Seekers of the Way was blurred, its outline barely visible through the wet glass. The image from the camera was clear enough, but standing at the window I could see little or nothing. Sybil had been inside the building with Slakey for over an hour. The room was closing in on me.

"I'm going out," I said, pulling on a billed cap with the logo *Cocaine-Cola* spelled out on the front.

"You'll get soaked," Bolivar said.

"It'll look suspicious if you lurk about near the church," James added. I twisted my lip in a sneer.

"Thanks for the solicitude—but your old Dad is not quite senile yet. This cap not only advertises a repulsive drink, it also contains a hydro-repeller field—and I was lurking unseen near churches before you were born."

When they didn't even smile at my strained witticism I knew that they were as uptight as I was. I needed the air.

The hotel lobby was empty—of human life that is. The managerbot bowed and dry-wiped its gloved hands for me. The doormanbot pulled open the door as I approached and drops of rain blew in dotting its metal features.

"A filthy night, sir," it smarmed. "But it will be a sunny day for sure tomorrow, begorra."

"Is that what you are programmed to say whenever it rains?" I snarled.

"Yes, sir, a filthy night, sir, but it will be a sunny day for sure tomorrow, begorra."

My nerves must be going if I was trying to have a conversation with a mindless robot. I went out, bone-dry of course as the electrostatic field repelled the raindrops.

Angelina . . . .

The pain in my chest, my throat, was real. I had been putting all thought of her out of mind—or I wouldn't have been able to function. But she was there at the edge of my consciousness all of the time. I let her in for the moment, relished the memory. Remembering how many times she had saved my life; keeping weapons tucked in with the twins in their baby carriage had been most important more than once. With what joy we had held up banks, relished the excitement—not to mention the money. And the way we saved the universe together, defeating all of those slimy monsters! Memories, memories. We had had our low moments, but at this moment I wanted to be like the inscription on the sundial. And record only the sunny hours. And the fun . . . .

I cut off this train of thought. Feeling sorry would not help—only action could get her back. That was why I was here, the boys as well, and this was the reason why Sybil was possibly risking her life. This was going to work. It had to work.

My walk was not without a purpose; I had seen a cafe just across the square from the Church of the Seekers of the Way. It had a row of tables outside protected by an awning. And a hydro-repeller field as well I realized as I entered; this field and mine flickered with glints of light where they interacted. I touched the brim of my cap and turned mine off, sat at a table with a clear view of the church.

"Welcome, welcome, sir or madam," the table candle said as its wick flickered and lit up.

"Sir, not madam."

"How can we be of service . . . sir not madam?"

The world was full of moronic robots and computers tonight.

"Bring beer. Big, cold."

"Delighted to be of service, sir not madam."

The table vibrated, then a hatch slid back and the beer emerged. I reached for it but could not lift it.

"Two kropotniks, fifty," a colder mechanical voice said. I pushed three coins into the slot and the clamp on the glass was released. "Thank you for the tip," the voice said, keeping my change. I drowned my incipient growl with a swig of beer.

The rain lashed down on the square, thunder rumbled in the distance. An occasional car swished by; the door to the Church of the Seekers of the Way remained closed. The beer was flat. I waited.

Time passed. I finished the first beer and ordered another one.

"Two kropotniks, seventy," the table said.

"Why? The last beer was two fifty."

"That was during the happy hour. Pay."

I fed in the exact amount this time and the glass was released. "Cheapskate," the computer muttered and emitted an electronic raspberry.

The rain finally slackened, stopped, and one of Vulkann's three moons appeared briefly through a gap in the clouds. Then there was flicker of movement across the way and three women emerged from the church. They talked together for a moment before separating. Sybil came towards me and I felt a certain relaxation; at least she was safe. She did not look at me but must have been aware of my presence because she turned and entered the cafe. I took a few minutes to sip my beer. She did not appear to have been followed. I finished my drink, put the glass down and went inside.

She was in one of the rear booths with a cocktail glass before her; she nodded slightly and I went to join her. She took a large swallow, then a second one—and sighed.

"Jim, that was an experience I find difficult to describe. There were three of us and we joined Father Marablis—or Slakey—I'm beginning to be unsure of a lot of things. There were no machines that I could see. He talked to us for a bit then touched his hand to my forehead. Something happened. I can't tell you what. I didn't black out or anything like that. I can only repeat what Vivilia VonBrun said—it was indescribable. But I can clearly remember what happened next. We were walking through a field of very short grass, following Marablis. He stopped and pointed upwards and at the same moment I heard the sound of chimes, most distinctly. He was pointing to a white cloud that drifted towards us. The chimes, the music, was coming from the cloud and when I heard it I felt, well, an elation of some kind. Some sort of spiritual upwelling. Then—and don't laugh—I swear I saw a little flying creature behind the cloud. Just a glimpse."

"A bird?"

"No . . . a tiny pink baby with little wings on its shoulders. Then it was gone and it was over."

"Just like that?"

"I—I just don't know. I remember that Marablis touched my arm, turning me, and I was back in that room in the church again along with the other women. I felt, well just sad, as though I had lost something very precious."

There was little I could say. She had a distant look in her eyes, looking at something I could not see. A tear ran down her cheek and she sniffed, wiped at it and smiled.

"Sorry. I'm not being much help. I know it has to be a con of some kind. I don't believe in day trips to Heaven. But something *did* happen to me. My emotions, they are real."

"I believe you. But there are, well, drugs that can affect the emotions directly."

"I know that. But still . . ." She stood and smoothed down her dress, touched a finger to the brooch. "Instead of listening to me blathering on let's take a look at this recording."

"You've done a great job. Thank you."

The twins had seen us in the street and had the door open as we came down the hall. I heard Sybil telling them about the experience, basically just what she had told me. But she was much more in control of herself now and beginning to get angry at being got to in some way. By the time she had finished her story I had the piece of electronic jewelry clamped into the activation module. The screen lit up with a view of the church moving closer.

The pictures were silent and so were we as we watched her meet the other two women. They talked, then turned to face Slakey when he entered. He was certainly in his Father Marablis mode, brown cassock and unctuous gestures; I was rather glad I couldn't hear what he was saying.

"Up to this point I remember everything," Sybil said. "He is telling us about the joys to come and, see his hand, collecting a few extra checks for the pleasure of our outing. There, that part is done. Here we go."

Slakey must have said something for they all turned and walked after him. The screen went black.

"Is the recorder broken?" Bolivar asked.

"I doubt it." I fast-forwarded the machine and the image reappeared.

"We are back in the room," Sybil said. "Without a record of what I saw. I'm so sorry."

"Don't be." I ran a quick analytical probe. "You did everything that you could. So did the recorder. It worked fine—but there just is no record. I don't know why or how this happened. The electronics appear to have been operating but they, well, just didn't record anything." I scowled at the machine. "And I do not believe in miracles."

"No one's thinking about miracles," James said. "We're thinking technology. Whatever field of force or electronic pervasion created the Heaven trip, well, could it have interfered with the recording?"

"Pretty obviously," I said.

"I have an idea," Bolivar said. "This was a good try—but it just did not work out. Next step. We need a long look around that place. You will remember that there was some kind of machinery that was blown up in the first church. I would like to see if there are any of the same kind of gadgets here . . ."

"No," I said.

"Why not?"

"I don't mean no let's not do it. I mean no you don't do it. Because I do this particular job." I raised my hand to quiet their protests. "I say that not because I am older and wiser, which is true, but because I have had much more experience at this sort of thing. Bolivar, I wouldn't think of making high-profit high-risk investments if you were there to do it for me. After watching that last karate tournament I wouldn't dare face up to your brother in an even fight. It has always been the age of the specialist. Do any of you believe that you can do an unseen breaking and entering and searching job better than I can?" Silence was my only answer. "Thank you," I said—with some warmth. "But you will all have to help. This is the plan."

We had that night and part of the next day to make our preparations. It was going to be a joint effort. The church service for the Seekers of the Way was due to begin at noon. We met for a final rehearsal an hour earlier.

"You first, Sybil," I said.

"I go in with the others. Talk, act naturally and keep my eyes open. If everything goes as it usually does, then I have only one thing to do. I know that the outer door is always locked before the service begins. So when Father Marablis begins his sermon, I squeeze this." She held up a tiny wafer of plastic.

"That is a one-shot communicator," I said. "The battery shorts through the chip, which sends a millisecond-long signal before it burns out. It is undetectable both before and after use. I'll be waiting nearby. As soon as I get the signal I go in through the front door." I held up a modified lockpick. "Sybil took a close look at the lock—which is a make called Bulldog-Bowser. I know it well and it is very easy to open. James, you're next."

"I'll be driving the delivery van, a rental with new identification numbers and fake signs. When Dad goes through the door I drive around and park in front of the church. Bolivar."

"I'm inside the van with passive tracking equipment, magnetometer and heat detectors. I should be able to follow people moving inside. I also have a warning alarm receiver."

I nodded. "Which I can activate in one of four ways in case of emergency. Bite hard on my back tooth, tap one toe quickly two times or—pull off the top button of my shirt."

"That's only three," Sybil said.

"The fourth I have no control over. It will be activated if— my heart stops. Should the alarm go off, the boys break their way in with all guns firing. Any remarks or questions?"

"Stun grenades and blackout gas as well as the guns," James said.

That was it. We had some tall and nonalcoholic drinks and discussed the Vulkann weather. After a time Sybil looked at her watch, stood and went out. We followed.

I waited out of sight around the corner, apparently looking at the gaudy items in a tourist shop window while I patted, one by one, the various lumps in my clothes; weapons, detectors, tools, alarms, that sort of thing. I had no idea of what I would find inside the church so I had visited a number of electronic stores and stacked up on everything I could or might possibly need.

The phone taped behind my ear clicked sharply. I turned about, strolled around the corner and up the two steps to the church door. My left hand on the knob concealed the rapid twisting of the lockpick with my right. It was as fast as turning a key; I do have some experience at this sort of thing. The door opened and I went through without breaking pace. Closed and relocked it behind me.

I was in a dimly lit vestibule with draperies covering the far side. I parted them a hairsbreadth and looked through. Father Slakey-Marablis was behind a high lectern and in full throat, unctuous vapidities washed over the attentive audience below.

". . . doubt shall be taken from you and will be replaced by reassurance. It is written in the Book of Books that the path to salvation leads through the Land of Good Deeds. Good deeds and love must be your guiding stars, the beckoning fingers of the hereafter. A hereafter that lies ahead of you, restful and satisfying, calm and filled with the effervescence that passeth all understanding."

Very good. Not really very good, but really very bad. But good for me. For as long as he burbled on I could penetrate his holy of holies. The staircase was behind the door on the left, as Sybil had told me. She had no idea where it led; that was for me to find out. I went through and closed the door silently behind me, bit down gently on the microlight I held between my teeth. Dusty stairs wound upwards. I climbed them, walking with my feet close to the wall to prevent them from creaking. There was another door at the head of the stairs that opened into a large room, dimly illuminated by a single window.

I was over the main hall and could hear the rumble of the sermon dimly through the floor. I walked silently between the boxes and stacked chairs to a door on the far wall. This was to the rear of the building and should be over the mysterious antechamber that might very well be the entrance to Heaven. This was also roughly the same location as that of the electronic equipment that had been destroyed in the Temple of Eternal Truth. As I opened the door the rumble of the voice on the floor below stopped.

So did I. One foot still raised. Then I relaxed and stepped forward when the organ music began and the women began to sing. A spiral stairway led down. I took it, slowly and silently. Stopped before what I hoped was the last door.

It was stuffy and warm and I was beginning to sweat. From the temperature alone. My pulse rate was normal and my morale high. No more waiting—a time for doing. I turned the light off and pocketed it, then opened the door into darkness and stepped through.

Bright lights came on. Slakey was standing just before me. Smiling.

I had only the briefest of glimpses because at the instant that the lights flared I had dived to one side. Biting down hard with my back teeth.

At least I tried to bite. But as fast as I had been, something else was much faster. I could see and hear—but that was all. My body was flaccid, my eyes open and staring. At the greasy floor because I had landed heavily facedown. My jaw dropped open; I drooled. I felt the panic rising as I realized I could do nothing, could not control a single muscle. But at least I was breathing and my heart was still beating, pounding loud and strong in my ears. A shoe tip appeared in front of my eyes and my vision swirled, settled, staring up at the bright light. Slakey must have rolled me over; I could not feel a thing. His face blotted out the light.

"You can see me, can't you? And hear me as well? My neural neutralizer allows that. I know all about you Jim diGriz. I know everything for I am all-powerful. I know how you invaded this holy place of worship. I know who you came with."

His hands reached down, my head turned. Sybil was lying next to me, sprawled and unmoving. My vision swirled again and Slakey was straightening up. Dressed in full regalia, I saw now. Bright robes with strange symbols covering them, with a high collar, a crown of some kind on his head. He raised his arms and shook his fists on high in a triumphant gesture. Both fists. The right one worked very well indeed and there was no sign of any scar on either wrist when his loose sleeves fell back.

"You are a pitiful mortal and shall be destroyed. You seek enlightenment but you shall not have it. You and this female creature you sent to spy. You wish to see Heaven—then you will go to Heaven. You shall, you shall!"

There was motion, my vision rocked. Stopped. My head was raised and I realized that he had dumped me across Sybil's unresistant body.

"Go, both of you, go. Go to Heaven."

He laughed, choked, laughed even louder.

"Well—not quite Heaven as you shall discover."

Blackout

CHAPTER 5

SOMETHING HAPPENED.

I couldn't remember it, could not begin to describe it. I did not want to think about it. I had far more important things on my mind. Like the fact that I was still paralyzed and lying face-down in red grit of some kind. I couldn't feel it but I could smell it. A rotten, sulfury smell.

Smell! Yes, it certainly was there, and growing stronger and stronger. Which meant something important. After I had been zapped I couldn't smell or feel anything: I could now. Which must mean that the paralysis must be wearing off, because I was vaguely aware of a scratchy pressure on my cheek. I concentrated, struggled hard, harder—then felt my fingertips move ever so slightly.

Recovery did not end quickly, not the way the onset of the paralysis had, but slowly and soon very painfully. Waves of red agony that ran through my reviving body that threatened to block my vision. My eyes were watering, tears ran down my cheeks as I writhed in agony. Slowly, very slowly it died away and I managed to roll over.

Blinking away the tears to stare up at a gray rock ceiling above. There was a low moan and with a great deal of effort I turned my head to see that Sybil was lying on the ground next to me. Her eyes were closed and her body twisted with pain as she moaned again. I knew what she was experiencing. Slowly and exhaustingly, with a great deal of grunting and gasping, I crawled to her, took her hand.

"The pain," I managed to say, "it goes away."

"Jim . . ." Whispered so quietly I could barely hear it.

"None other. You're going to be all right."

This was a pretty pathetic reassurance but was about all that I could think of at the moment. Where were we? What had happened? If this was Heaven it was pretty different from the place that she had described. Sharp volcanic gravel instead of grass; rock instead of sky. Where was the light coming from? And what was the last thing that Slakey had said? Something about not quite being Heaven.

With some effort I managed to sit up and saw the opening in the rock wall: we were in a cleft or a cave of some sort. And beyond the opening was a red sky.

Red? There was a distant deep rumble and I felt the ground beneath me tremble; a cloud of dark smoke roiled across the sky. Clutching to the rock wall I managed to drag myself to my feet and stumble over to Sybil. I helped her sit up with her back to the wall.

She tried to speak, starting coughing instead. Finally squeezed out the words. "Slakey—he was one step ahead of us all the time."

"What do you mean?"

"He was playing with us, and must have known that you were in the building. He cut his sermon short, made some kind of excuse about an unexpected meeting, turned the organ on instead, along with a recording of everyone singing. Asked us all to leave. Everyone except me. He took me aside, said that he had something most important to tell me. I was curious of course, besides the fact that I couldn't think of anything else to do except do as he had asked. Then, as soon as the others were gone, he pointed something at me. I had only the quickest look at something like a silver spiderweb, before I fell down. It was horrible! I couldn't move a muscle, not even my eyes. I was aware of him dragging me into that back room in the darkness—and the worst part was that there wasn't a thing I could do about it. I couldn't move, do anything at all, couldn't warn you that was the worst part. Then the lights were on, and you were there, falling. I remember him talking to you. After that—nothing.

"That's about all that I can remember—until I opened my eyes here."

I patted my side pocket, felt the lump of the communicator, felt a slight touch of hope at the same time. I put it to my ear, turned it on. Nothing. The same went for every other device on my person. All dead. Batteries and power packs drained. I couldn't even open the blade on my Schweitzy Army Knife; it seemed to be welded into a lump. I looked at the small pile of metallic debris and felt the urge to kick it across the cave. I gave in to the urge and did just that. It clattered nicely.

"Just junk now. All dead. Nothing works." I turned and stumbled towards the light.

"Jim, don't leave . . ."

"I'm not going far. I just want to look out, satisfy my curiosity, find out where we are."

Leaning one hand against the rock so I wouldn't trip, I took step after shuffling step until I was at the entrance and staring out. I felt my jaw fall open with shock as I dropped to my knees. For long moments I could only stare. With an effort I turned away, managed to stand again and went back to Sybil. She was sitting up now and very much more in control.

"What's out there, Jim?"

"Certainly not Heaven. The sky is red, not blue, no white clouds and certainly no grass. A geologically unstable area with an active volcano nearby. Plenty of smoke, but at least no lava. And there is a big and swollen sun like no sun—or star—I have ever seen before. It is light red in hue, not white or blue, which explains the russet coloring of the landscape."

"Where are we?"

"Well—" I groped for something intelligent to say. "Well

we know now that we're not on Vulkann," was the best I could come up with. "And . . ."

She noticed my hesitation. "And?"

"I just had a glimpse."

"Some glimpse! You should see your face—you've gone all gray."

I tried to laugh at this, but it came out as a pathetic gurgle. "Yes, I saw someone—or something. For just the shortest instant I could see sort of a figure, going away, fast. Biped, erect." My voice ran down and she looked very concerned. "Sorry. I'm just being stupid. It really moved too fast for me to see any details. But I think, no I'm sure, that it had a tail. And . . . it was bright red."

There was a long silence before she spoke.

"You're right. We're certainly not in Heaven. How is your theology?"

"Not too good—but good enough to know that I should not be thinking what I am thinking. Before you arrived I did a little theological digging in the net about the Heaven concept and all the afterworlds and afterlife, to find out more facts, to get some insight as to what it was all about. I'm afraid that my early religious education was more than neglected. Here is how it goes. There are as many concepts of Heaven as there are different religions. What I did was outline the Heaven as seen by the attendees at the Temple of Eternal Truth and search for comparisons. I found a really interesting assortment of religions with a great variety of names. I narrowed these down to the ones that featured a dichotomy of Heaven and Hell, which are places that are occupied after you die. There is an object called a soul, which you can't see or find or anything like that. It comes from somewhere unspecified. The description was pretty vague at this point. This soul, in some undescribed manner, is supposed to be you. Or the essence of you. Don't look at me like that—I'm not making it up! Anyway, this soul wants to end up in Heaven. There is a mention also of a sort of halfway house called Purgatory. And, I'm sure that you have heard of it, a direct opposite kind of place called Hell."

She looked shocked. "Then you think that . . . perhaps we have ended up in this place called Hell?"

"Well, until a better idea comes along—and I hope it will—that seems to be the conclusion . . . ."

There was a distant rumbling roar, the ground shivered beneath my feet. A sudden weight seemed to press down and I dropped to my knees, put my hands out to break my fall. I was heavy, suddenly very heavy; Sybil was sprawling on the ground again.

Then the strange sensation passed, as quickly as it had come, and I stood again, shakily.

"What—was that?"

"I haven't the slightest idea. I never felt anything like it before. It was like, what? A gravity wave passing over us?"

"There is no such thing as a gravity wave."

"There is now!"

She tried to smile, but shivered instead.

"Don't," I said. "We're someplace strange, and it might very well be a place called Hell. But we appear to be alive—so let us get out of this cave and find out just where in Hell we are!"

She pulled away and straightened up, running her fingers through her hair. And even managed a small smile. "I bet I even look like Hell," she said. "Let's go."

Our little burst of enthusiasm did not last very long. As we walked on, the air grew hotter, uncomfortably hotter. We passed around a spur of rock and found out why. We recoiled from the blast of heat and looked on aghast at the scene before us. Directly ahead ran a wide river of turgid lava. Darkened slag formed on top, cracking and breaking apart as it flowed by to reveal the glowing, turgidly liquid stone below. We retreated. Retracing our steps.

"We'll try the opposite direction," I said, then coughed. Sybil did not answer, just nodded in agreement. Her throat must have been as dry as mine; she would have been just as thirsty. Was there any water in this parched landscape? The answer did not bear thinking about.

Something else did not bear thinking about. Angelina.

Slakey must have sent her someplace just the way he had sent us. To Heaven I hoped. I hoped even harder that it was not to this terrible planet that she had gone.

We retraced our path past the cave mouth from which we had emerged and stumbled on through a landscape of rolling gravel dunes. It was still hot, but not the ovenlike furnace that we had just left.

"A moment," Sybil said, stopping and sitting on a wide boulder. "I'm a little tired." I nodded and sat beside her.

"Not surprising. Whatever that paralysis web was it certainly didn't do us any good. Physically or mentally."

"I feel beat—and depressed. If I knew how to quit I would."

Looking at the despair in her face, hearing the echo of exhaustion in her voice—I grew angry. This fine, strong, attractive agent should not be reduced like this by one man.

"I hate you Slakey!" I shouted. Jumping to my feet and shaking my fist at the sky. A rumble of a distant volcano was not much of an answer. I got even angrier. "You will not get away with this. We are going to get out of this place, yes we are. The air on this planet must have come from someplace, from living green plants. We'll find them—and you cannot stop us!"

"You are wonderful, Jim," Sybil said, standing and smoothing down her wrinkled and filthy dress. "Of course we will go on. And of course we will win."

I nodded angry agreement. Then pointed down the valley. "That way, away from the lava and the volcanoes. It will be a lot better."

And it was. As we walked the air became cooler. After a bit, when the valley widened out, I caught a glimpse of green far ahead. I did not want to mention it at first—but then Sybil saw it as well.

"Green," she said firmly. "Grass or trees or something like that ahead. Or is it just wishful thinking?"

"No way! I can see it as well and it is a very cheering sight indeed. Forward!"

We almost ran as the verdant landscape opened up ahead. It was grass, knee-high, cool and slightly damp as we pushed

our way through it. There were clumps of trees farther ahead,
then more and more of them, almost a small forest.

"Good old chlorophyll," I exulted. "Bottom of the food
chain and from whence all life doth spring. Capturing the sun's
energy to manufacture food . . ."

"And water?"

"You better believe it. There has to be water somewhere
around here—and we are going to find it—"

"Shhh," she shhhsed. "Do you hear that? A sort of rustling,
like dry leaves."

I did hear it, a light crackling sound that was coming towards us from the forest. Then something small came out from
under the trees and moved hesitantly into the grass.

"Well, Hello," I said to the tiny reddish-brown form that
emerged. It looked up at me with button-black eyes and
squealed with fright.

The squeal was echoed by a louder and more angry squeal
from the forest. There was a thunder of running hooves and a
giant avenging form burst out from under the trees, snorting
with massive maternal protectiveness. A good two meters from
snuffling nose to twitching tail. Covered all over with protective spines now rigidly erect.

Sybil gasped with horror.

I smiled and cried out, "Sooooy, pig, pig, pig!"

"Jim—what is it?"

"One of the most endearing and lovely creatures in
the galaxy, friend of my youth, companion to man. It is a—
porcuswine!"

She looked at me as though she thought I was going mad.

"Endearing? Is it going to attack?"

"Not if we don't threaten her swinelet." The tiny creature
had lost its fright when its monster dam had appeared and had
nosed aside the protecting quills to find some refreshing milk.

I moved slowly, bending over to pick up a windfall branch.
Beady and suspicious eyes followed my every movement.

"That's a good girl," I said, stepping forward and making
reassuring clucking noises. She quivered a bit but held her

ground. Turning her head to follow me as I approached. A drop of saliva formed on a protruding, sharp tusk, then dripped to the ground.

"There, there," I murmured. "Little Jimmy doesn't hurt porcuswine. Little Jimmy *loves* porcuswine."

Reaching down I brushed a handful of quills slowly aside between her ears, reached out and prodded with the end of the branch, then rubbed it strongly through the thick bristles.

Her eyes were half-closed as she burbled contentedly.

"Porcuswine just love to be scratched behind the ears— they can't reach the spot themselves."

"How do you know about these terrible creatures?"

"Terrible? Never! Companions to mankind in his quest to the stars. You should read your galactic history more closely. Read about the strange beasts and deadly creatures that were waiting for the first settlers. Monsters that could eat a cow in a single bite. They learned fear from the faithful porcuswine, let me tell you. An artificial genetic mutation between giant pigs and deadly porcupine. Tusks and hooves to attack, spines to defend. Loyal, faithful and destructive when needs be."

"Good pork chops too?"

"Indeed—but we don't speak about that in their presence. I was raised on a farm and let me tell you, my only friends were our herd of porcuswine. Ahh, here's the boar now!"

I shouted joyous greeting to the immense and deadly form that lumbered out of the forest. He glared at me with red and swiney eyes. Grunted aloud with pleasure as the end of my stick scratched and scratched at his hide. I grunted with the ef- fort—and pleasure as well.

"Where did they come from?" Sybil asked.

"The forest," I said scratching away.

"That's not what I mean. What kind of a place is this with volcanoes, lava flows, gravity waves—and these creatures?"

"A planet that had to have been settled by mankind. We'll find out soon enough. But first let us follow the pigpaths into the forest and find some water. Drink first, cogitate later."

"Agreed," she said leading the way. I followed her and our

newfound porcine friends followed me. Grunting expectantly for more delicious scratching attention. We lost them only when the path led through a clearing surrounded by storoak trees. The boar slammed his tusks into the trunk of one heavy-laden tree and shook it mercilessly. Acorns as big as my head rained down and the little family munched on them happily.

We emerged from the forest into a water meadow that had been stirred up muddily by sharp hooves. It bordered a small lake. The far side was shielded in mist that obscured any details. We left the muddy path and found a shelf of rock that led to the water. Sat at the water's edge and drank cupped handfuls of the clear and cool water until we had drunk our fill.

"Find a few dry sticks, rub them together and it could be pork for dinner," Sybil said, smacking her lips.

"Never! They're friends." My stomach rumbled enticingly. "Well maybe later, much later. And only if we can't find another source of food. I think a little exploring is in order. This is—or was—a settled world. Mankind took the mutated porcuswine and storoak to the stars. There should be farms here."

"I wouldn't even know what one looked like. I was a city girl, or rather a small-town girl. Food was something that you bought in the shop. My mother and father—everyone there—worked at teleconferencing or programming or computing or whatever. No factories, no pollution, that sort of thing was confined to the distant robot construction sites. Our town was just low and ordinary, just a lot of landscaped buildings and green parks. Utterly and totally boring."

I squinted across the lake where the mist appeared to be clearing. I pointed.

"Like that place over there?"

CHAPTER 6

"WHAT PLACE?" SHE ASKED, STANDING and shielding her eyes with her hand. I pointed in silence.

"Seen one, you've seen them all," she muttered, frowning. "They must be factory-produced, stamped out like cereal packages. Fold the thing and glue it and plop it down, hook up the electricity and it starts to work. I couldn't even bear to go to school in Hometown—that is really what it was really called, would you believe it? I graduated first place in my kiddy class, got a scholarship, went away to school and never came back. Knocked around a bit, got involved with police work, liked it. Then I was recruited by the Special Corps and the rest is history."

"Do you want to take a look at this hometown?"

"No, I do not."

"It might be fun—and there should be food there. Unless you want a pork roast so badly that you want to kill a porcuswine with your bare hands?"

"No jokes, please. We'll take a look."

It was not a large lake and the walk was a short one. Sybil, who had started out in good spirits, grew quieter and quieter as we approached the low buildings. She finally stopped.

"No," she said firmly.

"No, what?"

"No it's not a place I really want to visit. They all look exactly alike, I told you, central design, central manufacture. Plug the thing in and watch it go to work. I hated my childhood."

"Didn't we all? But the porcuswine, they were the best part of it. Probably the only part that I remember with any feeling. Now let's go see if we can find a McSwineys and get a sandwich in this bijou townlet."

There was nothing moving in the streets or the buildings ahead. A single road came out of the hamlet and ended abruptly in the grass. There was a billboard sign of some kind beside it, but it was end on and we couldn't read it until we got closer. We walked at an angle as we approached so we could see what it said. Sybil stopped suddenly and clasped her hands so tightly together that her knuckles turned white. Her eyes were closed.

"Read it," she said.

"I did."

"What does it say?"

"Just a coincidence . . ."

Her eyes snapped open and she bit out the words. "Do you believe that? What does it say?"

"It reads, in serifed uppercase red letters on a white foreground, it reads . . ."

" 'Welcome to Hometown.' Are we mad or is this whole planet mad?"

"Neither." I sat down and pulled a blade of grass free, chewed on it. "Something is happening here. Just what we have yet to discover."

"And we are going to discover what by sitting on our chunks and chewing grass."

She was angry now—which was much better than being frightened or depressed. I smiled sweetly and patted the grass beside me. "To action, then. You sit and chew the grass while I scout out the scene. Sit!"

She sat. Because of the force of my personality—or because

she was still tired. I climbed to my feet creakily and wearily and strolled forward into Hometown.

Found out everything I needed to know in a very short time and went back to join her sitting and chewing.

"Strangest thing I have ever seen," I said.

"Jim—don't torture me!"

"Sorry. Didn't mean to—just trying to come to grips with this particular reality. Firstly, the town is empty. No people, dogs, cars, kids. Anything. One of the reasons that it is empty is that everything seems to be in one lump. As though it was made that way. The doorhandles don't turn and the doors themselves appear to be part of the wall. The same with the windows. And you can't look in. Or rather it looks like you're looking in but what is inside is really in the glass of the window. And nothing really seems right or complete. It is more like an idea of Hometown instead of being Hometown itself."

She shook her head. "I have no idea of what you are talking about."

"Don't worry! I'm not so sure myself. I'm just trying to pick my way through a number of very strange occurrences. We arrived here in a sort of a cave. With volcanoes and lava streams and no grass or anything else." I glanced up at the bloated red sun and pointed. "At least the sun is the same. So we went for a walk and found green grass and porcuswine, the porcuswine of my youth."

"And the Hometown of mine. It has to mean something . . ."

"It does!" I jumped to my feet and paced back and forth in a brain-cudgeling pace. "Slakey knew where he was sending us and it wasn't to Heaven he said. So he must have been here before. Not quite Heaven, that's what he said. Maybe he thought he was sending us to Hell. And the spot where we arrived was very Hellish what with the red creature, the volcanoes and lava and everything. Could it have been Hellish because he expected it to be? Because this Hell is his idea of Hell?"

"You lead, Jim—but I just can't follow you."

"I don't blame you, because the idea is too preposterous. We know that someplace named Heaven exists someplace, somewhere. If there is one place there could be others. This is one of the others. With certain unusual properties."

"Like what?"

"Like you see what you expect to see. Let us say this planet or whatever it is was a place that was just a possibility of a place—until Slakey arrived. Then it became the place he was expecting to find. Maybe the red sun got him thinking about Hell. And the more he thought the more Hellish it became. Makes good sense."

"It certainly does not! That's about the most flakey theory I have ever heard."

"You bet it is—and more than that. Absolutely impossible. But we are here, aren't we?"

"Living in another man's Hell?"

"Yes. We did that when we first came here. But we didn't like it and wanted to leave it. I remember thinking that the barren, volcanic world was just about the opposite of the one where I grew up. . . ."

It was my turn to wonder if this whole thing wasn't just institutionalized madness. But Sybil was more practical.

"All right then—let us say that was what happened. We arrived in this Hellish place because Slakey had come here first and everything—what can we say—lived up to his devilish expectations. We didn't like it and you wished very strongly we weren't there but in a place with a better climate. You got very angry about that, which may have helped shaped what we wanted to see. Then we walked on and came to it. We drank, but we were still hungry. Rather I was, so much so I must have thought of my earliest gustatory delights. Which just happened to be in Hometown. Given that all this is true—what do we do next?"

"The only thing that we can do. Go back to Hell."

"Why?"

"Because that is where we came in—and where we must be if we want to get out. Slakey is the only one that knows how to pass between these places. And another thing . . ." My voice was suddenly grim.

"What, Jim? What is it?"

"Just the sobering thought that Angelina may have been sent to this place before we were dispatched. If so, we won't find her in my youth or your youth. She would have to be in Slakey's particular Hell."

"Right," she said, standing and brushing the grass from her dress. "If we are thirsty we can always find our way back here. If we are hungry—"

"Please save that thought for awhile. One step at a time."

"Of course. Shall we go?"

We retraced our steps back through the field and into the forest. A distant, happy grunting cheered me up a good deal. As long as there were porcuswine in existence this galaxy would not be that bad a place. Out of the trees and across the field of grass. That grew sparser and shorter until it disappeared. Volcanic soil again and more than a whiff of sulfur about. The mounds were getting higher as we walked and we labored to climb an even higher one. When we reached the summit we had a clear view of a smoking volcano. It appeared to be the first of very many. And behind it the red sun, which was hovering just above the horizon.

The dunes ended in foothills of cracked and crumbled stone. Red of course. The cleft of a small canyon cut into them and we went that way. A lot easier than climbing another hill. We both heard the scratching sound at the same time; we stopped.

"Wait here," I whispered. "I'll see what it is."

"I go with you, diGriz. We are in this together—all the way."

She was right of course. I nodded and touched my finger to my lips. We went on, as slowly and silently as we could. The scratching grew louder—then stopped. We stopped as well. There was a slurping wet sound from close by, then the scratching started again. We crept forward and looked.

A man was standing on tiptoes, reaching above his head with a shard of rock, scratching at something gray on the cliff face. A piece of it came away and he jammed it into his mouth and began chewing noisily.

This was most interesting. Even more interesting was the fact that he was bright red. His only garment a pair of ancient faded trousers with most of the legs torn off. There was obviously a hole in the seat of these ragged shorts because his red tail emerged from them.

That was when he saw us. Turned in an instant and gaped open a damp mouth with broken black teeth—then hurled the piece of rock in our direction. We ducked as the stone clattered into the stone wall close by. In that instant he was gone, swarming up the sloping cliff face with amazing agility, vanishing over the rim above.

"Red . . ." Sybil said.

"Very red. Did you notice the little red horns on his forehead?"

"Hard to miss. Shall we go see what he was doing?"

"Doing—and eating."

I picked up a sharp fragment of stone and went over to the spot where he had been working. There was a gray and rubbery looking growth protruding from a crevice in the canyon wall. I was taller than our rosy friend and could easily reach it; sliced and chopped at it until a piece fell free.

"What is it?" Sybil asked.

"No idea. Vegetable not animal I imagine. And we did see him chewing it. Want a bite?"

"I wouldn't think of depriving you."

It tasted very gray and slimy, and was very, very chewy. With all the taste and texture of a plastic bag. But it was wet. I swallowed and a piece went down. And stayed down. My stomach rumbled a long complaint.

"Try some," I said. "It's pretty foul but it has water in it and maybe some food value." I tore off a chunk and held it out. Very suspiciously she put it into her mouth. I looked up—jumped and grabbed her and pushed her aside.

A boulder thudded into the spot where we had been standing.

"Angry at losing his dinner," I said. "Let's move out away from the rocks, where we can see what's happening."

We had a quick glimpse of him climbing higher still and finally moving out of sight.

"You stay here," I said. "Keep an eye out for Big Red. I'll get more of this gunge."

The sun did not seem to be appreciably higher in the sky when we had finished our meal. Stomachs full enough, and thirst slaked for the moment, we rested in the shade because the day was growing measurably warmer.

"Not good, but filling," Sybil said, working with her fingernail to dislodge a gristly bit that had lodged between her teeth. When it came free she looked at it disparagingly, then dropped it to the ground. "Any idea what we do next?"

"Put our brains into gear for starters. Since we woke up in this place we have been stumbling from one near-disaster to another. Let's check off what we know."

"Firstly," she said, "we've gone to Slakey's version of Hell. We'll call it that until we learn better. We are in another place—on another planet—or we have gone mad."

"I can't accept that last. We *are* someplace else. We know that machines are involved in this—because they were carefully destroyed in the building on Lussuoso. Angelina was sent someplace from that temple. We were sent someplace from the one on Vulkann. We know that for certain—and we know something even more important. A return trip is possible. You went to Heaven and came back. And we must consider the possibility that Angelina could have come here before us."

"Which means that we need some intelligence—in the military use of the word."

"You bet. Which in turn means we have to find Big Red with the horns and tail and find out all that he knows. About Angelina, about this place, how he—and we—got here. And how we are going to leave . . ."

A sound intruded, a soft, shuffling sound that grew slowly louder. Coming up the canyon floor towards us. Then we could hear the susurration of muttered voices.

"People—" I said as our recently departed devilish friend walked into view. He was followed by a small group of companions, at least twelve of them. Men and women. All bright red. All carrying sharp rocks. I had never seen any of them before—and one glance told me that Angelina was not in this motley crowd. They stopped when they saw us—then started forward when their leader waved them on.

"You can flee, should you wish, but we'll come after you. Run or stay, it makes no difference." He shook the rock at us.

"We are going to kill you. Kill you and eat you.

"Hell is a very hungry place."

CHAPTER 7

I HELD MY HAND UP to them, palm out, the universal sign of peace. Maybe. "Wait," I said. "If you attack us we will be forced to defend ourselves. And we are very dangerous. You will all be hurt, killed if you dare resist us. We are not normal humans but are ruthless killers . . ."

"Dinner!" Red Leader foamed. "Kill!"

I cupped my raised hand, raised the other in defense-offense position, balanced forward on the balls of my feet.

Sybil was at my side, hands held in the same way. "You didn't mean that about killing them—did you?"

"No—but I want them afraid so we can finish this quickly. Now!"

We screamed loudly in unison and attacked. Big Red shrieked and dropped his weapon when I chopped his wrist with the edge of my hand, following through with stiff fingertips into his solar plexus. Went on without stopping and kicked the legs out from under the two people behind him.

I was aware that Sybil had moved to the side to take her antagonists off guard and off balance. Two sharp kidney punches sent two women screaming to the ground.

The stone swung down and I went under it and hit the

wielder on the side of the neck, stepped aside as he fell.

A few more brisk blows and it was all over. The ground was covered with writhing, moaning, red figures. A hand reached out for a rock and I stepped on the wrist. That was the last resistance.

"They are a sorry and feeble lot," Sybil said, dusting of her hands disgustedly.

"No other way to handle it. No broken bones that I can see, and no blood." We picked up the stone weapons and threw them aside. Looked more closely at our battered assailants. They were dressed, if it could be called that, in a tattered and faded collection of clothing fragments. Bits of anatomy, normally concealed, poked out. All of them were bright red with neat little horns and, now flaccid, tails. They drew cravenly aside as I walked between them and picked up their unconscious leader, propped him against the rock wall and waited for him to come around. He groaned and opened his eyes—shrieked and fell over and tried to scrabble away. I straightened him up again.

"Look," I told him. "All the killing and eating was your idea. We were just defending ourselves. Can we call it quits? Just nod your head, that's better. I think we started off on the wrong foot so let's try again. My name is Jim . . ."

There was a thud and a cry of pain from behind me, proof that Sybil was covering my back.

"My name is . . . Cuthbert Podpisy, Professor of Comparative Anatomy, University of Wydawnietwo."

"Please to meet you, Professor. Aren't you a long way from home?"

He rubbed at his sore midriff, looked up at me with bleary red eyes. And sighed.

"I suppose I am. I haven't thought about that very much of late. The hunger and thirst tend to dominate one's consciousness. All we wanted was a bit of protein." He whimpered a bit, feeling very sorry for himself. "The diet is monotonous and not very filling. Lacks many amino acids I am sure. As well as minerals and vitamins."

"The gray stuff you were eating off the rock. That's your diet?"

"The same. It is called colimicon. I don't know what it means. I was told the word when I first came here."

"How did you get here?" Sybil asked, coming over to stand beside me—but not taking her eyes off the battered execution squad.

"I have no idea. I was on term leave, I went to this holiday world. To enjoy myself on the Vulkann beaches. It was all very nice and I had a good tan, not red like this, and I was putting on weight from overeating, destroying my liver with over-drinking, you know. . . . All I can remember is that I went to bed one night—and woke up here."

"How about the others?"

"The ones I have talked to say just about the same thing. The others are mad, they don't talk. It seems that the longer you are here . . . are you going to kill me?"

"Don't be foolish. I've eaten some strange meals in my time but draw the line at professors."

"You say that now, but—"

"I promise, all right? And speaking of professors—have you ever heard of a Professor Justin Slakey?"

"No. Rings no bells. Mine is a small university."

"All right. Now tell me about your red relations here. You said that people arrive here. Do any leave?"

"Only as dinner!" He cackled and drooled a bit around his blackened teeth, not as sane as he had first appeared to be. I changed the subject.

"If you are an anatomy professor perhaps you can explain your interesting skin color. Not to mention your little horns and tail."

He pinched a handful of loose skin at his midriff and blinked at it. "Very interesting," he said in a distant voice. "I used to study the phenomena, take notes, tried to take notes. Not pigmentation at all. I believe the color change to be due to enhanced capillary growth beneath the skin. Ahh, the tail." He groped for his and caressed it. "Might be added bones to the coccyx. Not possible, bone growth though, yes, or cartilage . . ."

I left him mumbling there and waved Sybil to one side where we could keep an eye on the others. Not that they appeared to be any threat. Some were still unconscious while the others sat or lay placidly as though drained of energy. One young man dragged himself to his feet and looked at us with obvious fear. When we did nothing he stumbled away, around the bend in the canyon and out of sight.

"I don't like this at all," Sybil said.

"I never liked it—and I like it even less the longer we stay here. These people aren't natives. They've been brought here. Dumped in this place for some unfathomable reason. At least we know who is responsible. We've got to find our way back— before we end up like these. Am I beginning to turn red yet?"

"No—but you're right. We've got to resist. But what can we do? Is there any point in going back to Hometown—or to your porcuswine?"

"None that I can think of at the moment . . ."

The sky darkened for an instant and we staggered, suddenly heavy. The phenomenon passed as quickly as it had begun. Gravity waves? I didn't let my thoughts dwell on it. What could we possibly do to save ourselves?

"Collect as much of the colimicon as we can carry," I said firmly. "Food and drink will keep us alive, give us a chance to take the next step. . . ." Inspiration failed me, but Sybil was thinking too.

"Go back to the cave where we woke up. We were in such bad shape we didn't search it well. Looking for what—I have no idea."

"But you have a good idea. Whatever brought us here dumped us on that particular spot. It needs a much closer look." I pointed to the sprawled, scarlet figures. "What about this lot?"

"There is nothing we can do for them—not now. Perhaps when we get back, get some answers. Maybe then we can do something. They are alive, so at least they know how to survive. And they did try to kill us."

"Point taken. Let's get moving."

We found some more colimicon and pried rubbery chunks from the rock crevasses. They were difficult to carry until Sybil turned her long skirt into a mini by ripping off a great length of the fabric. "And it's cooler like this," she said as she neatly knotted our food and drink into a bundle. I took it from her and pointed.

"Lead the way."

I did not dare think how long the days here were since the sun appeared to be just as high in the sky as it had been when we first saw it. Perhaps the planet did not rotate on its axis at all and this day was a million years long. We plodded on. Back towards the opening in the rocks where this whole depressing action had begun.

We started up one of the gravel dunes and I stumbled over a largish fragment, fell forward.

Saw the eruption of fragments from the sudden, small pit, heard the missile ricochet away.

"Move!" I shouted. "Someone's shooting at us!"

Sybil was running towards some broken boulders as I did a sideways roll and scrambled to my feet. More shots followed us, but a fast-moving target is hard to hit. I slid, gasping, into the lee of a giant boulder, saw that Sybil had reached shelter as well.

"Where's the sniper?" she called out.

"Top of the slope we were climbing. I had a quick glimpse, just something moving."

"Any particular color?"

"The local favorite."

"Next?"

"Get our breath back. Then spread out and hunt the hunter. Sorry but I dropped our supplies. We'll worry about that later. After we find this redskin. All right with you?"

"Agreed. Whoever it is I want him in front of me rather than behind."

I made the first rush, slanting across the hill then sheltering behind a boulder. A shot hit the rock, sending fragments clattering; another hit the ground. But even as our ambusher was firing Sybil was running just as I had done.

In rushing spurts we slowly made our way up the hill. Our attacker kept shooting; he appeared to have plenty of ammunition.

We were approaching the summit when I saw him. Big, red, running for better cover, a sack over one shoulder, carrying a long-barreled weapon of some kind. I sprinted in his tracks, going fast. I dived again for the shelter of a boulder when he turned and fired. I saw Sybil angle away around the top of the hill while he blasted shot after shot in my direction.

The end came suddenly. I heard him fire in the other direction; he must have seen her. I put my head down and plowed up the slope as fast I could. There he was a few meters away, turning the gun towards me—when a fast-thrown rock caught him in the back. He squealed, jumped—tried to aim.

And I was on him. Twisting the gun away and kicking him hard in the chest. He shrieked again as he fell; the sack dropped from his shoulder, spilling out shiny tubes.

Sybil stumbled up, as exhausted as I was, and looked down at our fallen adversary. He was fat and he was red, with the now normal horns and tail. But he was very familiar. He scrambled backwards, turned to look for a way to escape and I saw his profile.

"It can't be! But he looks like—" Sybil finished the sentence for me.

"It could be Slakey!"

"Or Master Fanyimadu or Father Marablis."

He was that familiar. But of course this could not be. He looked at us with wide eyes, trembling, frightened. Spoke.

"Have we . . . met before?"

"Perhaps," I said, "My name is diGriz. Is that familiar?"

"Not really. Any relation to the Grodzynskis?"

"Not to my knowledge. And your name is . . . ?"

"That's a good question. It might be—Einstein?" He looked hopeful, then stopped smiling when I shook my head *no*.

"Wrong answer. Do Mitchelsen or Morley sound familiar? Epinard?"

"Yes, those names are familiar," Sybil said. "They were all physicists. They're all dead."

"Physics!" He brightened up at that and pointed in the direction of the bloated sun. "Burning continues always. But the nucleus isn't stable, you see. The core, a Fermi sphere. Then the nucleus, lithium not stable . . ."

"Professor . . . ?" I called out.

"Yes? What? But those nuclei simply break up again."

He closed his eyes and swayed slowly back and forth muttering to himself softly all the time.

"He's mad," Sybil said firmly. I nodded agreement.

"Like the others—only more so. But he's saying something about physics. And he did respond when I called him professor."

"There are a lot of professors around."

"Too true." I picked up the gun and turned it in my hands. "And where did he get this? It's in good condition, fires all too well." I tapped a dial on the butt, fully charged, then pointed to the spilled tubes on the ground. "You recognize the weapon?"

"Of course. Linear accelerator gun. The military calls them Gauss rifles."

"Exactly. No moving parts, lots of juice in the nuclear battery—with plenty more steel slugs in these tubes. How did it get here? Do you remember what happened to all that gear that I brought with me, mechanical and electronic? None of it would work. We've seen no other artifacts—until this."

Our demonic friend stopped muttering, saw the gun and jumped to grab it. Sybil put out a foot and he sprawled onto his face. I held the gun up so he could see it.

"Professor—where did you get this?"

"Mine. I gave me the . . . " He looked around bewilderedly. Lay down and closed his eyes and appeared to be asleep.

"Not exactly a bubbling font of information," Sybil said.

"I think this madness is catching—or grows on you the longer you stay here."

"Agreed. So let's go back to the original plan. The cave."

"The cave." I retrieved and shouldered the bag, seized up the gun and ammunition. We looked back as we walked but he never stirred.

"Do you get the feeling that the longer we are in Hell the more questions there are to ask—and the fewer answers?" Sybil nodded glum agreement. Then pointed.

"Isn't that it ahead? The opening in the rocks?"

"Looks like it."

I felt more depressed than I had ever been before in my life. Which says a lot since I have been in some very depressing situations. This search for the cave was a token gesture born of desperation. If there had been any device, any machine—anything at all in the cave—we would have seen it before we left. This was a dead end.

As we approached the cave entrance there was a cracking explosion of sound inside, accompanied by a sudden burst of bright light. Sybil dived aside and I raised the gun, flipped on the power.

Scraping footsteps sounded from inside the cave, something horrible coming towards us. I sighted along the barrel, put steady pressure on the trigger as a man appeared in the entrance.

"Throw that away and come with me—quickly!" my son said.

"Coming, Bolivar!" Sybil shouted as she ran. "We're right behind you!"

CHAPTER 8

I DROPPED THE GUN AND the bag of ammunition, the colimicon, and ran—with Sybil right behind me. Bolivar led the way, stumbled to a halt towards the rear of the cave. He looked around, shuffled his feet. "No, more to the left," he mumbled. "Back, back. Good."

"Fast!" he shouted, raising his arms. "Take my hands!"

We weren't arguing. He seized our hands and, with a powerful muscular contraction, pulled us tight against his chest. I opened my mouth to speak—

It was a completely indescribable sensation. It was like nothing I had ever experienced before, had no relation to heat or pain, cold, emotions, electrocution.

Then it ended; bright light flared and there was a thunderous sound.

"Get down!" someone shouted and Bolivar dragged us after him to the floor of the room. Rapid explosions sounded, gunfire. I had a quick glimpse of a man firing a handweapon, clumsily, for when the gun recoiled he dropped it. From his left hand; his right arm was bandaged. He turned then and ran, followed by other running footsteps.

"James!" Bolivar cried out.

"Fine, fine," a muffled voice answered. He came out from behind the ruins of the burning machine. His face was smeared black and he was brushing glowing embers from his shirt. "Very close. Good thing he wasn't shooting at me. He did a good job on the electronics though."

"Thanks, boys, for getting us back," I said, then coughed raspingly. "My throat hurts like Hell."

There was a hiss of white fumes and the fires were blotted out by the automatic quenchers. An alarm was ringing in the distance.

"Explain later," James said. "Let's get out before anyone else shows up."

I didn't argue. Still numb from the events of the past day. Day? We ran out of the church, it was night, the van was parked at the curb just where we had seen it last—how long ago?

"Into the back," James ordered. He started the engine as the rest of us struggled in through the open rear doors. Barely had time to close them before he kicked in the power. We sprawled and rolled and heard the sound of sirens getting louder—then dying away as the van broadsided around a corner. He slowed after that, drove at what must have been something like normal speed. Turned a few more times and stopped. James spun his driver's seat around to face us and smiled.

"Drinks, anyone?"

Through the windshield a large rotating sign was visible. RODNEY'S ROBOT DRINKING DEN with CHEAPEST AND MOST ALCOHOLIC DRINKS IN TOWN in smaller lettering below. A robotic face appeared at the window. "Welcome to this drunkards' paradise. Orders, please," it grated.

"Four large beers," I told it, then coughed uncontrollably.

"Tell us what happened," Sybil said when I had gasped into silence.

"Sure," Bolivar said. "But first—are you guys all right?" Looking at us intently, relaxing only when we had nodded our heads. "Good, great. You gave us a scare, Dad, when the alarm went off."

"I didn't think that I had time to actuate it."

"You didn't. We only knew something was wrong when your heart stopped. We hit hard then."

"It never stopped!" I said defensively, grabbing at the pulse in my wrist. A nice solid thud-thud.

"That's good to hear. But we didn't know that at the time. We must have broken in just seconds after you went to Hell. Marablis, wearing some kooky outfit, was still working the controls. Bolivar got him with the stunner as he was turning around."

"I dropped him—but you were both gone. That explained the stopped heartbeat. You had been moved, transported, sent—to Hell as we found out. James took care of that. Advanced hypnotism, he's very good."

"Been a bit of a hobby for some years. Marablis was an easy subject. Stress and shock. I eased him under and took control. He told us that he had sent you both to Hell. Bolivar said that he would go after you. I had Marablis work the machine and you know the rest. It was a long five minutes but it worked out fine in the end."

I should have been immune to surprises by this time. I wasn't. "Five minutes! We were in Hell for hours—most of a day at least."

"Different time scales?" Bolivar said. "And I'll tell you something else just as outré. When I was in Hell I was here at the same time, I mean I could see what Bolivar was seeing, hear him speaking."

"And vice versa—"

"Beer," a tinny voice said and Sybil and I leaped forward.

"Four more," Bolivar said as we drained our glasses. He handed us the two remaining full ones.

The cold liquid helped. Gasping with pleasure, my brain got back into gear and I remembered something else. "James! The shooting when we arrived—what happened?"

"Just that. As you were coming back through, this guy burst in waving a gun. I dived for cover while he shot up the machinery. Then he and Marablis ran for it."

"I had a quick look at him," I said. "It couldn't have been, but . . ."

James nodded solemnly. "I could see him very clearly. It was Professor Slakey—with a bandage on the stump of his right wrist."

"Then who, who—?" I said, doing a stunned owl imitation.

"Who was at the controls, you mean? Who sent you to Hell and brought you back? That was also Professor Slakey. Working the controls with his good right hand."

"I have more news," I said. "There is a bright-red, long-tailed and behorned Slakey in Hell."

The silence got longer and longer as we considered the implications, or lack of them, in this information, until Sybil spoke. "James, whistle for the waiter if you please. Order up a bottle of something a bit stronger for the next round."

Nobody argued with that. Everything had happened so fast—and so incomprehensibly—that I had trouble pulling my thoughts together. Then memory struck hard.

"Angelina? Where is she?"

"Not in Hell," James said. "That was the first question I asked Marablis when I put him under. He admitted that much under stress. Fought hard not to answer where she was, almost surfaced from the trance. I put him deep under to bring you two back from Hell. When you were back safe I was going to press him really hard for an answer. But—you know what happened. Sorry . . ."

"No sorry!" I shouted happily. "Angelina is not dead—but has been sent somewhere. Maybe Heaven. We'll find out. Meanwhile, you got us back. Sorry is not the word to use. We'll have to try and work out what happened, what all these puzzles and paradoxes mean. But not right now. There are two things that we must urgently do now. We have to get help. And we've been compromised enough. Slakey knew about Sybil and me when he knocked us out. Now he knows the whole family is after him. He might try and fight back so we have to stay away from the hotel room. And we must contact the Special Corps at once."

"All I need is a phone," Sybil said. "I have a local contact number that will be spliced through directly to Inskipp."

"Perfect. We outline what has happened. Tell him to order a tight guard around that church. No one is to go either in or out. Then tell him to get Professor Coypu here soonest. Anyone who can build a working time machine as well as many other scientific miracles certainly ought to be able to figure out just what is going on with these Hell and Heaven machines. We'll stay out of sight until the professor has arrived—along with the Space Marines. Never forget—we have been to Hell and we came back. We're going to find Angelina and get her back with us the same way."

I suppose that I should have enjoyed the days of forced relaxation at the Vaska Hulja Holiday Heaven, but I had too much to worry about. Always lurking behind all the pleasures of swimming and sunbathing, drinking and eating, was the knowledge that Angelina was still missing. There was some reassurance in the fact that her kidnappers had admitted that she was alive, though not where she was. Small consolation; she was still gone and that could not be denied. A dark memory that would not go away. I knew that the twins shared these feelings, because behind all the horseplay and vying for Sybil's attention was that same memory. I would catch a bleakness of expression when one of them did not know he was being watched.

Nor was it all fun and games. We went to work. The first thing that we had done after checking into this hotel, with false identities, was to list everything we knew, had seen, had experienced. None of it seemed to make sense—yet we knew that it must. We forwarded all of this material to the Special Corps where, hopefully, wiser heads than ours might make sense of it.

They did. Or it did, a wiser head I mean. Our little trip to Hell seemed to have had a scrambling effect on my brain so at times my thoughts would dribble away. I also kept looking in mirrors to see if I was turning red. After awhile I stopped doing this—but I still felt the base of my spine when I was showering to see if I was growing a tail. Disconcerting. This feckless state of affairs ended next morning when I came down early for breakfast and saw a familiar figure at our table.

"Professor Coypu—at last!" I called out in glad greeting. He smiled briefly with his buckteeth popping out between his lips like yellowed gravestones.

"Ahh, Jim, yes. You're looking fit, skin tanned but not red. Any signs of a tail?"

"Thank you, no, I have been keeping track. And you?"

"Fine, fine. On my way here I examined the remains of the destroyed machines at the church and have analyzed all your notes, examined the clothing you wore in Hell, thank you. It all seems fairly straightforward."

"Straightforward! I see nothing but confusion and obfuscation where you . . ."

"See the forest as well as the trees. I can inform you in full confidence that inventing the temporal helix for my time machine was much more difficult." His teeth snapped off a piece of toast and he chewed it with quick rodent-like enthusiasm.

"You wouldn't care to chop some of that metaphorical wood for me—would you?"

"Yes, of course." He patted his lips with his napkin, giving his protruding teeth a surreptitious polish at the same time. "As soon as I discovered that Jiving Justin was involved in this matter, the shape of future things to come became clear . . ."

"Jiving Justin?" I burbled with complete lack of comprehension.

"Yes," he cackled, flashing his teeth at me. "That's what we used to call him at university."

"Who, who?" I was in owl overdrive again.

"Justin Slakey. He used to play the slide trombone in our little jazz quartet. I must admit to being fairly groovy myself on the banjo as well—"

"Professor! The point of it all, please—would you kindly return to it?"

"Of course. Even when I first met him, Slakey was a genius.

Old beyond his years—which considering the state of geriartrics might have been far older than he appeared. He took the theory of galactic strings, which as you undoubtedly know has been around as theory for a long time. No one had ever come close to tackling it until Slakey invented the mathematics to prove their existence. Even the theoretical wormtubes between galaxies were clear to him. He published some papers on these, but never put everything together into a coherent whole. At least, until now, I thought he hadn't completed his theory. It is obvious that he has."

He washed some more nibbled toast down with a quick swig of coffee. I resisted more owl imitations.

"Stop at once!" I suggested. "Start over since I haven't the slightest idea of what you are talking about."

"No reason that you should. The reality of the wormholes between one universe and another can only be described by negative number mathematics. A nonmathematical model would be only a crude approximation—"

"Then crudely approximate for me."

He chewed away, forehead furrowed in thought, unconsciously brushing away a strand of lank hair that floated down in front of his eyes. "Crudely put . . ."

"Yes?"

"*Very* crudely put, our universe is like a badly cooked fried egg. In a pan of equally badly cooked and stringy eggs." Breakfast had obviously inspired this imagery; I had eaten the eggs here before. "The frying pan represents space-time. But it must be an invisible frying pan since it has no dimensions and cannot be measured. Are you with me so far?"

"Yoke and all."

"Good. Entropy will always be the big enemy. Everything is running down, cooling down towards the heat death of the universe. If entropy could be reversed the problem would be easy to solve. But it cannot. But—" This was a big *but* since he raised an exclamatory finger and tapped his teeth. "But although entropy cannot be reversed, the rate of entropic decay can be measured and displayed, only by mathematics of course, and can be proven to proceed at a different rate in different universes. You see the importance of this?"

"No."

"Think! If the rate of entropy in our universe were faster than the rate of entropy in universe X, let us say. Then to a theoretical observer in that universe our universe would appear to be decaying at a great rate. Right?"

"Right."

"Then, it also becomes obvious that if an observer in our universe were to observe universe X, the entropy rate there would appear to be going in the opposite direction, what might be called *reverse* entropy. Though it does not exist it would be observed to exist. Therefore the equation is closed."

He sat back and smiled happily at his conclusions. I hadn't the slightest idea of what he was talking about. I told him that and he frowned.

"I do wish, diGriz, that you had taken a little more mathematics instead of playing hooky from school. To put it even more simply, a phenomenon that is observed to exist *does* exist and can be mathematically described. And what can be described can be affected. What can be affected can be altered. That is the beauty of it. No power source is needed to manipulate the wormholes between the universes, although energy is of course needed to establish the interface. The wormholes themselves are powered by the differences in their entropy rate. Justin Slakey has discovered that and I will be the first man to take my hat off to him."

He lifted an invisible hat from his head, then patted it back into place. I blinked quickly and cudgeled my brain hard, trying to understand just what he was talking about. With great difficulty some sort of order began to emerge from his flights of physical fancy.

"Tell me if I have this right. Different universes exist, right?"

"Yes and no . . ."

"Let's settle for the *yes*—just for a moment. Different universes exist, and if they exist they could be connected by wormholes in space. Then the difference of entropy between these universes might be used to travel through the wormholes from one galaxy to another—and Slakey has invented a machine to do just that. Okay?"

He raised the finger, frowned, shook his head in a very negative no. Thought a bit more, then shrugged. "Okay," he said in a most resigned manner. I hurried on before he changed his mind.

"Hell is a planet in a different universe, with different laws of physics, maybe a different chemistry, where time passes at a different rate. If that is so then Heaven is a different universe connected to ours by wormholes in space and time. There could be more . . ."

"The number of theoretical universes is infinite."

"But with Slakey's machine they can obviously be contacted, over and over again. And what he can do—you can do?"

"Yes and no."

I resisted the temptation to rip out a handful of my hair. "What do you mean yes and no?"

"I mean yes it is theoretically possible. And no, I cannot do it. Not without the mathematical description of the entropy relationships that was recorded in the machine. The one he destroyed."

"There will be other machines."

"Get me one and I'll build you an intergalactic wormhole subway."

"I will do just that," I promised. Not rashly but because I had to do just that to get to Angelina. Which led to the next obvious question. "Who has these machines?"

"Slakey."

"Which Slakey?"

"There is only one Slakey."

"I can't believe that. I saw three at least. One bright red with a tail. Another with no right hand—and a third with a good right hand."

"You saw the same man—only at different times. Just as if you were to take a time machine to visit a baby being born, then went on in time to see the same baby grown—then saw him again as an old man. The mathematics is quite clear. In some manner he has managed to duplicate himself at various times during his existence. He, they, him, are all the same individual, just observed at the same time though he is from various different times. Since they are all the same person they have to share the same thoughts. That's how Slakey no-hand knew that Slakey right-hand was in trouble and came to the rescue. You saw this same phenomenon with your own sons, the twins. Since they are biological twins and divided from the same original egg, they were at one time exactly the same person, or egg. So when they were in different universes they shared the same thoughts. It is all very obvious."

"What's obvious?" Sybil asked as she came into the breakfast room.

"What is obvious," I said, "is that we now know how to get to Heaven and Hell—or wherever else we want to go. The good professor appears to know all about these various universes."

She nodded. "If you know that Professor—do you know how Jim found his porkuswine in Hell?"

"I do. I read your notes concerning that visit and I agree completely with your first conclusions. Hell is obviously a malleable and unformed universe. It must have been geologically active when Slakey first found it. He mistook it for Hell—so it became Hell. You both found his Hell, but also formed a little bit of your remembered worlds there as well."

"Then a question, please?" Sybil asked. "If we did that— why didn't the other people we found there do the same thing?"

"Also obvious," the professor pontificated, always happy with an expectant audience. "They were normal people—not supernormal Special Corps agents. The force of your personalities and your mental strength enabled you to force your memories upon the fabric of that universe, to bend it to your will. Where normal people might run in fear you turn and growl savagely and rend your enemies."

"You make us sound like feral terriers, wild dogs!" I growled savagely,

"You are. Any more questions?"

"Yes. What happens next?" Sybil said.

"I can answer that," I answered. "With Professor Coypu's help we will build a machine to travel to these distant universes. And we will get Angelina back."

"That is wonderful news. But let us not do any of that until after breakfast," she added with womanly practicality. "I'm sure that we will need all our strength to do all of that."

CHAPTER 9

I WAITED UNTIL JAMES AND Bolivar had joined us at the breakfast table, and had eaten their stringy eggs, before I brought them all up to speed.

"Meeting come to order." They all looked intently at me—with the exception of Professor Coypu who was muttering to himself as he scrawled mathematical equations onto a large scratchpad. "The professor will not mind if I simplify drastically what he revealed to me this morning. Heaven and Hell are in different universes and we can get to them. Plus there are other universes we can reach—and Angelina is in one of them. With a little help from us he can build a machine that we can use to get her back. Understood?"

Everyone nodded and smiled. Except for Coypu, who sniffed miffedly. He could apparently do two things at one time because, while still noodling his equations, he spoke.

"Your simplification is utter nonsense. These equations prove . . ."

"That you know what you are doing," I broke in before everything got murky again. "And we know what we are going to do. We are going to find one of the Slakey clones. Unless they used their machine to leave this planet, they must still be here.

I had the Special Corps put the pressure on the local military to seal this planet tight. Like a roach motel they can come in but they can't go out. An intense and thorough search has been going on at this moment . . ."

"Let the Slakeys go," Sybil said.

Silence descended. Even Coypu stopped writing. Sybil smiled sweetly at her stunned audience. "Think latterly," she said. "Think subtly. The trouble with you men is that all the testosterone and other hormones you have whizzing around your systems tend to make your actions very predictable. So try to be a little more devious, just this once. These men you are looking for, Slakey and Company, are just as masculine as the rest of you and will be expecting you to do what you are planning to be doing."

"Then what should we do?" I asked.

"Ease up, allow for loopholes and human error. Let them test the doors until they find one unlocked. When they get out have them followed."

"That won't be easy . . ."

"Yes it will," Coypu said. "I have been considering a new and unique theory about the effects of inter-universe travel," he held up his pages of equations, "that I have now proved to my satisfaction is true. It is called entropic delimitation."

He smiled with scientific satisfaction, so pleased with himself that he tapped happily on his teeth with his fingernails, looked around at our glazed stares.

"I will elucidate. When you were in Hell you observed that certain changes occurred to people there. Skin color became encarmined, new appendages grew, insanity progressed. These equations prove positively that the changes are not physical in the sense that they are made by chemicals in the atmosphere and so forth. No indeed. These changes are caused by entropic delimitation, the basic incompatibility of material taken from one universe to another. Once I had realized this it was simplicity itself to construct an E-meter. A machine that embodies immense possibilities while remaining simple in construction. Here it is."

He dug around in his shirt pocket, took out something small and placed it carefully on the table. We all leaned close.

"It looks like a stone tied to a piece of string," I said.

"It is. When I analyzed your reports and saw the direction in which my researchers were going, I took the precaution of obtaining some Hell-matter. From your discarded clothing, Jim. There were bits of gravel in your pockets, from all that slithering about on the ground I imagine. Now—the proof of the pudding is in the eating."

He picked up the string by the loose end, stood and walked over towards me. Stopped and held this complicated scientific device out so that the stone was suspended just before my nose. I looked at it cross-eyedly.

"Is it moving?" he asked.

"It seems to be swinging towards me."

"It is. You were in Hell long enough for entropic delimitation to affect your body, if ever so slightly." He held the thing out over Sybil's hand and nodded happily. Then walked to the twins, held it in turn behind one head and then the other. He pointed at James.

"You are the brother who operated the machine and did not pass through to Hell."

James could only nod in silence. Coypu admired his invention. "If I can get this strong a response after such a brief transit—just think how Jiving Justin will light up in the dark! As soon as I have manufactured a few thousand meters, simple enough to do, all the restrictions on free movement will be lifted. No attempt will be made to apprehend the miscreants or stop them from leaving—"

"Great!" I cried aloud gustily. "They can run but they cannot hide. Every train, bus, spaceship, scooter, rickshaw, every form of transportation, will have a meter close by. We'll follow them and they will lead us to another of their machines and we will grab it and the good guys will win!"

Of course it didn't happen that easily. Instead of trying to run, Slakey and Slakey had apparently gone to ground. When they didn't walk into any of our traps, the good Professor

Coypu went back to the workbench and improved upon his original model. Which, all things considered, was pretty crude. He built larger ones with amplifying circuits that would work over greater distances. Then military jets quartered the skies over the islands—and had a trace within hours.

"Here," the Special Corps technician said, opening up a large map and tapping his finger on a red-marked site. We all leaned close. "The pilot of the search plane took off, circled for altitude—and all the bells went off."

"That is right in the middle of a city," I said.

"It certainly is. In fact it is the center of the capital of this planet, Hammar City. The first reading we had almost blew the needle off its bearings. And it hasn't moved since we spotted it. But there are two other, weaker traces in the city—and one of them is moving."

"Is it possible—that there could be another machine, which would explain the strong trace? And the other contacts might be a couple of Slakeys?"

"Professor Coypu is of the same opinion. He says if you plan to take any offensive actions you must speak to him first."

"No problem. Where is he?"

"In the nightclub downstairs doing research."

"Research . . . ?" It was mind-boggling time again. "But which club? There are seven in this hotel."

"The Green Lizard. Very ethnic."

I wondered what could be ethnic about lizards; I soon found out. The sound of jungle drums filled the hot, moist air, while the screams of nocturnal animals cut through the semidarkness. I ducked under the low leaves of the trees and almost choked myself on a vine.

"May I be of service, human visitor?" a large green lizard said, smiling fangedly before me. While the head was that of a lizard the green body was human and enthusiastically female. Painted green I realized, this fact was visible even in the dim jungle light. Also visible was the even more interesting fact that paint on skin was all that she was wearing; nothing else. I wondered just what kind of research the professor was doing here.

"Coypu," I said. "I'm joining him. Small man, gray hair, good teeth . . ."

"This way, please, dear human visitor." She led me through the jungle—a fine figure to follow!—to a log table. Coypu sat on a chair stump just as naked, though not as attractive, as my leading lizard. He was sucking at the straw of a tall drink in a section of bamboo while he scribbled equations on a large leaf.

"I'll have whatever he has," I said, then forced my gaze back on the professor when she slithered away.

"Ahh, Jim, sit down."

"I don't want to interrupt your work."

"You're not. I have just finished with all of my research. So that tomorrow I'll be able to finalize my scientific paper titled 'Saurian Substitutions for Reenhancing Subliminal Sexual Inhibitions.' "

"Sounds fascinating."

"Indeed it does. I'm also writing a shorter and more popular version for the Internet called 'Chicklist for Hungry Hunters.' "

"You're onto a winner. What did you want to talk to me about?"

"Plans. We must find a fail-safe way of getting our hands on an intact model of Slakey's universal differentiator. My research cannot proceed until that has been done. Twice now his machines have gone up in flames before they could be examined. Let us try not to let that happen again. I have constructed a device that will make that possible."

"What is it?"

"A temporal inhibitor. An intellectual offspring of my temporal helix. Which you will remember, since you traveled on it, when you traveled back in time and had some interesting adventures while you were busy saving the world. You deserve some credit in this invention as well. You will also remember that when you saved the Special Corps from time attack you met those time travelers from the future, who gave you a machine. It froze everyone around you with a time stasis. Once I knew it could be done the rest was easy."

"You're a great man, Professor."

"I know that. Finish your drink and sally forth. You'll find the temporal inhibitor, or TI for short, on the table in my room. It works just like the one you used before. Turn it on and everything around you freezes in time. Except for you, of course. Go, Jim, go forth with the TI and use it to get the dimensional machine. Leave me now for I have important research to do here and you are a married man."

I went. Picked the lock on his suite and looked at the flashlight on the table. I picked it up and turned it on. Instead of lighting up it hummed industriously. Nothing else appeared to have happened that I could see. I turned it off, dug a coin out of my pocket and threw it into the air, turned on the flashlight. The coin hung in midair, dropped only when I turned the TI off.

"Next stop Hammar City!"

I used the room phone to call the suite where the boys were staying. There was a recorded message for me suggesting that I join them in Waterworld, the most popular nightspot in the hotel. I slipped the TI into my pocket and left, and found the nightspot easily enough, following the sound of wet music and splashing waves. But I hesitated at the entrance, having had more than enough of nightclubs after the Green Lizard. This one was better lit and provided more clean-cut fun. With the lighting effects and almost nul gravity field, the illusion of being underwater was very good. The waitresses had mermaid tails and swam laden trays of drinks and food to the floating tables. The happy customers danced a few feet off the floor, twining themselves sinuously about to the happy beat. I could see Bolivar dancing with Sybil, both enjoying themselves greatly. He didn't seem to mind when James cut in—or was it the other way around? Not that it mattered. They were young and in high spirits and deserved every bit of relaxation they could get. I could take care of getting the machine myself while they danced the night away.

I was picking up some needed devices from my room when the phone pinged and turned itself on. Inskipp glared out of the screen at me.

"What do you think you are doing, diGriz?"

"Just running a little errand. Picking up something for Professor Coypu," I said innocently. A scowl replaced the glare.

"No you're not—at least not alone. I know everything, remember. Including exactly what it is you are getting for Coypu. There have been too many mistakes made of late. Sloppy work. That practice ends now. Captain Grissle of the Space Marines has his squad waiting for you in the lobby at this very moment."

"Thank you, thank you, you are kindness itself. I'll join him right away."

I would of course exit from the back entrance of the hotel and avoid the noxious military presence of the marines. There was a loud hammering on the door.

"While the squad is waiting in the lobby that will be the captain coming for you now. Go."

I seized up the TI and thought of using it on the marine, but the snarl from the phone changed all that.

"I'm watching you, diGriz—no games!"

I muttered a few favorite profanities under my breath as I opened the door. A burly marine with nasty tiny red eyes and a jaw like an anvil was standing outside. He saluted a quivering tense salute. I touched the flashlight-TI to my brow.

"Transportation to the airport is waiting," he shouted. "After you, sir."

It was all very well organized; at least the Special Corps could get this kind of thing right. Marines stamping, guns waving, sirens wailing; the usual. Captain Grissle briefed me on the way, ticking off the points with a raised finger.

"One. The Hammar City police have the area where we are going under close observation. Investigation has shown that the machine you are looking for is in a meeting hall owned by an organization called the Circle of Sanctity. Very exclusive, bigwig politicians and industrialists. Some of the members of this group are being interrogated right now."

"Do you know what this whole operation is about?"

"I do, Agent diGriz. I have been in on this investigation from the very beginning. Point two. Unlike the other churches involved in this investigation, this operation appears to be all male. Instead of looking forward to Heaven, this lot is into money—and power. An industrialist named Baron Krümmung seems to be in charge."

"They get rich, he gets richer."

"That's it."

"Identification?"

"Positive. A bit older, fatter and balder. But he's Slakey, no doubt at all."

Another incarnation. How many of them were there knocking around the galaxy? Depressing thought—there could be any number, armies of the same man, images clicked at different points in time. And all of them sharing the same thoughts and memories. That didn't seem possible—I decided not to even think about it.

"How do you want to handle this operation?" the captain asked.

"Am I in charge?"

"Completely. Orders received from the highest level."

"Inskipp?"

"None other."

"He's getting mellow in his old age."

"I doubt that. We follow your instructions exactly. As long as I and my two sergeants are with you at all times."

CHAPTER 10

THE FLIGHT IN THE BALLISTIC-ORBIT SST did not take very long at all. Plenty of G's at each end, acceleration and deceleration, with free fall in between. I slept when we were weightless, found it to be very relaxing indeed. And I had plenty of sleep to catch up with. Ground transportation, and another marine officer, a lieutenant this time, were waiting for us. There was a lot of snapping of stiff salutes, so dear to the military heart. I waited impatiently until all thumbs were back on seams on trouser legs.

"Tell me, Lieutenant, has anything changed since the last report?"

"Negative, sir. The detectors are keeping track of the two individuals just as before. They have not moved again and we have kept our distance from them. Neither of them is in the vicinity of the machine."

"Do they have any idea they are being tracked?"

"Negative. We have never approached them—never even seen them in fact. Our orders were to keep distant observation until you had secured the machine."

"I'll do that now. Lead the way."

I was keeping this operation as simple as possible since I

didn't want a third goof-up. The front door to the building was already open and secured; more marines were keeping out of sight inside. My armed guard trotted behind me when I trotted, stopped when I stopped.

"Tell me again," I whispered. The lieutenant pointed to high, double doors at the end of the hall.

"That's it, where they meet. It is a conference room, circular, about twenty meters across." He handed me a small metal box with a collection of dials on it. "Your detector, sir."

"Give it to the captain to carry. Is the door unlocked?"

"Don't know, we haven't been near it. But I have the key here."

"Good. Here's what we do. We walk *quietly* up to the door. You put the key into the lock. You try it. If it is locked then you unlock it. As soon as you are sure it is unlocked you give the nod—and pull the door open." I held up the TI. "This is not a flashlight but is a temporal inhibitor. You open the door and I turn it on. Everything in that room will be fixed in time. Nothing there, human or mechanical, will be able to move until I turn it off again. Which I will not do until the machine is secured. Do you all understand?" Their eyes were glazed—and with good reasons. I shrugged.

"You don't have to. Are you all ready?" They nodded enthusiastically. "Then let's do it."

They all saluted again and at least they were quiet about it with no stamping boots this time. Grissle and his two sergeants were breathing on my neck as we crept forward. I readied the TI. The lieutenant put the key in the keyhole, turned it slowly— then pulled hard and the door flew open.

"Zapped!" I shouted as I switched on the TI. It was pitch dark inside and I couldn't see a thing.

"Can you turn on the lights?" I asked. There was no answer. Frozen in time. The lieutenant was strangely off balance and still pulling on the door handle. My glassy-eyed squad were as still as statues. I stepped back a bit and as soon as the field enveloped them they could move.

"We're going in there," I said. "But I can't see a thing—and I don't dare turn this device off to find a light switch. Suggestions?"

"Battle torches," Captain Grissle said, shifting the detector to his left hand and unclicking his torch from his belt. A bright beam flared out, followed by the others.

"Stay close," I said. "Hold hands, hold my arms—or you'll look like him." I pointed to the crouching and immobile lieutenant; they all cuddled together. We shuffled forward slowly like competitors in an eight-legged sack race, towards the far end of the room.

"Reading steady," Grissle said, "and the needle is pointing at that door over there."

The door was open so at least I didn't have to worry about that. Shuffle-shuffle we went, lighting up the interior of the adjoining room.

Revealing the rack of electronics. A duplicate of the last one I had seen—except that this one was intact.

"There!" I pointed. "That's what I want. Cuddle, clutch and shuffle. All right, stop here. Because we have a problem. I will have to turn this TI off if we are going to disconnect this thing." I pointed at a glowing light on the control panel. "We'll have to turn its power supply off as well if we are going to take it away with us. Any suggestions?"

"The sergeants will draw their weapons to protect us," Grissle said. "You and I grab the machine, move it, look for any switches, power lines, whatever. There's nothing else we can do."

I thought about it for a bit and could not think of any alternatives.

"Let's do it. Get your guns out. Shout if you see anything. Or better yet—try to shoot first. I'll turn the time-freezer off and restore the status quo. Ready?"

Grim nods of agreement; the sergeants with guns pointed, the captain taking a firm grip on the machine.

"Here goes . . ."

I touched the switch.

And everything happened at once.

The machine burst into life, lights flickering in quick patterns. With a terrible shriek someone appeared next to me, seized me and pulled me off balance. I grabbed him with my free hand . . . .

We were going. Going someplace, somewhere, the sensations that weren't sensations again. Going.

All I was aware of was my heart thudding louder and louder in an empty silence. Fear? Why not? Back to Hell? Or Heaven . . .

White light, strong, warmer air. And the tinkling, clanking, crash of broken glass.

I was on the ground, sharpness under my back, with a fat and older version of Slakey stumbling away from me. The temporal inhibitor was still in my hand.

"Got you, Slakey," I called out, pointed and pressed the switch.

He ran on, stopped and turned, swaying dizzily, laughing.

"That weapon, whatever it is, won't work here. No imported machine will. You fool, haven't you learned that yet?"

I was learning, but very slowly. And my punctured legs hurt. I put the inoperable TI against the broken crystal on the ground, used it to push against the sharp shards as I stood up. I pulled a sliver of glass from my leg and watched blood stain the fabric.

"We're not in Hell," I said, looking around me. "Is this your Heaven?"

It might very well have been because it was—incredible. I gaped, very much in awe. But not so much that I didn't keep Fat Slakey inside my field of vision. What I saw was like, well, like nothing I had ever seen or imagined before.

A world of transparent beauty, crystalline, exuberant, colored and transparent and rising up around me. Shrubbery of glass, analogs of trees and leaves, transparent and veined, reaching out on all sides.

But not where I was standing I realized. Here it was all broken shards, a circular area of destruction. Broken and fragmented.

"No, not Heaven," Slakey said.

"Where then?"

When he did not answer I took a step towards him and he raised his hands.

"Stop there! No closer. If you stay where you are I'll answer your question. Agreed?"

"For the moment." I was making no promises. But I knew so little that anything that kept him talking would be of help. "If not Heaven—then where are we?"

"Another place. I don't come here often. It is of little or no use. Whimsically I used to call it Silicon Valley. Now—I call it Glass, just Glass."

"You're Professor Slakey. And perhaps you might also be the one who runs the operation we just left—Baron Krümmung."

"If you like." Surly, looking around. I took a tentative step which got his attention. "No!"

"I'm not moving, relax. And tell me what this is all about . . ."

"I tell you nothing."

"Not even about yourself in Hell?"

He slumped when I said that. "A tragic mistake. I won't make that kind of mistake again. I can't leave of course, too long in Hell. Too long. Certain death if I left now."

"The gun? Why the gun?"

"Why? What a stupid question. To live of course, to eat. The colimicon contains little or no nutrition. A slow death that way. A gun to hunt with, a gun for a hunter."

It was a sickening thought, for there was only one other food source in Hell. I was in the company of a madman—and I understood so little of what was happening. But he was talking and I had kept the important question aside, spoke it now as casually as I could.

"That woman on Lussuoso. Where did you send her?"

"That woman?" He laughed, a laugh devoid of humor. "Come now, diGriz, do I look that stupid? Your wife? Your Angelina—and you call her That Woman."

He saw the expression on my face, turned and ran. Down a path of broken crystal through the magic forest. And I was right behind him and gaining.

But he knew where he was going. Running—then stopping, looking down, shuffling sideways. I reached for him. Just as he vanished. Saved by himself, pulled out of this universe.

I was very much alone. Stranded on an alien planet in an alien universe. And not for the first time. I tried to cheer myself up with the thought that I had been in Hell and had come back.

"You'll do it again, Jim. You always win. You're the original good guy and good guys always win."

Thus cheered, I looked around. The crystal forest glinted in the sunlight; nothing moved in the warm silence. The path of broken shards led away from the clearing. Where it went to I had no idea. I walked slowly down the path beneath the glass foliage. It turned and skirted the edge of the cliff now. There was water below, stretching away to the horizon. Off to the left, in the direction the path led, there were some offshore islands. Above me crystalline branches reached out over the water; waves were breaking over the rocks below. There was scud on the water, foam roiling and surging.

I stopped. Slakey was gone and I was very much alone. This was not a very nice thought and I rejected it. It would just be a matter of time, that's all. Captain Grissle and his marines would have the machine disconnected by now and rushed to that dear genius Coypu. Who would analyze and measure and operate the thing to come and find me. I hoped.

What next? Alone in this crystalline universe was very alone indeed. I smiled at the thought and started to laugh. At what? Nothing was funny. I shook my head, suddenly dizzy.

"Oxygen—lots of it," I said aloud to reassure myself.

There was no reason at all that the atmosphere on this alien planet should match the atmospheres of the terraformed and settled planets. Quite the opposite, if anything. Slakey was obviously seeking out and visiting worlds where humans could live and breathe. I held my breath for a bit, then breathed shallowly.

The oxygen high died away and I looked around at the glass forest—with the trampled path through it. The path that now led along the cliff edge. Should I really follow it? I was not used to indecision, so was undecided about it.

But it really was decision time. My trip to Hell had proven that there was a cartographic coordination between leaving and arriving positions when flitting between universes. Sybil and I had arrived in that cave—and gone back from it. So should I go back to the place where I had arrived? Or try to find out more about Glass?

"The answer to that one is obvious, diGriz," I said to myself. I believed in taking advice from someone very intelligent whom I trusted. "Sit on your chunk and wait to be rescued. And quietly die of thirst and/or starvation. Get moving and find out more about this place. For openers—is that ocean fresh water or is it loaded with chemicals? Or is the liquid really water? Go forth and investigate."

I went. Along the glass-sharded path. Happy that the soles of my shoes were made of seringera, an elastic compound that is supposed to be as strong as steel. It had better be.

The crystalline trees were higher along the coast, with meadowlike areas of bluish grass between them. I came around a bend in the path and in the middle of the next meadow was the statue of a glass animal.

Up to this point I had just accepted the presence of crystalline growths. Too much had happened since I arrived here to question the landscape. I did not query their existence; they just were. Maybe natural mineral structures, or perhaps some living creature like coral had secreted them.

Or had all of this been made by some incredible artist? The orange and yellow little creature in the field certainly was a work of art. Glassy fur covered it, each hair separate and clear. The open mouth had two rows of tiny and precisely formed teeth. I looked beneath the tree next to it and jumped back.

An animal, twice as big as I was, stood poised to jump. Unmoving. I relaxed. Admired the knifelike teeth with their serrated edges; giant claws stretched out from each foot. Glass grass crunched underfoot when I walked closer to it. Looked up and admired the artistic construction. The thing's eyes were on a level with mine and were certainly most realistically formed.

Particularly since they were moving ever so slowly to look at me.

These creatures were alive!

I went back and bent over the smaller one, the hunted. Yes one foot was definitely lower, the one on the other side raised a fraction.

I wasn't looking at sculpture or artifacts. I was in a world of slow-moving crystalline life.

"Well why not?" I reassured myself. "You're not mad, Jim, you have just finally used your exquisite powers of observation to observe what should have been obvious from the first."

I tried to remember my chemistry. Glass was neither basically a liquid nor a solid when in a disordered state. And wasn't water glass a liquid? As we are carbon based, so there could be—there certainly were!—life-forms based on silicon. There would surely be some exotic chemical compositions and reactions involved. But all around me was living proof that it could happen.

With the side of my shoe I cleared away enough broken fragments from the path to make a space to sit down. I rested my chin on my arms, braced on my kneecaps, held the position as long as I could.

Yes—the two animals were moving. Slow metabolism and slow life. Entropy obviously moved at a different speed here, at least with these glass creatures. Too bad I couldn't stay and see who won the race. Maybe if I came back in a day or two I would find out. But exploring had better take precedent over sight-seeing; it was hot and I was already beginning to feel thirsty.

The path along the cliff edge was dropping down towards the ocean below, until it eventually ended on a glassy beach. With all the fancy glass this planet sure had great sand. The water—if it were water—was clearer here. It was a tidal sea and the tide was going out. Ahead, in a finger of eroded rock, were sparkling tide pools. I went and bent over the first one—and something scurried into a crack.

It wasn't the only thing living in the pool. Tiny fishlike creatures with trailing appendages flitted away from my shadow. And they didn't look like glass. They were living in the water which maybe wasn't water.

"Try it, Jim, you might like it," I advised myself. I scooped up a handful and sniffed. Smelled like water. Took a drop on my fingertip and touched my tongue to it hesitantly. Water. Slightly tangy but still water. I sipped a bit of it and it went down well with no obvious ill effects.

But that would be enough for now. That tang could be anything—and I wasn't terribly thirsty yet. I would wait and see if there were any bad reactions. I walked on along the beach towards the small islands just offshore. These were little more than sandbars. There were larger ones, also green and farther out, but these were close enough to see in some detail. There was growth of some kind on them. Green, unlike the crystalline forest and plants. Chlorophyll? Why not—anything was possible. Water and possibly food. Things were beginning to look up.

They looked like bushes—and something was moving in them. Not the wind, there was scarcely any to speak of.

Living creatures? Animals of some kind? Edible or intelligent? I would settle for either or both. I strode out knee-deep in the sea towards the closest one. The water was very shallow and I might be able to reach it without swimming.

"Hello!" I called out. "Anyone there? I am a kind and peace-loving stranger from far away and mean you no harm. *Mi vidas vin. Diru min—parolas Esperanto?*"

The figure moved out of the shade, waved and called out.

"About time you showed up."

"Angelina!"

CHAPTER 11

I WAS PARALYZED BY JOY, petrified by pleasure. Standing stock-still, shouting her name aloud. Smiling foolishly while she waved and blew me a kiss.

Then she dived into the water, being far more practical than I was and not just standing there shouting and waving. A half-dozen strong strokes and she rose up out of the water beside me like a goddess from the sea. Damp and solid with her clothing dripping wet and in my arms. Laughing aloud with pleasure, kissing me with an excess of loving enthusiasm.

Forced to stop from lack of breath, still holding to each other, not wanting to be separated.

"You feel all right—feel great," I finally said. "You are all right, aren't you?"

"Couldn't be better, particularly now with you here. Bolivar and James—?"

"They're the same. We've all been working hard to find you. I won't lie to you and say we weren't worried. I'm sure that you can well imagine our feelings."

"I certainly can! But you got here so fast. It hasn't been much time at all. How long have I been away? It can't be more than two, maybe three days at the most. The days are so short here that it is hard to tell."

We started back to the beach. I shook my head. "You were here only a few days—from your point of view. I'm glad of that because that means that you didn't have much of a chance to really get worried. But we are beginning to find out that time seems to move at a different rate in each different universe. Different entropy rate, that's what Professor Coypu says."

"I don't understand—different rates? And different universes?"

"That is what this whole thing appears to be about. Slakey has found a way of moving between these universes. So while only a few days went by here for you—it has been well over a month that has gone by since you vanished. I'll tell you in great detail what fascinating things have gone on during that time, but first, please, what happened to you?"

She was no longer smiling. "I made a mistake, Jim, and I'm so sorry that I got everyone all worried and involved. I thought I could do this on my own. I really thought that the Heaven thing that the other girls believed in was all some kind of crooked scam. And I know all about crooks—and scams. Master Fanyimadu seemed such a greasy slimeball I never thought he would react like he did—or that he would be helped by his twin brother . . ."

"Wait, my love—please start again, and from the beginning I beg of you. Sit beside me in the sand, that's right, arms entwined. Big kiss or two, right. Now from the very beginning if you will. All I know about what happened is that message you left for me in my computer."

"I was pretty cocky when I recorded it. Rowena and all the other girls were so excited about seeing Heaven that, I, well, wanted to see for myself. It took a good deal of convincing—as well as a lot of money—to set up the trip. I didn't want go unarmed so I had my gun, a grenade or two, the normal items. I planned to take a look at Heaven—then find out what kind of con job Fanyimadu was playing. But it never got that far. We met him at the temple and he gave us a theological pep talk, then told us that it was time to go. He took us by the hands and Rowena and I were following him when there was some kind of movement, some kind of thing happening, I can't describe it."

"Neither can I. It's the going through or over or to a different universe."

"Then you'll know what I mean. But it ended suddenly and we were still in the temple when this stranger appeared, looked just like Fanyimadu, and was shouting some kind of warning and pointing at me. Well, you understand, I just worked by reflex then—"

"Reflex involved a certain amount of gunfire, some explosions, a little self-defense?"

"Of course, you know how it is. Rowena was screaming and fainting, I was knocked down, but I still did plenty of damage you will be happy to hear. Then, I don't know how it happened, we were here in this crystal world, the three of us. The two men and me. They ignored me; one of them seemed to be hurt and the other was bandaging him. I was just diving towards them when they were gone. Just like that. Bang. When I found myself alone I, well, just looked around."

"Was anyone else here?"

"No one that I could see. It was lonely of course, and I missed you, and it was sort of frightening and depressing at first. But that was easy enough to ignore once I started exploring. There was really nothing else that I could do. I followed that broken-glass path to the ocean—isn't this the most incredible place you have ever been! I drank the ocean water and it seemed all right. There is a kind of grass and some shrubs on the little islands. They bear tiny orange fruity things too—but they are poison. I found that out the hard way . . ."

"But—you're all right?"

"I am now. I was getting hungry so I sniffed the fruit, it seemed all right. That was when I took one little bite and was very sick for a very long time. So I just stayed there on the island and took it easy until I felt a little better. I was thinking about seeing what was on the bigger islands as soon as I had the strength. There is the ocean of water here, but no food. I was beginning to get a little worried—and that's when I heard you calling. Now tell me what is happening, what it all means."

A little worried! Any woman other than my Angelina would be a basket case left alone like this. I kissed her passionately which was very good.

"Things have been very busy since you vanished. The boys helped me, but we couldn't get the job done alone. So we called in the Special Corps and Inskipp sent in the troops. As well as Professor Coypu and an agent named Sybil who penetrated another fake church with still another Slakey. He seems to have multiplied himself over and over again. We had a plan to find the machine he uses but Sybil and I were caught before we even got started. We ended up in a place called Hell. It's Coypu's theory that each of these places is in a different universe. Heaven is one, and Hell and this Glass are others. Then we set up a plan and I managed to get into another one of Slakey's front operations, trying to lay my hands on one of the machines for the Professor to examine. It didn't quite work out as planned— which is how I ended up here."

"You have been busy. Now tell me more about this Hell place and your companion, what was her name? Sybil?"

I recognized that tone of voice and told her in greater detail about my visit to Hell. Sybil had only a brief mention and I think that I came out of it pretty well, certainly Hell had not been the time or the place for romance of any kind.

"Good," she finally said. "And the last time you saw the boys they were enjoying themselves with this female agent. How old is she—about their age, you think?"

There were daggers behind her words and I walked ever so carefully. Yes, would you believe it, exactly the same age as the boys. Mutual interests, nice to see. But it was even nicer to be with her here. Which led to some enthusiastic cuddling and no more talk of Sybil.

"Enough," she said finally, standing and brushing the sand off her clothes. "With James and Bolivar in good health and enjoying themselves, Inskipp in charge of the investigation and

Coypu busy inventing his brains out, we have no need to worry about any of them."

"Correct—we worry about ourselves. Only we don't worry. One can die of thirst in three days, but we have an ocean full of water so that's not going to happen."

"Yes—but you can also die of starvation in a month. And I'm beginning to get hungry." She pointed out at the larger islands. "There could be food out there. Why don't we take a look? I have had plenty of time to think about the situation here and I was going to do just that. Did you notice how all the crystal life-forms stay away from the shore?"

I hadn't—but I did now. "I'll bet you know why."

"I do. I made a simple experiment. Whatever the living crystals are, they are not glass. They dissolve in water. Not right at first, it takes awhile. Then they get sort of soft and swell up, and eventually melt completely."

"What happens when it rains?"

"It never does. Look—no clouds."

"And the water doesn't bother the other kinds of life here? I saw things swimming around in a rock pool."

"Some of the green growths extend roots or something into the water. Meaning they are a water-based life-form like we are . . ."

"And might very well be edible," I said with growing enthusiasm. "While we can't eat the glass creatures, we might find something we can nosh on the islands."

"My thinking exactly."

I rubbed my jaw and looked over at the sandy beach on the nearest island, no more than two hundred meters away. Beyond the beach there were green growths of some kind, much bigger than the shrubs that covered the small island that Angelina had explored.

"But we also have to think about leaving Glass," I said. "We should go back to that spot where I appeared. So Coypu can find us when he gets his machine working."

"He can only get it working after he invents it and builds it," she said with great practicality. "I suggest that we leave a message there telling him where we are. Then do a little exploring. If we are going to be here any length of time we are going to need food."

"My genius," I said, kissing her enthusiastically. "Rest and save your strength. I'll trot back and do just that."

While I trotted, then slowed down as the oxygen got me giggling, I considered a vital problem—how was I going to leave a message? By the time I reached the clearing I had the problem solved. My wallet was still in my pocket and was filled with unusable money and valueless credit cards. With my current name on each one.

In the clearing I used my shoes to kick and scrape clear a circle in the sand. In the middle of it I placed the wallet. Then, picking up the pieces of glass, with great delicacy using a fragment of shirttail, I constructed an arrow of colored fragments that pointed back down the path. With other pieces I spelled out the single word ISLANDS.

"Very artistic, Jim," I said, stepping back to admire my handiwork. "Very artistic indeed. When our rescuers arrive they will figure that out instantly."

I stepped over my announcement and went back to join Angelina. It was growing dark and she was sound asleep. It was warm and the sand was soft—and it had been a busy day. I sat beside her and must have fallen asleep as well, for the next I knew it was daylight and she was lightly patting my shoulder.

"Rise and shine, sleeping beauty badly in need of a shave. Rise and drink your fill from the ocean, then let's swim over and see if we can find some breakfast."

"Let me show you something," I said, removing the cloth bundle from my pocket. "Used my shirttail. Wrapped another piece of shirt around it to make a handle."

"You are so practical, my darling," she said, taking up the glass dagger and admiring it, then handing it back. "But won't it dissolve when you go into the water?"

"Not if I hold it over my head and swim with one arm."

"My husband, the athlete. Shall we go?"

It took her only a few strokes to reach the first, smaller island, where she waited patiently while I thrashed over to join her. When we started across to the other side she stopped and pointed.

"There," she said, "under that thing that looks like a cross between a sick octopus and a dead cactus. Those are the shrubs I told you about. The ones with the orange fruit. Pure poison."

"Let's see if we can find something better on that larger island."

It was a tiring swim for me but I did it without getting a drop of water on the blade. I emerged from the water panting and puffing and looked around.

"There may be other berries or fruits or such that aren't too obnoxious," I said. "That looks like a path over there."

"If there is a path—then something made it. And that something could be dangerous."

"Remember my trusty knife," I said, unwrapping it and brandishing it happily.

"In that case you may lead the way."

The path really was a path, trodden flat and turning and twisting through the strange growths. There were analogs of trees, shrubs and bushes, even a green groundcover halfway between grass and moss. But nothing was in any way familiar. Or looked in any way edible. It was Angelina who saw a possibility first.

"There," she said, parting the fronds of a feathery growth. "Those bluish bumps on the trunk."

The bumps had a nasty resemblance to blue carbuncles. I bent and prodded one with my fingernail; a thin skin split and blue juice oozed out.

"Possibly edible?" Angelina asked.

"Possibly," I said with deep suspicion. "And there is only one way to find out. It's my turn to be guinea pig."

I reached out gingerly and poked my finger into the juice. Brought it to my nose and sniffed.

"Yukk!" I said. "Even if it is edible it will come up even faster than it went down. Press on."

I wiped my finger in the soil until it was filthy but cleansed of the juice, then started warily down the path again. It wound around the larger growths but always continued in the same direction. Uphill and away from the shore.

"Wait," Angelina said. "Do you hear anything?"

I stopped and cocked an ear, then nodded. "A sort of booming sound, coming from up ahead."

"Jungle drums. Perhaps the natives are restless."

"We'll soon find out."

I tried to sound more cheerful than I felt. Stranded on an alien planet in an alien universe. No food to eat, unknown dangers to face. Most depressing. But at least I had Angelina again and that was incredibly cheering. I grabbed the mood swing as it went up and tried to hold onto the good feeling. I still walked slowly and silently with the knife probing out before me.

The booming was louder and the beat most irregular, slowing then quickening in an unpredictable manner. Well why not? We couldn't expect a big-band sound here. Now the larger growths were thinning out and I could see what appeared to be a clearing beyond the bole of the last, much larger, one. The path turned there and appeared to go on, skirting the clearing and not crossing it.

"Very suspicious," Angelina said. "Whatever creature made this path it appears that it didn't want to cross that clearing."

"It might be shy—or nocturnal or something like that."

"There also might be something in the clearing that it didn't want to get near. And that's where the sound is coming from."

We stopped behind the big, bulging growth that appeared to be covered with thick green hair; then cautiously looked out.

"Wow!" Angelina gasped.

Wow indeed. In the very center of the clearing was a single grayish, lumpy thing like a great pile of slumped mud. A long growth emerged from its summit and hung down almost to the ground. Growing on this, like fruit on a branch, were glistening red spheres.

"Fruit maybe," I said. "Possibly edible."

"Possibly dangerous," she said. "I don't like the way that

thing is out there alone—and the way the path circles around it."

I did not like it either. "Two choices then. We follow the path and stay away from the thing. Or we get closer and find out more about it."

"Knowing you, Jim diGriz, your mind is already made up. But I'm going with you."

"A deal—as long as you stay behind me."

When we stepped into the clearing the drumming sound stopped. It knew we were there. In a moment the sound started again, faster and not as loud as before. This continued as I walked slowly in its direction. Stopped and looked at it closely and shook my head. Indeed, I thought, it sure is ugly.

A wet orifice opened in the center of the bloated form and a deep and rasping voice spoke.

"*It . . . sure is ugly,*" it said.

CHAPTER 12

"IT CAN TALK!" ANGELINA SAID.

"Not only talk—but it can read minds too. That is just what I was thinking before it spoke."

"*I wonder if it can read my mind too . . .*" the thing said hoarsely.

Angelina stepped back. "That is what *I* was thinking. I don't like this thing, not at all. Let's get out of here."

"In a moment. I would still like to find out what those globes are."

I did find out—far faster than I really wanted to. With incredible speed the branch-like growth whipped towards me. Before I could jump back it wrapped around my neck and pulled me forward.

"Grrkk . . ." was all I could say as I sawed at the thing with the glass knife. Yellow ichor dripped from the wound; the thing was incredibly tough to cut and I was still being pulled forward.

"Hack it off!" Angelina shouted, seizing me around the waist and pulling back as hard as she could. It helped a bit, but I was still being pulled towards the opening that had emitted the voice.

It had stopped speaking now as the opening gaped wider and wider, moist and filled with sharp, dark ridges.

I sawed and choked. I couldn't see very well. I kept on sawing.

The opening was just in front of my face when I cut the last fibrous strand and fell backwards.

I was vaguely aware of Angelina dragging me along the ground away from the thing which was now booming out loudly and hoarsely.

"I wonder if . . . it sure . . . read my ugly . . ."

I sat up and rubbed my sore throat. "That was . . . too close."

"How do you feel?"

"Bruised—but all right." I looked down and realized that the knife and my right hand were covered with the thick and sticky liquid. And I was still clutching the severed end of the stalk, with a red globe attached to it, in my other hand.

"Let's go back to the ocean," I said, as hoarsely as our opponent who was still talking, feeding back a mixture of our thoughts to us. "I want to wash off this gunk—and see what this red thing is."

"I'll carry it," Angelina said. "Move—before this monster pulls itself out of the ground and comes after us."

She meant it as a jest, but I did walk that much faster. Back to the shore where I scrubbed and cleaned off the congealing liquid. Angelina was beside me dunking the globe into the water.

"Let me have the knife," she said. "It's my turn to try the local cuisine."

"The knife is getting soft."

"I'll be quick."

Before I could stop her she had sliced the thing open to reveal wet and even redder tissue inside. It looked uncomfortably like flesh. She cut off a sliver and sniffed it.

"Doesn't smell too bad."

"Don't!" I said, but I was too late. She had popped it into her mouth, chewed quickly—and swallowed it.

"Not too bad," she said. "Tastes sort of like a cross between seafood and candy."

"You shouldn't have done that . . ."

"Why not? Someone had to. And as I said—it was my turn to do the testing. And I still feel fine."

"Well, at least we know why the path went around the clearing, Ouch!" I had touched my sore neck. "We stay on the path from now on. You were right about that. That thing, it's like an angler fish."

"A what?"

"A fish that lives at pelagic depths in the ocean. It has sort of a fishing-pole organ growing out of the top of its head that dangles in front of its mouth—hence the name. It has a lump at the end that glows in the dark and attracts other fish. They snap at it—and get eaten."

"But why the mind-reading stunt?"

I sighed and shrugged. "Anyone's guess. It must work well on the local life forms—what are you doing?"

She had cut off another piece of the red globe and was chewing on it.

"Eating, of course. I still feel fine, and I am more than a little hungry."

I watched the shadows move and tried to estimate how much time had elapsed. Angelina looked at my face, then reached out and patted my hand.

"Poor Jim. You look so worried. I'm fine, but still hungry."

"Let me try some before you eat any more of it. Maybe it is a sex-specific poison."

"What a charming thought," she said and scowled fiercely.

"Sorry, shouldn't say things like that. This place must be getting me down." I cut, chewed and swallowed. "Not bad. But after we finish this fruit I'm not going back for a second try at that thing."

"Agreed. And you have noticed that it is getting dark again?"

"I have. I suggest we doze here until dawn and then press on along the path. Second the motion?"

"Absolutely."

When the sun woke us we were alive and well and hungry. We divided up the fruit and ate it all. Washed off the juice, yawned and stretched and looked at the path.

"Can I have the knife today?" Angelina asked. "So I can break trail."

"Gone," I said, pointing to a damp knife-shaped spot in the sand.

"I'll see if I can find a rock that will do."

She found one shaped not unlike a hand ax, traditional tool of mankind. I looked for another one, then put a few more rocks in my pockets. Angelina led the way since she was as strong and fit as I was, possibly with better reflexes. And I was not about to start discussing the equality of the sexes with her at any time.

With our stomachs full, our bodies rested, we made good time. And followed the path around the clearing. I stopped just long enough to throw a rock at the creature there; I had carried it all the way from the beach just for this moment. It thudded nicely and the tentacle thrashed violently.

"I wish . . . I had a power saw . . ." the thing said.

"Did you think that?" I asked.

"You better believe it."

We struggled up the last and steepest part of the path to the ridge at the top. And stopped.

"Quite a change," Angelina said.

All the green growth ended sharply. As though a line had been drawn along the summit. A bowl in the hills stretched out ahead of us. Completely devoid of life. Sand and rock and nothing more; an empty, barren desert.

"You said that it never rains on this planet?" I asked.

"Never."

"If it did that would also be a sloppy end for the glass lifeforms. It also means that the carbon and chlorophyll life can't get too far from the ocean. I'll bet they dip their roots into it or get dew from the air. So up here—no water, so no life."

"But the path goes on," she said, pointing.

"Interesting. So I guess that we do too."

We followed it as it twisted and turned between boulders as big as houses, on to a central flat desert of sand.

"What on earth is *that?*" Angelina asked. I could not think of an answer.

In the sand was a small pyramid apparently made of rock. It was seamless—but hollow. That was obvious because the top was broken off and we could see inside. It was empty. But what was most interesting was the slightly larger pyramid close by. Also with an opening in the top. And the next and the next. Stretching out in a straight line across the desert. Each one with an opening in the top, each larger than the one before.

"An alien enigma," I said brightly; Angelina just sniffed, not considering this worth an answer. We left the path and walked along the line of pyramids. There were over thirty of them, the final one taller than we were.

"The last one," Angelina said, pointing. "The top. It comes to a point—and it is solid. Any explanations?"

For a rare moment I was silent.

"Shall I tell you what is happening?" she said.

"Speak, I beg of you."

"This has obviously been constructed by a silicon life form. It digests sand and excretes rock, thus building a pyramid around itself. When it grows too big for the pyramid it cracks out, moves along and builds another one."

"Highly interesting," I said, dazed by her logic. "But how did it get to build the first one in the first place—and how does it build a pyramid from the inside?"

"You can't expect me to know everything," she said, with impeccable logic. "Let's get back to the path."

"Let's not quite yet," I said pointing. "Isn't that something following the path and moving towards us?"

"Some things not a thing."

"You're right. Any reason we shouldn't stay out of sight until we see what they are?"

She nodded and we stepped into the shadow of the largest pyramid where we might see and possibly not be seen. Angelina cocked her head, then pressed her ear to the side of the pyramid. "Listen," she said. "Isn't there a kind of crunching sound coming from inside?"

"Please, not now. Possibly later. One alien mystery at a time if you don't mind."

The marching file of creatures was surely mystery enough. There were eleven of them and they were roughly man-size. But the resemblance ended right there. A fringe of legs or tentacles or something twitched quickly against the ground and carried each creature along. These moving parts supported a solid trunk the color and texture of tree bark—it could be a tree trunk for all we knew. A single stalk, very much like the one on the creature that had tried to eat me, emerged from the top of the trunk with what looked like a bulbous eye at the end. The eyes bobbed and looked about, apparently not seeing us pyramid-lurking in the shadow.

They shuffled by in silence, stirring up a quickly settling cloud of dust, climbed over the rim and vanished down the ridge on the other side.

"Now will you listen to the pyramid?" Angelina asked.

"Yes, of course, sure." I listened and perhaps I did hear a distant crunching. "I can hear something . . ."

"They're coming back," she said.

And so they were. Whether it was the same bunch or a different lot it was of course impossible to tell. Different ones, surely, because in the brief time they had been out of sight they had changed completely. The ribbed trunks had become globe-shaped and transparent, expanded from within so the ribbing now formed irregular stripes on the surface.

"They're filled with water," Angelina said, and I nodded dumb agreement.

"Possibly, possibly," I muttered.

"They march out of the desert and fill with water from a spring or from the ocean. Then march back with it. Why?"

"There is only way to find out—follow them."

Perhaps it was not wise. Possibly dangerous. But there were too many curious and unsolvable puzzles on this planet. We both had the desire to see if we might possibly solve at least one of these. When they were out of sight we followed them down the path.

Nor did we have far to go. The path led to a row of large boulders and vanished between two of them.

"Suspicious," I said. "Those rocks have been placed there."

"It could be a natural formation."

"It could, but the problem is the same. Do we stay out—or go in to investigate. And you will recall what happened the last time I got nosy . . ."

"Behind you!"

I took one look and jumped aside. Another string of water-carriers was approaching—and they were almost upon us. We stood by the path tense and ready to fight.

And while they were aware of us, our presence was completely ignored. The string shuffled on by in silence, each eye focusing on us in turn as they passed.

"They don't seem too interested in us," I said.

"Well I'm interested in them. Let's go."

We did. Slipping between the large boulders, then following the path between a second row to walk inside a circular, rock-girt area. Where we stopped—and did our best not to gape and bulge our eyes as though we had a joint IQ about that of body temperature.

It was so alien that it was hard to make out just what was happening here. One thing at least was certain—we knew where the water was going. The creatures we had been following wandered through a green labyrinth spraying water and shrinking their bodies at the same time. When this was finished, one walked away from the growth, then another and another. They milled about in a little group until, with sudden decision—or obeying some unseen signal—a line formed and they shuffled through the exit and were gone.

We walked closer to the confused growth, stopped when we saw movement under the broad, leaflike structures. In the semi-darkness, spiderlike creatures were climbing about, apparently tending the growth. Fragments of green fell down to the ground where other creatures cleaned them up. Another dropped down on the end of a cord or tentacle clutching something red.

"Very much like that fruit you got your neck squeezed for," Angelina said.

"Could be, could be—and look where it's going."

A tall opening in the rock led to some kind of cavern beyond. I bent to try and look inside when there was a light pulling at my leg, a feathery touch.

"What is that?" Angelina asked.

As always on this world there was no easy answer. It was like a soft bundle of sticks, or a complex insect made of twigs. Whatever it was it was plucking at my trouser leg. Then it stopped and shuffled towards the cave. Stopped and waited. Then returned and rustled the fabric once again.

"It's trying to communicate," I said. "I think it wants me to follow it. Well—why not?"

"No arguments. We've come this far."

When we started forward it scurried ahead. Stopped and waited, then moved ahead again. Sunshine filtered through the mouth of the cave, more than enough to see the sprouting creature that sprawled inside.

That was the only way to describe it. It was covered with complex structures that were apparently growing from its green hide. Some I recognized; there was the top half of a water carrier. Another was a bristle of growths bundled together like our guide. And there were others that were totally incomprehensible. Then one of the working creatures hurried by with a red globe which it dropped into an opening in the thing's side.

"It's looking at us," Angelina said, pointing. A group of whip-like tentacles, each ending in a bulging eye, had turned towards us.

"Hello," I said.

"Hello," it boomed out in return.

CHAPTER 13

"TALKING—OR MIMICKING?" ANGELINA SAID.

"Talking—talking—talking."

Which wasn't much of an answer. The eye-stalks still swayed in our direction—as did another organ or mushrooming growth that started to form under the eyes. It began as a swelling, then opened up into a sort of trumpet-shaped flower. This moved back and forth as though searching for something, then turned and pointed directly at me. I stepped back—

Color, sound, movement, terror.

Pain and red sounds, sharp memories.

A scream . . . a shout . . .

Then it ended and I realized that the person shouting was me. Hands on my arms, I blinked my eyes clear, saw that Angelina was holding on to me.

"What happened?" she asked.

"I . . . don't know. What did you see?"

"You closed your eyes and, well, just dropped to the ground. Then you just sort of scrunched up, shouting and twisting. It only lasted a moment."

"That thing," I said, my breathing rough. "It was in my brain, trying to communicate or something. Big and strong—"

"Did it try to hurt you?"

"Not at all, quite the opposite. There was curiosity there but I had no sensation of threat or menace. Whatever it wanted it, well, didn't find. It just pulled out. Perhaps I'm not in its intellectual league."

While I was talking the flower growth closed and disappeared. Next to it the water-carrier that had been growing larger stopped and began a sort of twisting motion. Then, with a plopping sound, it pulled free of the surface. Jumped to the ground and hurried away.

"It's the queen thing," Angelina said. "Growing parts of the colony."

"Or maybe it is the colony."

After that one attempt to communicate the creature never tried again. The eyes were withdrawn as though it had lost all interest. But it knew we were there because one of the leg creatures came hurrying into the cave with two of the red fruit we had seen growing outside. It plopped one into an opening in the giant creature's hide—then dropped the other one in front of us before rushing outside again.

"Thanks, Queenie," I said. "Very kind of you. Is it chow time? Looks like the one we ate before—and our friend here just ate one. Shall we give it a try?" I squatted down to look more closely at it. I prodded it with my finger and it split open. I licked the juice from my hand. "Tastes very much like the other one we had to fight for."

"Why not? If that murderous thing in the clearing is offering tempting goodies I suppose they must be edible. Give me a piece, if you please."

We finished it between us. Then, feeling very much ignored, we went back out of the cave into the alien garden.

"What about another one?" I asked.

"You're on."

None of the scurrying creatures came near us—nor took any notice when I reached up high and plucked another red fruit. We sat comfortably against the rock wall and ate it. It was very pulpy and liquid, food and drink at the same time.

"Now what?" Angelina asked, licking the last drop of juice from her fingers.

"A good question. And I suggest that we sleep on it."

"One of us at a time though. I still don't trust this queen-of-the-hive creature."

"Then we'll get out of here, find a secluded spot away from the path. We can always come back when we get hungry."

Angelina yawned gracefully. "You are on, husband mine. It certainly has been a long day."

We did this for two of the short days and nights. Sleeping, then going back for more fruit, mulling over our options, very limited indeed, and trying to figure out just what we should do next. With great effort at cogitation, we managed to never reach any important conclusions. Then we would sleep and start the whole process over again. On the third daylet Angelina came up with an observation that finally forced us to make a decision. She had been on this exotic world longer than I had—and had gone much longer without a decent meal.

"You are losing weight, Jim. And so am I." Which was true, but I just did not want to mention it to her. "The fruit is filling all right—but do you notice how quickly you get hungry again after eating?"

"I have been thinking about it, wondering really."

"Stop wondering. Water is water, hydrogen and oxygen. Since we don't get thirsty we must have been getting enough to drink from the fruit. But the food is a different matter. Who knows what kind of elements and molecules make up this fruit. I don't think we are ingesting any nourishment at all. If we stay here and keep on eating this stuff—we are just going to curl up and die of starvation in the end."

I sighed unhappily. "I'm forced to agree. The idea was tickling at my brain but I thought I was being stupid. It's been sort of fun here in a completely alien way. Back to Glass land?"

"Nothing else to do. And you have strange tastes if you think our stay here was fun. I say back to civilization and some good food and a hot bath. Let's head for that clearing where we arrived. We'll see if anyone has found your message yet."

I waved as we left. "Bye. Thanks for the hospitality." Of course there was no response. We went down the hill, skirted the killer angler, and swam back to the mainland.

"Onward—to the glass forest," I said, trying to be as cheerful as I could. "Coypu will have the machine analyzed by now and will quickly build one of his own. Which he will then use to track us down and rescue us. We'll be settling down to a steak dinner before you know it."

After three more of the local days had gone by I wanted to eat those words—since there was nothing else to eat on this world of Glass. My wallet was just where I had left it, my glass arrow and message undisturbed. I ground the crystal fragments to smithereens, growling darkly.

After that—it was just waiting. The crystal glade in the forest remained empty. No one came, nothing happened at all. We stayed there, making only the briefest of forays back to the ocean to drink. Time dragged by so sluggishly that we felt we were making about the same progress as the crystalline carnivore. It was catching up on its fleeing prey, but so slowly, slowly. Another night fell and was followed by another sunny day. And another. I took a second notch in my belt and tried to ignore the growing thinness of Angelina's face. By the fifth day I began to worry.

"There must be something else we can do," I complained.

"I don't see what. You're the one who told me that all we had to do was wait. You must be patient."

"I'm not!"

"You never were. But you must make the effort or you will worry yourself into an ulcer."

"I would rather drink myself into an ulcer!" The thought of strong spirits and cold beer got my spittle flowing. I spat into the forest and watched a stem of grass dissolve. Good thing it never rained here.

I awoke with the sun on the morning of our sixth day of waiting, watching its green-striped disk shining through the multicolored foliage. It was no longer exciting to look at, nor did I wonder anymore what made the stripes. Angelina was pale and drawn, moaning under her breath as she slept. I didn't want to wake her; sleep was our only escape from hunger. And the endless waiting. I walked down the path a bit and looked out over the ocean. The waves surged turgidly against the cliffs; nothing else moved. Depression struggled onto the back of depression. I sighed mightily and went back to the clearing.

When Angelina did wake up we talked a bit. I was thirsty but she wasn't, so I walked down to the beach to drink. There was nothing that we could carry water in. Therefore we took turns drinking so that someone would always be in the clearing. Waiting.

The walk was tiring—but it had to be done. I drank my fill, then a little more. Filling the stomach helped for awhile with the hunger. The walk back, uphill part of the way, was particularly exhausting. And I had to walk slowly or I would have an oxygen jag.

"Home is the drinker, home from the sea!" I called out. A feeble attempt at humor. "Hello!"

Maybe she was asleep again. I shut up but walked faster.

Stopped. Frozen.

The cleared area was empty.

"Angelina!"

This was the blackest of blackest moments that I had ever experienced. If Coypu had his machine working—he could have saved her. That had to be it. Coypu had done this, not Slakey. Could that be it? But Coypu was an unknown. If the marines had grabbed a machine, and if it were intact, and if Coypu had built a machine. . . . An awful lot of ifs. But Slakey had plenty of machines and knew that we were here. He could have returned and seized Angelina and left me here to starve quietly. Was it Slakey who got here first and grabbed her off this world?

"Who did this? Where are you?"

I shouted aloud, brimming over with frustration and anger. And fear. It must be Coypu. It had to be him.

I hoped.

But if it had been him why had he taken just Angelina and

left me here? There should have been a message, at least a message. I frantically kicked about among the broken crystal. No note, no traces of anything.

For a very, very long time nothing happened. I was giggling with fear. Too much oxygen. Slow down, Jim, take it easy. I sat in the cleared area where we slept and breathed more slowly. With one last snicker the laughter died. Depression took over.

The days on Glass were short—but this was the longest one I had ever lived through. It was growing dark and I must have nodded off with my head slumped on my chest. Fear, worry, hunger, everything. Too much, far more than too much.

"Dad—over here!" Bolivar said. I blinked my eyelids, still half asleep, dreaming.

"Are you all right? We have to move fast."

No dream! I set a new record for the broken glass sprint. Slammed into him and almost knocked him from his feet. We were falling—

—backward into a brightly lit hotel room, onto a soft, carpeted floor. I just lay there, looking up at Professor Coypu seated before a great mass of breadboarded electronics.

And Angelina smiling down on me.

"I hope they gave you something nice to eat," I said, inanely, still not believing that it was all over and she was all right. She knelt and took my hands in hers.

"Sorry it took so long. The professor says that he has trouble aligning the machine."

"Calibration errors, cumulative, entropy slippage," Coypu said. "Gets better each time though."

"Something to eat, Dad," Bolivar said, helping me to my feet and handing me a giant roast meat sandwich. Saliva sported as I growled and tore off an immense bite, chewed; paradisical. I took the proffered beer bottle by the neck and drank and drank until the back of my nose hurt from the cold.

"Here, sit at the table," Angelina said, pulling out a chair. "And don't eat so fast or you'll make yourself sick—"

"Warfle?" I said.

"—and don't talk with your mouth full. Eat slowly, that's better, while I tell you what happened. It was Bolivar who came for me. No time to wait, he said. The alignment was difficult—just seconds. I held back but he grabbed me and that was that. It took so long to get through to you again, I knew what you were feeling. But it is all all right now. We are all together this time. The end of worrying."

"The beginning of a lot of big worrying for some of us," Inskipp snarled in his friendly and ingratiating way as he walked into the room. He dropped into a chair and glared menacingly. "All right for you people to relax and cheer each other up with stories of your strange adventures. You forget that the rest of us are weighed down with responsibilities. Since this whole mess began we have been behind the eight ball, stuck in the mud, up the creek paddleless and getting nowhere as fast as a turgid turtle."

Instead of pointing out the tangled syntax of his mixed metaphor I reached for another sandwich. Priorities exist. He chuntered on.

"We have been tottering from calamity to calamity, our hand forced at every turn. Not one of the Slakeys has been apprehended. As soon as we close in on one of them another pops up and whips him away. All of our efforts so far have been spent in getting you out of trouble, diGriz. And the costs keep growing. I imagine it was your smart idea to rent this entire hotel, the Vaska Hulja Holiday Heaven, as center of this operation. Do you know how many millions of credits it has cost so far?"

"More than the gross annual income of a rich planet—I hope!" I belched rotundly. "Sorry. Ate too fast. Another beer? Thanks, James. And every credit well spent, Inskipp, you old skinflint. Rockets have roared, Space Marines have exercised furiously, news broadcasters have been working overtime, the galaxy is an exciting place and zillions of happy citizens have been entertained delightfully. You should bless me as a galactic asset instead of whining about your overdraft. Nothing but good has come out of this operation."

He turned bright red and bulged his eyes, opened his mouth. But Angelina spoke first.

"You are both right and wrong, Jim. It looks like Slakey has been put out of business. The search is still on, but it has been a long time since the detectors found any trace of him—on any civilized planet that we have contacted. The search is now spreading to every recorded world, as our great leader, H. P. Inskipp has kindly pointed out."

She smiled but Inskipp was immune to the kind word and the gentle touch. "I'm going to pull the plug and cut our losses," he said. I was suddenly very angry.

"No you are not, you monetarial moron! All of the civilized planets pay large sums to keep the Special Corps in business—and they never ask you for any kind of accounting. We are now faced with one of the biggest threats that mankind has ever faced—and you want to cut and run."

"What threat? What can one man do that can threaten a thousand worlds?"

"Think!" I said, grabbing up another beer to hold down the sandwiches. "Professor Justin Slakey may have started out as a top scientist and a genius. But this popping back and forth between universes has not only addled his mutual brains but in some way has multiplied his numbers. Do you want these madmen to go on multiplying and causing more and more trouble? We know he has sent people to Hell to provide lunch for his insane personification there. At the very least Slakey is a massmurderer. Who will go on committing murder and who knows what other forms of insane evil until he is stopped. And more than that . . ."

I really had their attention now. All eyes were on me, all mouths mute as I raised the bottle and drank in dramatic silence. Then raised a hortatory finger.

"Much *much* more than that. Look at all the lengths he went to, all the churches and organizations he created. All the masses of money he has collected. And why did he do all this? For the money, that's obvious. The sums involved are staggering. So ask yourself—what does he want the money for?

"What are his plans?

"Anyone who thinks they are for the mutual benefit of mankind may leave the room. All who stay will have the pleasure of hearing how we can find Slakey and stop him.

"Now—would you like to know how that can be done?"

CHAPTER 14

"OF COURSE WE WANT TO hear your plan, darling." Angelina said, then leaned over and kissed my cheek. "My husband the genius."

Facetious or not it was heartwarming. Bolivar and James were giving me cheerful thumbs-up signs, Sybil did the same and even Coypu was nodding in reluctant agreement. The only glum one was Inskipp, still counting his mounting debts. I rapped on the table with my beer bottle.

"I hereby declare this meeting of the Galactic Salvation League to be open. Who is taking the minutes?"

"My recorder is running," Sybil said, sitting down and putting it on the table before her. "Welcome home, Jim diGriz. You had us all very worried."

"I had myself very worried. What Slakey did to you and me in Hell—or to Angelina and me on Glass—is reason enough to pursue him to the edges of the galaxy and put him out of business. But we have more reason to go after all the hims other than simple vindictiveness."

Inskipp sneered lightly. "And just what is that?"

"I never thought that you would ask. I notice that while I

was away you managed to lose track of him completely. Is that correct?"

"Loosely speaking, why possibly, yes."

"Speaking very tightly I would say that now is the time for a plan that cannot miss. Professor—how goes your universe machine?"

"Very well, thank you. The little matter of calibration will soon be licked."

"I'm cheered to hear that. How many universes do you have access to?"

He clattered his fingernails against his teeth, forehead furrowed in thought. "Theoretically of course the number is infinite. Perhaps we even create these universes when we enter them, as you suggested when you came back from Hell. But, as of this moment, we have investigated or entered a little over forty-one."

"Is one of them Heaven?"

"No—but we are still looking. While the machine we captured has settings for different destinations I have no way of identifying them without activation and entry."

"What about Hell?"

"We very definitely can go to Hell. You will remember that your son James hypnotized a Slakey and made him send Bolivar there to find you."

"Well that's it, then." I sat back and sighed with satisfaction. "I could do with just a bit more to eat, if the sandwiches aren't all gone."

"Stop toying with us, Jim diGriz, or you'll get more than a sandwich in your gob!" Angelina suggested.

"Sorry, my love. I don't mean to make light of the situation. But it has been pretty grim of late and I was indulging myself."

"You're forgiven. What's so important about Hell?"

"Slakey is there. In his red, fat, insane, well-armed condition. Don't you think that if the other Slakeys could get him out of there—that they would? But they don't. Probably because it would certainly kill him, that's what Slakey on Glass told me. So we launch a little expedition to find him. And talk to him. An expedition in force because what one Slakey knows they all know. They won't kill him—that would be too much like committing suicide. But they will have no compunction about polishing the rest of us off when we try to talk to him. But if we get there fast, maybe use a bit of hypnotism on him, ask a question or two, right, James?"

"A piece of cake, Dad."

"We will then ask him to answer two incredibly important questions. Where is Heaven—and what is the overall plan? It is imperative that we find out what the snakey Slakeys want all the money for."

"Do it," Inskipp said, a man who always makes his mind up quickly. "What are you going to need for this job?"

It was a good plan, and a tight one. As soon as Slakey found out what we were up to he would react. Violently. And he was well ahead of us technically. Coypu still had not found a means of getting any operable machines into another universe. But Slakey in Hell had a working gauss rifle. I just hoped that there wasn't any more universally transportable weaponry in Slakey's hands.

Our advantage would have to be speed of attack. And numbers.

But our primary hit team had to be small so it could move fast. I would go because the whole thing was my idea. Then James had to be with me since he had to hypnotize the old red devil. And Angelina of course, she would not let me go alone. And of course Bolivar, who naturally would not permit a family outing without being present himself. We would go in fast and hit hard.

But our flank would be protected by two hundred very mean and obnoxious Combat Marines. They would be armed only with their hands and feet and combative know-how. Which should be enough. They would be guided by Sybil, who certainly knew her away around Hell. Also, I had caught a number of dark looks from Angelina whenever she saw me talking to the female agent. Which meant that life would be a lot smoother if Sybil led the troopers.

My old companion, Marine Captain Grissle, would be in charge of the troops and I received a message that he urgently wanted to see me. I sent for him.

"No guns?" he asked as he stamped through the door. "A marine is not a marine without a weapon."

"Unarmed combat, they're supposed to know all about that kind of thing."

"They do. But they would do better with a grenade or two."

"They would fuse into lumps and would not go off. I couldn't even open the blades on my pocketknife in Glass."

"Bayonets?"

"They will get stuck in their scabbards. And don't say leave the scabbards behind. I do not relish the thought of two hundred marines popping through into Hell and falling all over each other with naked bayonets in their hands. But, yes, I have thought about it and think that something can be done. We will all be carrying weapons."

"What?"

"I will work out the details and you will see just before we leave. Dismissed."

It took a few days to make all the preparations, which gave us a useful breathing period. Angelina had had a chance to put some weight back on, four good meals a day helped, and we were all raring to go. Coypu had been fiddling with his equations and his circuits and had built a superior model of his dimensional doorway.

"Basically its just a matter of power," he explained. "Slakey had to conceal his machines, keep them small and out of sight. We have no such restrictions."

The new machine was most impressive. At great expense he had tapped directly into the planetwide and international electrical grid. A large, red, insulated cable, over a meter in diameter, led into the main ballroom of the hotel, now converted into an electronic jungle. In the middle of the dance floor was a full-sized garage door mounted in a frame. I admired it—from the front only of course. Since it had no back. That is if you walked around it you couldn't see it or it wasn't there or something. But it looked sound and solid from the front.

"Take a peek and see what we have got," Coypu said, making some adjustments on his operating console. I turned the garage-door handle and opened the door a crack—then slammed it when the air began to whistle through.

"All black—with stars. And lower pressure. That's not Hell."

"But I'm very close, that's the adjoining one. Try it now."

A red sun burned down from the red sky. I sneezed when a whiff of hydrogen sulfide drifted out. "That's it," I said closing the door again. "Shall I call in the troops?"

"I'm ready when you are."

They were all waiting expectantly for the signal. Sybil and Angelina were the first to get there. Moments later the tramp of marching feet heralded the arrival of the marines. They stamped in, marched in position, faced front and thundered to a halt.

"Great," I said. "Stand them at ease and be prepared for issue of weapons."

"Weapons!" Captain Grissle's great jaw cracked into a unaccustomed smile.

"There!" I said as James and Bolivar drove in with the laden freight wagons. I opened one of the boxes and pulled out a bloated red form and waved it on high.

"A *salami* . . ." Grissle gasped.

"Very observant," I said. "A both deadly and edible weapon. Issue them to your men."

"You're not playing the fool again, are you?" Angelina said as she and Sybil looked on dubiously.

"Never, my love. This is a very serious decision and one that was worked out with impeccable logic. Instead of fighting with the inhabitants of Hell, we feed them. If they have been resorting to cannibalism, a redolent salami will make Hell a paradise for them. However, since most of them are a little insane we must expect trouble. Then, in any emergency, you will discover that a ten-kilo salami can wreak fearful damage. And if we overstay our leave we can always eat them ourselves."

The marines were issued one salami each. "And no nibbling," I warned. Sybil and the twins took theirs, but the look in Angelina's eyes warned me not to even wave one in her direction. I took mine and held it aloft.

"Are we ready, Professor?"

"Locked on."

"Then here we go!" I shouted, throwing open the garage door to Hell and pointing my salami. "Attack!"

It was a lovely sight. With their salamis at slope arms and in perfect step, the marines charged straight into Hell behind Sybil. My family followed.

As instructed, the marines had spread out in a long skirmish line. Sybil waved her salami and indicated the direction for them to take. Away from the lava lake and towards the foothills.

"This is a terrible place," Angelina said. The ground trembled as flame and smoke shot from a distant volcano.

"We'll get out as fast as we can. But it has to be done."

"Some trouble over there," Bolivar said. One of the marines had been ambushed by two of the locals who had leaped out of hiding and tackled him. He swung his salami with trained skill and bowled them both over. This broke the salami in two which must have released a deliciously garlicky smell that brought instant attention from the sprawled men. They scrambled in the sand, the marine forgotten, seized up their booty and fled.

"Well done," Angelina said, lifting her face and giving me a quick kiss on the cheek.

"Man down!" the captain shouted. "Take cover."

"Let's go," I shouted and led the rush.

Everything went according to plan; red Slakey would be easier to capture with so many marines involved in stalking him. It would be faster too.

Two of the marines carried their wounded comrade by.

"Flesh wound," one of them called out.

"Back through the door, the hotel doctor is waiting," I called after them.

We slowed to a walk, panting and perspiring. By the time we reached the scene the marines had done their job and Slakey had been captured and disarmed. He was being held fast by two of the largest marines. Bolivar and James grabbed the prisoner while the marines fanned out in a wide circular formation around us.

"We meet again, Professor Slakey," I said. He foamed a little and writhed in the twins' unbreakable grip but did not speak. I grabbed his arm so James could do his hypnotizing. Which, unhappily, did not seem to be working.

"I can't get his attention, sorry," James said. "I've never worked with anyone in this insane state before."

"Let me try," I said, breaking off a great chunk of salami and holding it close to the prisoner's nose. He stopped struggling and gaped; his nostrils twitched. Then he snapped at it and his teeth clacked together when I jerked it back. I handed the redolent salami to James.

"You've got his attention now."

"You're hungry," James said, "hungry and sleepy. Bite, eat, chew, that's it. Swallow, good man. Want more, nod, that's it."

"Quiet!" a dark-suited Professor Slakey said, running up the hill towards us. An attacking marine swung a powerful salami and felled him. He rolled down the hill and vanished from sight.

It was a good thing we had brought so many marines. One Slakey after another appeared—until at one point there were twelve attacking at the same time. The important thing was that they were all unarmed; apparently they had made only the single gun for Hell and we had caught them unprepared. Try as they might they never made it through the perimeter of muscular guardians. One of the Slakeys appeared almost on top of us, reaching for the now silent devilish form, but Angelina caught him and twisted and hurled him back down the hill.

Then the attack was over as swiftly as it had begun. Our prisoner was now sitting on the ground happily chewing his rations.

"They've stopped," I called out. "But stay alert—it could be a ruse—be ready for anything."

"They won't be back," James said around a chewy mouthful. "What one knows they all know. So they all know now that the prisoner let me down on the Slakey motivation for this entire thing. His brain is so addled that he had no idea of what I was talking about or what all that money is needed for. But he remembers Heaven, clearly, knows its importance. Once I had the information, the code sequence, the other Slakeys stopped the attack."

"You've memorized it?"

"Better than that." He held up the remaining half of his salami. "I scratched it on this with my fingernail."

CHAPTER 15

I WORKED OUT IN THE hotel's health club every day. The first day I was exhausted after an hour, the aftereffects of starvation on Glass saw to that. But the trainer sweated with me full time; weights, bike, hydrotherapy, 2G sprints and all the rest. It wasn't too long before I was able to put in a five-hour day and I was feeling fit and perky. My morale was also cheered on by the fact that I had put all of my lost weight back on as muscle. The layer of fat on my love handles, product of all dissolute and boozing living on Lussuoso no doubt, was gone. I jogged and I swam and realized I could no longer put off the moment of truth. Because I was sure that Angelina would not like it.

"I don't like it," she said very affirmatively. "No."

"My love—light of my life," I said clutching her hands in mine. The bar was empty and only the robot bartender was observing this digital act of passion. With a lithe twist she slipped her hands free, picked up her glass and sipped. I tried logic.

"If you look at the question from all sides you will see that this is the only possible answer."

"I can think of a lot more possibilities."

"But none that will work. We need to know what is happening in Heaven. The more people that go bumbling around there, the more chance there is of someone being spotted. One person must go in alone. One super-agent of superlative talent and experience, a lone wolf, he who slinks by night, lithe, handsome, unbeatable—the galaxy's best agent. And I can give you a hint about his name. Some call him 'Stalowy Szczur,' others 'Ratinox,' and even 'Rustimuna Stalrato'—"

"You?"

"How nice of you to say so! Now that you have spoken the truth aloud—can you think of anyone who is better qualified?"

She frowned and sipped her drink in silence, with perhaps the slightest gurgle from her straw when the last drop vanished. Stirred to life by this sound, the barbot whistled its wheels along the rails behind the bar and juddered to a stop. It spoke in a deep and sensual voice. "Does madam require a refill of her delicious drink, a Pink Rocket-popsy?"

"Why not?" A metal tentacle snaked out, curled around the stem of the glass and zipped it away out of sight. A door in the thing's chest opened and a new chilled glass appeared, brimming with drink.

"And for Sire? Drinkey?"

I was in training and not ready to get smashed to the eyeballs on booze. "Diet-whiskey with a slice of fruit."

"I can't argue with that," she finally said. "You are the best agent that Inskipp has. You know it and I can't deny it. Mostly because you are not an effete trainee new to the job, or a do-gooder officer of the law. Instead, you are basically a bent and twisted crook with a lifetime of experience in crime."

"You make it sound so good."

"I should know. But that still doesn't mean you go to Heaven alone. I'll go with you."

"No, you will not. You will keep the homefires burning, guard my back and . . ."

"One more word of that male chauvinist pig dreck and I will claw your eyes out."

When she used that tone of voice she meant it. I leaned back when I saw her fingers arch.

"I apologize, I'm sorry, I didn't mean it. Misplaced attempt at levity. I grovel at your feet," I said, dropping to the floor and doing a nice grovel and writhe.

She had to laugh and the air was cleared and I took her hands in mine again. "I have to go, and I have to go alone."

She sighed. "I know that, although I hate to admit it. But you will take care of yourself?"

"A promise—that I will keep."

"When do you leave?"

"I'll find out this afternoon. Our dear friend Coypu thinks he has finally licked the communication problem between us and the next universe."

"I thought he said that it was impossible."

"That was on a bad day. Today is a good one."

"I'll go with you."

The professor had tidied up all the breadboarded devices and looping wires that had made up his machine. Everything had now been integrated into a hulking black console that was all readouts and twinkling lights, tesla coils and glowing screen. Only the giant electrical cable was the same.

"Ah, James," he said when we came in, turned and rattled through a file drawer. "I have something for you."

He proudly produced a featureless flat black disk with a hole in the middle, dusted it off and passed it over.

"A music recording?" I asked, puzzled.

"You must not act like you have the intelligence level of plant life," he miffed. "What you are holding is a singularly re-markable invention. It is solid-state, has no moving parts, and even the electrons are pseudo-electrons, so they move at zero speed. It is impossible to detect it or affect it in any way. I've tried it in a number of universes and it works fine."

"What does it do?"

"When activated it signals the mother machine here. Which reaches out and brings you back. Simple."

"It certainly is. But how do I activate it?"

"Even simpler. It detects brain waves. You think at it and it takes you home."

I stared at the disk with admiration. What a wonder. I

spun it on my finger. All I had to do was to think *"Take me home . . ."*

Then I was across the room and slammed up tight against the machine, my hand held to its surface by the disk, my finger through the hole feeling as though it had been amputated.

"Can't . . . breathe . . ." I choked out.

Coypu hit a switch and I dropped to the floor. "A few little adjustments will take care of that."

I stood up, rubbing my sore ribs, still clutching the disk as I pulled my swollen finger out of the hole.

"Very impressive, " Angelina said. "Thank you, Professor. I'll have less to worry about now. When does he leave?"

"Whenever he wants to." He threw another switch and bolts of lightning coruscated deep inside the machine and the tesla coil snapped out loud sparks. "But there are a few other factors that must be considered before he departs. I managed to poke the tip of a universal analyzer through into Heaven. Some very interesting results. See." A screen lit up filled with rolling numbers and wiggling graphs.

"See what?" I said. "Makes no sense to me."

Coypu snorted with disgust and sneered with superiority. In that order. Then tapped the screen of the spectral gas analyzer. "It is obvious."

"Only to a genius like you, Professor. Explain, please."

I was sorry I asked. He explained at great and boring length. Gravity, air pressure, oxygen tension, speed of light, all that was okay. But there was too much more of electron spin, chaos dispersion, water quality, sewage disposal, fractal fracture and such. When he got on to analysis of atmospheric components I stopped him.

"What was that you said about some kind of gas?"

He pointed to the analysis bar on the screen. "This. A compound I have never seen before, so it has no name. I call it nitoxcubed. Because it acts somewhat like nitrous oxide."

"Laughing gas?"

"Correct. But with the pleasure factor cubed. So everyone goes around half-stoned. Then, if they leave Heaven, they get withdrawal symptoms, as is noted in the interviews in the record."

"I don't like that," Angelina said. "Could be habit-forming and Jim has enough bad habits right now. Can you do anything about it?"

"Of course." He held up a vial of purple liquid. "This will cancel the effects, an antidote. Roll up your sleeve, diGriz."

He filled a subdermal injector and gave my arm a spritz, blasting the antidote through my skin and right into my bloodstream.

"This is the only precaution you need take. Are you ready to go now?" He pressed a button and power surged through the machine.

"No rush!" I said, suddenly feeling rushed. "I need a good meal and a night's sleep first. We'll do it tomorrow morning, nice and early, at the crack of dawn. I will be off to Heaven."

We went out on the town that night, savoring the pleasures of this holiday world for the first time. Angelina and I held hands while Sybil had each of the lads by the arm and it was a great evening. The sound and light display was something else again, with an aurora borealis in the sky above and a two-thousand-piece orchestra in the pit below. Food, the best. Drink, better. Except for me; with morning getting ever closer I stuck to the diet-whiskey.

At dawn, leaving Angelina smiling in her sleep, I tiptoed out of the bedroom and headed for my appointment with destiny.

"You're late," Coypu said belligerently. "Getting cold feet?"

"Kindly knock off the pep talk, Prof. I'm ready whenever you are."

"Do you have the interuniversal activator?"

"Sealed inside my bootheel. We shall not be parted."

"Good luck, then." He threw more switches and the machine buzzed ominously. "The door is unlocked."

I opened the garage door and peeked. It looked good. I threw it wide and stepped through.

Nice. A warm yellow sun shone in the blue sky above, very different from the bloated red one in Hell. A small white cloud floated by at shoulder height. I poked it with my finger and it bounced away, giving off a pleasant chiming sound.

The landscape was most serene, low rolling hills covered with short grass. A grove of trees nearby shaded what looked like a paved road. I walked over and poked it with my toe. It was indeed a road, paved with soft cobblestones. It wound out of sight among the trees to the right. To the left it curled up a valley into the hills. Which way should I go?

There was a distant rumble like thunder from the direction of the hills. Curiosity, as always, won. I went that way. Curiosity paid off pretty quickly when I saw the road junction ahead with pointing-finger signs. I approached them with great interest.

"Three ways to go," I said, peering up at the boards. "I have apparently come from the direction of RUBBISH DUMP—which does not sound too exciting so I shall not retrace my steps. But, problems, problems, how do I choose between VALHALLA and PARADISE?"

Paradise sounded Paradisical, and brought to mind that fine planet named Paraiso Aqui. Which indeed did become Paradise Here after I had been elected president. I had dim memories of Valhalla from my religious research, something to do with snow, axes and horned helmets. Paradise sounded much better.

Then I noticed the piece of paper that had been nailed to the pole supporting the signs. It read PARADISE CLOSED FOR RE-PAIRS. Which, as you might imagine, made my decision much easier.

The road wound up into the hills and through a small valley. It ended at what appeared to be a high and crudely constructed wall. Large tree trunks, still covered with bark, were set into the ground. There was a metal door waiting invitingly, set into the wood. It was a false invitation. It had a handle that would not turn. I pushed against the metal, which resisted strongly. I was about to try my luck in Paradise when I noticed the sign above the door.

SERVICE ENTRANCE it read. Which implied strongly that there had to be another entrance. Which I would have to find. There was a path trampled in the grass and I followed it along the wall until it turned a corner.

"Now that's more like it," I said with sincere admiration.

No service entrance this! What looked like solid gold pillars held up a jewel covered pediment above a massive golden door. The precious stones glowed with inner light. There was the sudden blast of unseen horns, followed by loud and heroic music. Marching to its very enthusiastic beat I approached the entrance with great interest. When I came closer I saw that the jewels spelled out a message that I was unable to read. Probably because it was in some unknown language made up of strangely shaped letters that looked very much like crossed sticks. Not only strangely shaped but in an unknown alphabet, unknown that is at least to me. Above the jewels was an immense golden ax crossed with a golden hammer.

"Looks great, doesn't it?" a voice said.

I jumped, turned, landed ready for action. The music had covered the sound of his approach. But there appeared to be no threat from the newcomer. He was middle-aged and plump, wearing an expensive business suit and a white lace shirt with a blood-red necktie, and was smiling in the most friendly manner.

"You here same as me? Take a look at Valhalla."

"Sure am," I said, relaxing. And taking note that woven into his tie with gold thread was the same crossed axe and hammer that hung above the entrance. "Valhalla here we come . . ."

"Not yet!" he said quickly, raising his hand. "A look, sure, that's what I'm after. A quick look to see what the afterlife holds. Not quite ready for the real thing quite yet—"

His voice was drowned out by a blasting blare of horns and a tremendous drumroll as the golden door slowly swung open. As the music died away a woman's voice bid us welcome.

"I bid you welcome. Enter, good followers of the League of the Longboat and Life Friends of Freya. Enter and behold that which one day will be yours for eternity. As long as you pay your loyal tithe. Here is Valhalla! The mead-hall at rainbow's end. Come forward—and don't trip over the snake."

Some snake! It must have been a yard thick and vanished out of sight in both directions. It writhed slowly as we stepped over it.

"Uroboros!" my companion said. "Goes right around the world."

"Be quick," our invisible guide called out, "for you do not have much time. I shall part the veil, but can do this only briefly. Only by special dispensation of the gods is this possible. Thor always smiles upon warriors of the League of the Longboat, and Loki is away in Hel right now, so Thor, in his generosity, permits your presence for a quick peek at that which is yet to come. So look, breathe deep and enjoy for someday, one day, this will be yours . . . ."

The interior was veiled in darkness which slowly lightened. I stepped forward for a closer look and slammed my nose into an invisible barrier. It went down to the ground, stretched higher than I could reach. My companion rapped it with his knuckles.

"The Wall of Eternity," he said. "Glad it's there. You have to be dead to pass it."

"Thanks. I'll pass on passing. Zowie!"

The exclamation was pulled out of me by the bizarre scene that was suddenly revealed on the other side of the barrier. A fire roared in a massive stone fireplace and some entire giant beast was being cooked over it. At long wooden tables lots of big men with long blond hair and beards were really living it up. There was plenty of mad drinking and eating. Great mugs of drink were slopped onto the wooden tables, to be seized up and guzzled down. With one hand, because in the other hand most of the men held steaming meaty bones or the legs of very large birds. Their voices could be dimly heard like distant echoes, shouting and swearing. Some were singing. Great blond waitresses with mighty thews and even mightier busts were passing out the food and drink. An occasional shrill cry cut through the roar of masculine voices as buttocks were clutched; occasionally there was a thud as quick female action slammed a mug into a groper's head. Yet the large ladies laughed and tweaked many a Viking beard with more than a hint of orgies to come. In fact, dimly on a table in the distance, a meaty couple appeared to be doing just that, giggling in distant laughter. Which died away as darkness descended again.

"Isn't that something!" my companion said, eyes staring with admiration.

"Not for a vegetarian," I muttered, but not loud enough to spoil his fun. "I wonder if we belong to the same church?" I asked smarmily.

There was no answer—because he was no longer there. Opportunity missed; I should have been prying information out of him instead of goggling the joys of Valhalla. I went outside, but he really had gone back to wherever he had come from. Behind me the door slammed shut and the glowing jewels stopped glowing.

The show was over—and what had I found out?

"A lot," I reassured myself. "But this is surely not the Heaven as Vivilia VonBrun described it. Valhalla looks like a man's idea of a night out with the boys going on forever. Which means there must be more than one heaven in Heaven. Perhaps she saw the other one, Paradise. Which means I should take a look at it—even if it is closed."

Prodded by this stern logic I retraced my steps to the signboards, turned and followed the path to Paradise. It twisted its way through a thick stand of trees and brush.

Then I stopped as I heard the rumble of a vehicle's engine ahead. Putting caution before boldness I dropped to the ground and crawled forward through the bushes.

Parted the last one and looked out.

CHAPTER **16**

WHAT I WAS LOOKING AT was, or so it appeared, a normal building site that you would find on any planet. Beyond it were some low, temple-like buildings around a decorative lake. Just near me there was the framework of a half-constructed building, very much like the others. Earthmovers were landscaping around it, riggers swinging a steel beam into place. They were human too, not robots, for I heard one of them shout "*Bonega—veldu gin nun.*" Civilized Esperanto speakers talking about welding the structure. It was all so commonplace that I wondered what it was doing in this paradisical corner of Heaven.

Once I get the curiosity itch, I have to scratch. I stayed under the protective bush and watched the action. I wished, not for the first time, that Coypu could find a way for machines to be taken between the universes. I would dearly love to have had a telescope with me to watch the goings-on. And to take a much closer look at each of the working men on the site. If Slakey was one of them I would have to rethink any plans to investigate fuller on the site.

He didn't seem to be working here. All the builders I could see were lean and young. Though there was one older man in a hard hat, a foreman of some kind. Fairly fat—but he bore no resemblance to any of the Slakeys I had seen.

After a good time had passed I realized that it was pretty boring just lurking here in the shrubbery: I suppressed a yawn. I either had to do something positive or get out of there and do some research in the rubbish dump. But before I could make my mind up it was made up for me.

Older-and-Fatter looked at his watch—then blew loudly on his whistle. Everyone downed tools and turned off engines. At first I thought they were quitting for the day, until the roache coach came trundling up. Familiar from a thousand building sites and factory entrances around the galaxy. Filled with frozen food and armed with microwave. Selection of choice, porcuswine cutlets or deep-fried crustacean limbs, buttons pressed, steaming meal delivered.

The laborers lined up, shouting guttural oaths at one another and producing loud badinage as workers across the galaxy are wont to do, and received their meals as they were extruded from the delivery slots. Some sat down on the beams and boxes that littered the site. Happily a few of them decided to make a picnic out of the meal and strolled up the slope to sprawl on a patch of grass near me. Not near enough to hear what they were saying though, but close enough to start ideas curdling about in my brain. The fat foreman was one of the picnickers, tucking into a steaming and meaty rib that was big enough to have come from a brontosaurus.

I waited a bit, then rose and strolled towards them, whistling as I went.

"Lovely day, isn't it?" I said ingratiatingly. And was greeted by a sullen silence and surly scowls.

"Work going well?"

"Who the hell are you?" the foreman said, throwing his rib away and hauling himself to his feet.

"I'm an accountant. Work for the boss."

"For Slakey?"

"I call him Mr. Justin Slakey since he pays the bills. And you would be . . . ?"

"Grusher. I'm the gaffer here."

"My pleasure. Are you the one who reported the shortage in the cement supplies?"

"I reported nothing. What's this all about?" He was now eyeing me suspiciously—as were all of them.

"A minor matter . . ."

"Look bowb, who do you think you are just walking up here and asking questions? I worked for Slakey for years. I hire the roughnecks, chippies, brickies, the whole lot. I order building materials, build what he asks me to build like adding to this fun park here. He never asks questions—just pays the bills I send him. It's a cash deal."

"I don't like this guy," one of the workers growled. A particularly obnoxious one with bulging biceps. "You said there would be no trouble when we signed on, Grusher. Secret location for business reasons. Knocked us out before we came here. Good money and good hours and everything in cash."

"You from the tax people?" another equally ugly worker asked.

"He's the tax man," Bulging Biceps said as he pulled the spud wrench from the loop in his belt.

"Make him welcome," Grusher said, smiling coldly, as they moved in a circle about me. "He's interested in cement—well, we're pouring concrete today. Let's give him a closer look—from down inside."

I jumped aside so that the wrench whistled by me, then ducked under a wild punch. I'm good at self-defense—but not this good. Nine, ten to one and all fit and obnoxious. And closing in.

"You're right!" I shouted. "And you're all under arrest for tax invasion. Now go quietly . . ."

They roared in anger and hurled their muscled forms forward.

"Take me home!" I thought. *"Now!"*

I crashed into the metal panel on the machine, hung there spread-eagled.

"Professor . . . cut the power . . ."

"Sorry," Coypu said, "I knew I forgot something. Meant to make those adjustments before you came back."

He touched a button and I slumped to the floor. There was an open bottle of beer on his console; I stumbled over and drained it.

"What have you discovered?"

"Very little. My heavenly tour was just beginning. There is a suburb of Heaven named Valhalla with a pretty rough crowd and not my idea of heaven. Then there is Paradise, which is still being built. I better keep on looking. So I just popped back for a beer and to let you know what was going on. A little trouble there, nothing to mention. If Angelina should ask about me say that everything is going fine. Now—can you send me back, but not quite to the same spot if you don't mind?"

"Not a problem since I have calibrated the spherical locator during your absence. Would a kilometer laterally do?"

"Fine." I opened the garage door a crack, saw only blue sky and green grass. "This will be great. See you later."

I stepped through and felt the sun warm on my back. A light breeze was blowing and wafting some small clouds in my direction, drifting slowly above my head.

There were more of them appearing, some even drifting against the wind which was ominous. One of them floated by in the other direction. It tinkled—and more. Was that laughter coming from it? It drifted along and I drifted after it. Along a path of sorts that had been trodden in the grass. Then, far ahead, I saw a white structure of some kind that topped a distant hill. Another puffy cloud drifted after the first one, chiming pleasantly as well. Follow the path, that seemed obvious. It was made of yellow bricks that were resiliently soft. A cloud of birds was swirling about above the road ahead. At least I thought that they were birds. I quickly changed my mind about this when I got closer. They were pink and round, with little white wings that were surely too small to support them. They began to look very familiar.

When I had done my religious research about Heaven—and Hell—I had been most taken by the illustrations. It soon became clear that all of the religions of history, while being pretty divisive for the most part, had on the other hand provided plenty of artistic inspiration. Poems and songs, books and paintings, architecture, as well as some strange and interesting sculpture. Somewhere in all those data banks I had seen these pink pirouetters.

They circled ever closer until I stopped and bulged my eyes at them.

They were little, fat, pink babies hovering on hazy wings. All of them had golden curls of hair on their heads and were of indeterminate sex. I say this because they all had what appeared to be wispy lengths of silky cloth about their loins. They fluttered closer until they were circling above my head like a cloud of gnats; I strongly resisted the impulse to leap up and get one by the leg for a closer look. They circled and smiled and laughed aloud with a sound like tiny tinkling bells.

Then they pointed and stirred with excitement for coming towards us was another flock of the same little creatures. The new lot appeared to be carrying guns of some kind; I looked for cover.

"Shame, Jim," I said when they had fluttered closer. "You've got a nasty and suspicious mind." They weren't carrying guns but instead were armed with tiny golden harps. They strummed as they flew, swooping into a circling formation with the first lot. I sat down on the yellow brick road to watch. And discovered that the road was warm as well as soft.

After an arpeggio of plaintive pluckings, the entire airborne swarm burst into song. It was nice enough, though a little high-pitched for my liking, and sung in an unfamiliar language.

"*Die entführung aus dem Serail!*" one chirrupy lot sang as they swooped away. But another bunch had already fluttered into position to have a go of their own.

> "*Per queste tue manine,*
> *In quale eccessi, mi tradei,*
> *un bacio de mano . . . .*"

This was followed by a song in Esperanto. I could understand it, although I wasn't quite sure what it was about.

"Profunde li elfosis min
Bele li masonis min,
Alte li konstruis min.
Sed Bil-Auld estas foririnta . . . ."

And so forth. The singing was not bad, at first, but a little too tinkling and twittery for my tastes. They could have done with a couple of good bassos to back them up. It all finally ended on a high-piercing note that made my teeth hurt. They swirled upward and away.

"Great," I called after them. Then an afterthought. "Is there a good bar or cantina nearby?" Only the sound of high-pitched laughter sounded from above. "Thanks a lot," I muttered sourly. Stood and scuffed down the road trying to ignore my growing thirst. The white building on the hill appeared no closer and the sun was hot on my shoulders. But a turn in the road held out some promise of succor. A little plaid tent of some kind was set up beside the road. Gilt chairs with ornate arms were arrayed on the grass before it. A woman in a white dress sat on one of the chairs sipping from a golden mug.

She smiled broadly at me as I approached. A rather fixed smile that did not change—nor did her eyes move to follow me. More frosted mugs were on a table in the tent. I took up one, sniffed and tasted it; cold sweet and definitely alcoholic.

"Not bad," I said in my most friendly manner. She did not turn her head or reply. I went and sat in the chair next to hers. A very attractive woman, firm of breast and fair of brow. I was glad that Angelina wasn't here, for the moment at least. I leaned forward.

"Do you come here often?" I asked, all conversational originality. But at least it did get her attention. She turned her head slowly and fixed her dark and lovely eyes upon me, opened moist red lips.

"Is it time to go already?" she husked richly, put her glass down, rose and left.

"Well, Jim—you do have a way with women," I mused and drank my drink. Then blinked quickly as she stepped onto the yellow brick road and vanished. It was quite abrupt and soundless. I walked over and looked but there was no trace of a trapdoor or device of any kind.

"Slakey!" I said, spun about, but I was alone. "Was she here on one of your day tours, a quick look at Heaven then back to the checkbook?" I remembered what Coypu had said about the narcotic gas in the air here; she had really looked stoned, on that and the drink maybe. I put mine down without finishing it.

Refreshed enough, I went on. A twist in the road led through a flowered ravine and I saw that the building on the hill was now closer and clearer. Gracious white marble columns supported a gilded roof. As I came close I saw that stone steps led up from the road. I stopped as they began to move.

"A Heaven-sized escalator," I said, eyeing them with glum suspicion. "You have been observed Jim—or have actuated some concealed switch."

There seemed to be no point in retreating. My presence was known—and after all I was here to investigate. So I did. Stepping gingerly onto the steps that carried me gracefully up to my destination.

A large single room filled the interior of the building, with blue sky visible between the columns that framed it. A shining marble floor, dust and blemish free, stretched to the throne at the far end. A man sat there, old and plump with white hair, occasionally strumming a chord on the harp he held. If nothing else, Heaven was surely big on harps. A golden halo floated above his head.

As I walked closer, the noble head turned towards me, the halo bobbing and moving with it. He nodded and the lips turned up in a smile.

"Welcome to Heaven, James Bolivar diGriz," he said.

The voice was rich and warm, the profile familiar.

"Professor Slakey, I presume?"

CHAPTER 17

I WAS SORELY TEMPTED TO think *get me out of here and take me home* but restrained myself. I had a foolproof means of escape, or so Coypu had reassured me, and my escape from the building site had proved him right, so I should hang around for a bit. I wasn't being threatened, at least not yet, and this was supposed to be a reconnaissance mission.

"No hard feelings?" I asked.

"Should there be?"

"You tell me. The last time we met, or I met with a number of your incarnations, mayhem and murder seemed to be the name of the game."

"Of course. Hell." He nodded. "I wasn't there but of course I was aware of what was happening. That was very good salami—you must give me the name of your supplier."

This conversation was getting a little surrealistic, but I decided to press on. This was the first time I had talked to Slakey without some kind of instant violence in the offing.

"Where is Heaven?" I asked.

"All around you. Isn't it enjoyable?"

"Is this the Heaven the seriously religious hope to go to when they die?"

"Pleasant, isn't it? Did you enjoy the cherubs?" He smiled benignly. I decided to be a little more direct.

"Why are you here in Heaven?"

"The same reason you are."

"Let's get down to facts. You are a crook with a number of cons. A murderer as well, since you shipped all those people off to Hell. And you have been giving suckers daytrips to Heaven. To a variety of Heavens." He pursed his lips and nodded as though in thought.

"If you say so, dear boy. I want no dissension in Heaven."

"What is the purpose of all this? What are you doing with all the money you bamboozle out of people?"

This time the cold look in his eye was pure Slakey. "You are getting tiresome, Jim. And boring. And a bit of a nuisance—don't you think so?"

Now that he mentioned it I realized that I wasn't exactly being the life of the party. "I'm sorry, Professor. I'm not usually like this."

"Apology accepted, of course. It's so nice here in Heaven that we shouldn't quarrel. There—why don't you sit down there and rest?"

There was a chair beside me that hadn't been there an instant before. A good thing too since he was right, I really was tired. Very, very tired. I dropped into it. Slakey nodded again.

"Time to get comfortable, Jim. Take off your boots, stretch your toes . . ."

What a good idea—or was it? What was wrong with it? I couldn't quite remember. Meanwhile I was taking off one boot, then the other, and tossing them aside.

Slakey smiled toothily and snapped his fingers and my lassitude vanished. The boot heel! *Get me out of here!* I blasted the thought out so loudly that it rattled around inside my skull.

The boots were gone and nothing had happened. Or rather something not too nice happened, because when I jumped to my feet and turned to run I fell flat on my face. Staring at the golden bracelet around my ankle. Attached to a length of gilt chain that vanished into the ground.

"Good trick," I said sternly, although it came out a little squeakily. I climbed to my feet and sat down again in the chair. "Not really. You are a stupid little man and very easy to out-think. Didn't you realize that your undetectable device would be detected? An interuniversal activator indeed! I sneer at it. My science is so far ahead of yours that I hesitate to describe the difference. Not only my science but my intellect. More child's play to outwit you. First I used hypnotic gas to make you amenable, then it was only a matter of simple suggestion to control a simple mind. You were happy to turn over your boots to me. Along with your life, you must realize. I am the master of science, of life and death, time and entropy!"

Also one brick short of a load, one nut short of a nutcake, I thought grimly. It was not going to be easy to get out of this one.

"You are indeed," I said with all sincerity. "But you are also a man of mystery as well. With all your talents why are you going to all the trouble setting up your con games?"

He chose not to answer; insane or not he kept his secrets. And he was beginning to lose his temper.

"Wispy, time-shortened man—do you know how old I am?"

"No, but I'm sure that you will tell me. Not that I really care."

I turned away and yawned and watched out of the corner of my eye as his face turned purple.

"You have strained my patience, diGriz. You must show respect and, yes, awe for someone like me—who is over eight thousand years old!"

"Amazing!" I said. "I wouldn't pick you as a year over seven thousand . . ."

"Enough!" he raged, leaping to his feet. "I am tired of you. Therefore I now condemn you to Purgatory. Bring him."

This last command was directed at a hulking, man-shaped robot that came clanking up the stairs. It was dented and scarred, red with rust and coated with black dust. One electronic eye glowed balefully; the other had been torn out of its socket. It stamped towards me and I quailed back, so great was the thing's insensate menace. It hissed and bent, reached out and with its sharp-bladed fingers it cut the chain that secured me . I jumped away—but it caught me in midair with clutching hands the size of shovels. Grabbed me and crushed me to its metal chest, its grip unbreakable and painful. Fat and white-haired Slakey grunted with the effort as he pulled himself to his feet and waddled away, my captor clomping after him. Down the stairs we went and out onto the yellow brick road.

Slakey stamped his foot and there was a slathering, liquid sound as the road lifted up like a great yellow tongue. A dark pit was revealed from which rose a dreadful stench.

"The doomed enter Purgatory," he intoned. "None return. Go."

My captive robot, still clutching me, leaned forward. More and more.

Until we dropped face-first down into the pit.

There have been a number of times in my adventurous life when I have strongly wished I was elsewhere. This was definitely one of them. My past life did not flash before me, but the jagged stone walls certainly did. They were lit by a ruddy glow from below that we were rapidly approaching at what must be ter-minal velocity.

Was this the way it was going to end? Not with a whimper, but with a resounding crash when my metallic captor hit the ground. Which was rushing towards us far too fast. A bleak, black landscape lit by sporadic gouts of flame. I wriggled inef-fectively in the robot's iron grasp.

Then we juddered and slowed and I almost slipped out of the thing's embrace as deceleration hit it. But it just clamped harder on my chest until I couldn't breathe.

With a resounding clang we hit the ground and I crashed down as the thing let go of me. Before I could get my breath back it had me by the arm and was dragging me along. I had very little choice; I went. Limping because the stony ground was exceedingly hard on my stockinged feet. I wished that I was back in Heaven with my boots.

What I could see of the surroundings was far from inspiring. A miasma hung in the air that not only stank but irritated my air passages as well. I coughed and, as though in ghastly echo, there was the sound of heavy coughing from up ahead. We went around a mound of crushed rock and I saw the cause.

Stretching out and vanishing into the distance, barely revealed by the ruddy light, were long, low, almost table-like structures of some kind. Standing along both sides were bent figures with their arms extended. They were doing something, just what I could not say. As we passed close to one of the structures there was a rumbling sound and from the mouth of an apparatus there fell a mass of some dark powdered substance. A wisp of it came my way and I coughed again for this was the source of the stench and irritation.

It was difficult to see clearly what was going on since my metallic captor neither slowed nor stumbled, just dragged me forward steadily. Yet, since the scene repeated itself over and over, I began to see what was happening. I couldn't understand it—but I could observe it.

The dust was flowing, or being carried, slowly down the length of the table-like constructions. The laborers, they were all women I could see now, ran their fingers over the surface. That was all they did, slowly and repetitiously, never looking up, never stopping. One of them picked up something, I could not tell what it was, and dropped it into a container at her side. I dragged by.

By far the worst part was there total lack of interest or attention to anything other than their work. I would have certainly looked up if a giant, decrepit robot dragged someone by me. They did not.

We passed more and more of them. All engaged in the same mysterious task, silently and continuously. This went on for a very long time. There were hundreds, possibly thousands, of laboring women. Then we were past the last ones and I was being hauled off into the semidarkness.

"I say, good robot guide, where are you taking me?" It

plodded on. I pried at its clamped fingers. "Cease!" I shouted. "This is the voice of your master, your human master. Stop now you animated junkyard."

It neither slowed nor paid me any heed, dragging me along like a dead beast. I walked again, stumbling, which was somewhat better than being dragged. To a metal door set into the rock face. It opened the door and pulled me through. I heard it clang shut behind us although I could see nothing in the darkness. It started up an unseen stairway, apparently seeing all right with its single operating eye. I fell and banged my shins, fell again and again until I grew used to the stairs. I was reeling with exhaustion by the time it stopped again and opened another door. Seized me up and threw me through it.

Behind me the door clanged shut even before I hit the ground. Reality twisted, the sensation of passing from one universe to another. There was sudden light and I banged down hard onto a stone floor.

Cold light lit the even colder scene; my teeth began chattering. I was in a metal-walled room with a barred door set in the far wall. Snow and frigid air blew in between the bars.

Had I been hauled down to Purgatory, then tossed through the machine, just to be allowed to freeze to death? It didn't make sense. There certainly must be lots of easier and less complicated ways of disposing of me. My blue and bare toes, protruding from the ruins of my socks, kicked against something. I looked down at the heaped clothing, thick boots, gloves. This was a message that I was happy to receive.

My fingers were trembling as I pulled on the heavy socks and trousers, then kicked into the boots. They didn't fit that well—but they kept out the cold. Everything I put on was a depressing shade of ash gray which did not disturb me in the slightest. The clothing was warm and not too uncomfortable. I wound a scarf around my neck, popped on a seedy fur hat, then wriggled my fingers into the thick gloves.

Right on cue the barred door swung open and more snow blew in. I ignored it and turned around to see if there was any way of getting out the same way I had come in.

"I am called Buboe," a menacingly deep voice said. I sighed and turned to look at my newest tormentor.

Dressed like me. Almost of a height, but he was heavier and wider. In his hands he held a flexible metal rod that I looked at very suspiciously. Particularly when he waggled it in my direction.

"This is Buboe's bioclast. Bioclast hurts lot. It kills too. You do what Buboe say, you live. Don't do it, you hurt and die. This is hurt."

He flicked the thing at me. I jumped aside so that the tip barely grazed me.

This was a new kind of pain. It felt like my flesh had been sliced to the bone and boiling acid then poured into the wound. I could only stand, holding my wounded arm and waiting for the pain to pass. It did, eventually, and it was hard to believe that both clothing and arm were still intact. Buboe waggled the bioclast at me and I shivered away.

"Learn fast, live. No learn, die."

His linguistic abilities were not of the best but he had an unassailable and thoroughly convincing argument. And at least he could talk; I could only nod agreement not trusting myself to speak yet.

"Work," he said, pointing his weapon at the open door. I stumbled through it into blue-lit daylight, a desolate, snow-whipped frigid hell. Large machines were moving around me, but until my eyes stopped tearing at the sudden cold I could not see what they were doing.

I soon found out. This was an opencast mine, a great sunken pit of broken stone and heaped gravel. The black layers were being torn open by hulking machines; the rubble they heaped up was then carried away by many-wheeled devices. At first I thought that the machines were workrobots. Then I saw that each vehicle had a rider or an operator. The machines did the digging and carrying under the men's guidance.

"You go up," Buboe said, rapping on an immobile machine. The sight of his thin rod sent me scurrying up the handholds on its side. I wriggled into the bucket seat, looked out through the scarred and chipped window before me, wondered what to do next. A loudspeaker above my head scratched to life.

"Detection. Unknown individual. Identify yourself."

"Who are you?" I asked, looking around for an operator, but I was alone. It was my steel chariot that was speaking to me.

"I am Model Ninety-one surface debrider and masculator. Give identity."

"Why?" I asked angrily, having never enjoyed conversations with machines.

"Give identity," was all it would say.

"My name is none of your business," I said sulkily—then regretted the words the instant I had spoken them.

"State work experience with this Model Ninety-one, None-ofyourbusiness."

"I will give the orders. Now hear this . . ."

"State work experience with this Model Ninety-one, None-ofyourbusiness."

There was no way to win this argument. "None."

"Orientation instructions begin."

They did, and they went on for far too long in far too stupid detail, geared to the thought processes of a retarded two-year-old. I listened just long enough to find out how the thing operated, then looked around for some way out of this dilemma. Knowing that it was not going to be easy.

". . . now power is on, Noneofyourbusiness. Work begins."

It surely did. There were levers by each knee, along with the two pedals, controlled direction and speed. A single, knobbed control moved the hydraulically powered arm that projected forward from right below the cab. This was first pressed against the rock surface and the trigger pulled. Fragments of rock blasted out in all directions—including towards the cab, which explained the thickness and scars on the forward-facing window. When enough rock had been broken free I touched the glowing red button that signaled for the bucketbil. This trundled over on its two rows of heavy wheels and backed into position below. I worked the controls for the loading arms which stuck out just below my face.

The first time I dumped a load I I waved to the driver of the bucketbil. His grim expression never changed, but he was considerate enough to raise a thick middle finger to me. I loaded and he left.

Light was fading from the sky. Night approached and work would cease for the day. A nice thought, but not a very accurate one. Worklights came on above, the headlights of my Model 91 illuminated the falling snowflakes and the rock face: the work continued.

An indeterminate, but long, time later there was a warbling sound from the cab's loudspeaker and the machine's power was switched off. I saw the driver of the nearest stopped Model 91 climbing wearily down from his machine. I did the same, and just as wearily. There was another heavily dressed man waiting on the ground, who climbed up the machine as soon as I got down. He said nothing to me—nor did I have anything to say to him in return. I shuffled after the other shuffling man. Through a door in the canyon wall. Into a large and warm hall filled with men and redolent with the strong pong of B.O. My new home.

It was worse than any army camp or work camp that I had ever been in. There was an overlay of despair that could not be avoided. These men were condemned and bereft of any spark of will. Or hope.

The only note of interest came after I had found an empty bunk to dump my heavy outer clothing, then followed the others to the eating tables. I was looking at the appalling food on my battered tray when a large hand seized my shoulder painfully.

"I eat your kreno," said the overweight and obnoxious individual who was attached to the hand. Another hand of the same size reached for the purple steaming lump on my tray. I lowered the tray to the table, waited until the kreno was well-clutched—then grabbed the wrist.

This was the only decent thing that had happened to me since I had left for Heaven this morning. Or a week ago. Or something.

Since he was very big, obviously obnoxious and undoubtedly strong, I played no fancy games. As his thick head went by I cracked him across the bridge of the nose with the side of my hand. He squealed in pain so I generously gave him peace by punching his neck in the right place with stiffened fingertips. He kept on going to the floor and did not move. I picked up my tray and took the kreno from his limp fingers. Looked around at the other diners.

"Any of you lot want to try for my kreno?" I asked.

The few who had bothered to look up from their food quickly lowered their eyes. The man at my feet began to snore. The only other sound was the slurp and crunch of masticating food.

"It's really nice to meet you guys," I said to the tops of heads. Sat down and ate hungrily.

Forcing myself not to think about where I was and what I was going to do.

Or what the unforeseeable future might be like.

CHAPTER 18

A GREAT NUMBER OF STRENUOUS days passed, not to say nights, in endless, brainless toil. The food was disgusting but kept the body's furnace stoked. My kreno-clutching friend, whose name I had soon discovered was Lasche, was the barrack's bully. He stayed out of my way, though he glared at me from behind the pair of black-and-blue eyes I had given him, then found other, more vulnerable men to pick on.

The routine could not have been simpler—or more mind-destroyingly boring. There were two shifts, one worked while the other slept, and there were no days off. The day started when the lights came on and Buboe appeared to stir the laggards along with his bioclast. As we filed out of the barracks the other shift stumbled in. It was the hot-bed system with one worker getting out of bed just before the other one crawled into it. Since the rough blankets were never changed or cleaned this made for an unusual miasma in the sleeping quarters. That was the way the day began; it ended when the lights went out.

In between working and sleeping, sleeping and working, we ate the repulsive meals that had been prepared in the robot kitchen. There was very little talking among the inmates, undoubtedly because there was absolutely nothing to talk about.

The only change in this routine was when I operated a bucketbil rather than a Model 91. This was even more distasteful and boring since it involved only driving away with a full load, dumping it and coming back empty.

I had a spurt of interest when I went to dump my first load, trundling along in the wake of another filled machine. Our destination proved to be nothing more exciting than a giant metal hopper set into the ground. There was no indication at all where the crushed rock was going. Or why. Was there a cave or a conveyor underground? I didn't think so. I had come to this planet courtesy of Slakey's universe machine. The chances were that crushed rock was going somewhere the same way. I thought about this for a bit, but soon forgot to think about it under the pressure of work and fatigue.

It must have been the fatigue that put me off guard. I had concerned myself with Lasche for the first few days as his shiners turned from black to green and other interesting colors. He seemed to have forgotten about me as well.

But he hadn't. I was wiping up the cold remains of the evening meal when I noticed the expression on the face of the man across the table from me. He was looking up over my shoulder and I saw his eyes widen. It was reflex that made me jump aside—and just blind luck that my skull wasn't crushed. The rock that Lasche was wielding struck my shoulder a numbing blow, knocking me off the bench. I roared with pain and rolled aside, stumbled to my feet and stood dizzily with my back to the wall. I made a fist with my left hand, but my right arm was numb and powerless. I shuffled along the wall until I had a clear space before me. Lasche followed me, lifting the rock menacingly.

"Now you're gonna be dead," he said. I felt no desire to join in the conversation. I watched his beady and nasty little eyes, waiting for him to attack.

He did—but fell forward as the man at the table behind him stuck out his foot and tripped him. I made the most of it, bringing my knee up to meet his face as he went down. He screamed hoarsely and dropped the rock. I grabbed it up with my good hand, ready to slam it into his skull.

"If you kill him, or maim him so he can't work, Buboe will kill you," the man said. He of the tripping toe. I dropped the rock and satisfied myself with a quick kick in the thug's ribs and a punch in his neural ganglion that would keep him quiet for some time.

"Thanks," I said. "I owe you one."

He was thin and wiry, with black hair and even blacker grease on his hands. I kneaded my sore right arm with my hand as it tingled back to life.

"My name is Berkk," he said.

"Jim."

"Can you operate an arcwelder?"

"I'm an expert."

"I thought you might be. I have been watching you since you came here. You know how to take care of yourself. Let's go see Buboe."

Our brutal keeper had a room of his own, absolute luxury in this place. And a heating coil as well. When we found him he was stirring an unappealing orange mass in a battered pot. But it smelled all right and would surely be better than the slop we were fed.

"What you want?" He scowled at us. Probably found the effort to speak coherently a tiring one.

"I need help putting that Model Ninety-one back together. The one that fell off the rockface."

"Why help?"

"Because I say so, that's why. It's a two man job. Jim here can work a welder."

He stopped stirring and looked at us suspiciously, his bulging red eyes moving from Berkk's face to mine. It took some time; obviously coherent thought was as alien to him as articulate speech. In the end he grunted and went back to stirring his meal. Berkk turned to leave and I followed him out.

"Would you care to translate?" I asked.

"You'll work with me in the repair shop for awhile."

"All that from a grunt?"

"Sure. If he had said no that would have ended it."

"I want to thank you . . ."

"Don't. It's heavy and dirty work. Let's go."

He lifted a grease-stained finger to rub his nose—and it touched his pursed lips for a second.

He wanted silence, he got silence. There was more here than met the eye—and I felt the first spurt of hope since I had arrived in this terrible place.

We went down the corridor beyond Buboe's lair to a large, locked door. Berkk obviously didn't have the key, because he sat down with his back to the wall. I joined him and we waited some time in silence until Buboe finally appeared, still chewing some last gristly bit of his meal. He unlocked the door, let us in sealed it again behind us.

"Let's get started," Berkk said. "I hope you meant it about the arcwelder."

"I can work that and every kind of machine tool, repair printed circuits, anything. If it's broken I can fix it."

"We'll find out."

The wrecked Model 91 had its side stove in, in addition to a broken axle. I cut out the crumpled area while Berkk levered a steel plate onto a dolly and rolled it over. We used a chain hoist to lift it. Without any robots to help it was hard work.

"We can talk here," he said as he hammered the plate into position. "I've been watching you. You don't act as stupid as the muscular morons here."

"Nor do you."

He smiled wryly. "Would you believe it—I volunteered. Everyone else here got drunk or hit in the head or something. Then woke up in this place. Not me, no. I answered an ad in the net for an experienced machinist. Incredible salary. Looked really great. I went to this lab, met a Professor Slakey. Blackout—and I woke up here."

"Where is here?"

"I haven't the slightest idea. Do you know?"

"Some. I know Slakey and I know that you can get here from Heaven. No, don't look at me like that, let me explain. I was thrown into a room and ended up in a different one. In a different universe I am sure. The same thing must have happened to you when you came here."

While we repaired the machine I filled him in on Slakey's operations. It all must have sounded really far out, but he had no choice other than to believe it. When the repairs were done we took a break and he produced a jar filled with a very ominous-looking liquid.

"I got some raw krenoj from the kitchen, I go there to keep the machines running. Took scrapings from some of the vegetables and managed to isolate a decent strain of yeast. Fermented the krenoj, terrible! Alcoholic all right but undrinkable. But, some plastic tubing—"

"The worm! Heat source, evaporated, cooled and condensed, distilled and now waiting our attention." I swirled the liquid happily in the flask.

"Be warned. There's alcohol in there all right. But the taste—"

"Let me be the judge," I said rashly. Raised and drank, lowered the flask and retched dryly. "I think . . ." I gasped, and my voice was so harsh my words were almost indistinguishable. "I think that that—is the foulest thing I have ever drunk in— a lifetime of drinking foul beverages."

"Thank you. Now if you will pass it over."

It did not get any better with more drinking. But at least the ethyl alcohol began to take effect, which possibly made the entire exercise worthwhile.

"I can put some of the pieces together," he said, then wiped his finger across the coating on his teeth that the drink had deposited. "We had a guy here once, very briefly, with a big mouth. Said that he had helped repair the rollers in a pulverizing mill someplace. He thought that they were grinding up our rock."

"Did he say why?"

"No—and he was gone next day. He talked too much.

That's why we have to be careful. I don't know who or what is listening—"

"I know who. Slakey in one of his manifestations. He has this rock dug out here, then it is sent somewhere. Then it is ground up, then sent to the women who sort it and take something out of it."

"What?"

"I don't know what—except that it is terribly expensive. In money and in human lives."

"I'm sure of it. And we won't find the answer here. I want out of this place and I need help."

What music to my ears! I seized his hand and pummeled him on the back with joy. "You have a plan?"

"An idea. I don't think we can get out the way we came in. Through that barred room." I nodded agreement.

"That is undoubtedly a dimensional doorway operated by Slakey himself. But what other way is there to go? I have looked carefully and could not see any way to climb out of this valley. And even if we did—where would we go? This might be a barren planet at the end of the universe."

"I agree completely. Which leaves only the other way. Think for yourself—"

"Of course. The broken rock goes into the pit. We go with it and are crushed to death, right?"

"Wrong. I have been working on this for a long, long time. But I needed someone to help me—"

"I'm your man," I said. Slightly blurrily.

"Back to work," he said, climbing swayingly to his feet. "Gotta finish repairs first."

Work had a sobering effect and no more was said that day. An electric bell summoned Buboe who opened the large locked door that opened to the outside. I shivered and stamped my feet while Berkk drove the Model 91 out and parked it there. The door was sealed again and Buboe unlocked the other door that led us back to our quarters. And searched us ruthlessly before letting us out.

There was a backlog of repairs needed on the machines and we had plenty to do. Slowly. I would be back as a driver as soon as the job was complete. And Berkk never spoke again about his plan. I did not want to ask, figuring that it was his idea and he would know when the time was right. Life was work and sleep, work and sleep—with loathsome meals ingested briefly between. Berkk remained silent until the day when we were finishing the job of replacing a wheel on a bucketbil. We lay side by side beneath the thing, one holding, one hammering.

"This is the last repair you are going to do," he said. "Buboe says he is shorthanded and wants you back on the digging. I've been putting this off but we can't put it off anymore. You ready to go?" he asked. I did not ask where.

"Yes. When?"

"Now." He turned to look at me and I saw that his face was suddenly grim. "Have you ever killed a man?" he asked.

"Why? Is it important?"

"Very. If we are to go, then Buboe will have to be disarmed, maybe killed. I'm not much of a fighter—"

"I am. I'll take care of him. And hopefully not kill him. Then what?"

"Then these. We must get them into this bucketbil and out of here without being seen."

He kicked a tarpaulin aside, let the worklight play over them for an instant, then covered them again.

They were two frames made of rebar. They were shaped like coffins and were the same size as coffins. The finger-thick lengths of reinforcing bar were closely placed and crossed at right angles, then had been welded into place to form the cages. One side of each cage was hinged so it could be opened. Open this and crawl in. Close and turn the latch. Then—what he planned was obvious.

"Is this the only way?" I asked.

"Do you know of another?"

"It's suicide."

"It's certain death here if we don't try."

"We go into the hopper with the crushed rock, then through to—somewhere."

I took a deep breath, then let it out in a long, slow sigh.

"Let's do it," I finally said. "The quicker the better because I don't want to have time to think about it, or estimate our chances to get out alive instead of being pulverized."

CHAPTER 19

THIS WAS THE LAST BUCKETBIL in need of repair. We stretched the work out as long as we dared. Knowing that when it went back to work—so would I. In the rockpit. Before that happened we had to make our break together. One man could not do it alone.

All our preparations for escape had been made long since. It was just the idea of getting crushed along with the rest of the rocks that had been holding us back. I ran the file over the protruding bolthead. Stepped back to admire my work—then threw the tool onto the ground.

"Let's do it—and quick."

Berkk hesitated a moment, then nodded grim agreement. I dug into the scrap pile and found the cosh that I had made. I pulled its strap onto my wrist and slipped the thing up my sleeve. It was just a plastic tube filled with ball bearings but would surely do the job.

Berkk looked at me and I gave him what I hoped was a reassuring smile and a thumbs-up. He wheeled about and stabbed the button that would summon our keeper.

Who was very slow about arriving. Undoubtedly involved in some other sordid task. Minutes slipped by and I saw the beads of perspiration form on Berkk's forehead—even though the workshop was chill.

"Press it again," I said. "Maybe he didn't hear it the first time."

Again. And a third time. I slammed the cosh against my palm, testing it. Behind me the door rattled open and I just had time to get it back up my sleeve again as Buboe appeared.

"What you ring so much for?"

"Finished," Berkk said, slapping the metal flank of the bucketbil.

"Take out," Buboe said, turning his key in the lock. Cold wind blew in and he turned to glare at me. "You out of here. Go work." He continued to stare at me, his back to the bucketbil, slapping the bioclast against his trouser leg.

"Sure, whatever you say." I smiled insincerely instead of screaming.

This was not going right. He was supposed to be looking at Berkk so I could work my will upon him without getting a bioclast blast at full power. Behind him I could see Berkk climbing up the ladder and dropping into the control seat. The motor hammered and burst into life. And our captor still stared at me. And stepped forward.

"Out, go," he commanded. Lifting the bioclast towards me.

The bucketbil's engine idled roughly and died.

"Something's very wrong here," Berkk called out, staring down in horror.

We stayed that way as long seconds ticked by. The bioclast waving before me, the brute's eyes fixed on mine, Berkk clutching the steering wheel not knowing what else to do.

Luckily our thuggish warder's brain was incapable of entertaining two thoughts at one time. When the meaning of Berkk's words finally penetrated, he turned around.

"What happen?"

"This," I said, released from frightened paralysis, taking a single step forward. The cosh dropped into my hand, I swung—

—and he dropped heavily to the ground. I raised the cosh

again but he lay, unmoving. Not stirring even when I pried the weapon from his grip.

"Let's do it!" I shouted, pulling the tarpaulin from off our horde.

Berkk lifted the first rebar cage and heaved it up into the bucket. I used the prepared lengths of wire to bind the unconscious man, ankles and wrists, then wired his legs and arms one to the other. He could untwist the wire when he came around, but it would take time. While we, hopefully, would be long gone. I tied the gag into his mouth and dragged him back just as Berkk was heaving up the second cage. I pulled the tarp over the bound man and straightened up. Berkk had the big outer door partly open, held it that way as I clambered up the side of the machine and dropped into the bucket.

"Anyone out there?" I asked as he got into the driver's seat.

"No machines, no one in sight." He started the engine again and I could see his hands trembling.

"Slowly now, take your time. A deep breath, that's it. Now—go! And don't forget that you have to close the door once we're outside!"

The way he had revved the engine told me that he had forgotten the next step, driven now by panic and not intelligence. But having been reminded, he now did just as we had planned. Drove out through the door and stopped. Kicked the thing out of gear and locked the brakes. Climbed slowly to the ground and closed the workshop door. "Locked," he said as he climbed back up again.

As we drove into the darkness, I pulled myself up so I could look over the lip of the bucket. Lights and trundling machines were working in the open pit ahead.

"Did you . . . did you kill him?" Berkk asked.

"Far from it. Skull like rock. He'll have a headache—"

"And we'll be gone. There's a bucketbil dumping right now."

"Only one?"

"Yes."

"Go slower, take the long way. Don't get there until it's gone."

We slowed and rumbled on; I ducked back down as headlights washed over us. Moments later we stopped. The engine died but the headlights stayed on, illuminating the black bulk of the hopper.

"Let's go!" he shouted and jumped to the ground.

I realized I was still holding the bioclast. I threw it far out into the hopper and it vanished from sight. Then I heaved the first cage up and over the side onto the ground, bent and dragged up the other one. It followed the first and I went right after it.

We had planned this, step by step. And as long as we kept moving we did not have to think about what the last and final step was going to be. Berkk had clambered up onto the wide lip of the hopper, turned and reached down and grabbed the first cage when I pushed it up to him. Then the other. Only when I had climbed up beside him did I see that he was shaking from head to toe.

"Can't—do it!" He gasped, sat down and put his arms over his head. Beyond him I saw the sudden flare of approaching headlights.

"Too late to go back!" I shouted as I scrabbled at the steel frame and pulled the door open. "Get in!"

"No . . . ," He pulled back. I balled a fist and hit him on the jaw. Not enough to knock him unconscious—I hoped!—but enough to addle his thoughts.

It worked. I hauled his limp body into the cage and was closing the sealing hasp when he began screaming and tearing at me through the bars.

"Keep your hands inside!" I shouted as I kicked the cage off the ledge. It rattled down into the hopper and vanished from sight.

Now—could I do that to myself?

"Good enough for him, Jim. It better be good enough for you,"

Easy enough to say; harder to do. I opened the hinged side

and looked down into the cage. It was like looking into a rebar coffin.

I don't know how long I stood like that, unable to move, unable to commit myself to the destiny I had so easily tipped my partner into.

Headlights washed over me. "Bowb!" I grimaced between grated teeth. Dropped down, crawled in, locked the gate. Took a very deep breath.

Reached through the bars to grab the edge. Pulled myself over.

Dropped into darkness.

As we go through life we should learn from experience. Some of us never do. I have done a number of foolhardy and very dangerous things in my lifetime. One would think that I would have learned by experience. I never have. I cursed loudly as my cage banged and clattered down the wall, held tight to the inside handles.

The banging stopped and I was in free fall. I clung tight, bent my knees and braced my feet against the bars—and waited for the inevitable impact. There was the twisting interuniversely feeling and a red glow appeared suddenly below, grew brighter. I was falling into a furnace!

Panic possessed me. My heart began to beat like a triphammer and I knew this was the end. A mound of blackness suddenly slammed into the cage with almost deadly impact.

There would have been no *almost* with that *deadly* if the broken rock had not heaped itself into a conical pile.

Pain burst hard upon my body as the cage hit the piled rock at an angle, bounced and slithered down. More pain in my side as a rock point stabbed in between the bars. Clattering and banging, sliding, finally thudding to a stop.

I had to move, but I couldn't. The next load of rock would fall on top of me, crushing and entombing me. If I didn't get out now I never would.

With trembling fingers I pulled at the lock bar of the door. It would not move, had been bent inwards by the impact. Panic helped. I grabbed it with both hands, pulled and twisted with all my strength. Heard the roar of falling stone above me.

Pulled it free. Threw the door open and crawled out. Clambered across the broken surface as lumps of rock rolled by around me. One bounced off my leg, felling me. I crawled on. Until I noticed that the boulders were now moving out from under me, carrying me forward. There was just enough ruddy light to see that a wide, moving belt was carrying the rock—and me—to an unknown destination. Not a good one I was sure. Stumbling and falling I made my way to the edge, dropped off it onto the solid ground.

"Berkk!" I shouted. Where was he?

He was not being carried off with the crushed rock that I could see. But perhaps he had landed and bounced in a different direction, had gone down the pyramid of broken stone at a different place?

I was staggering, not walking. My leg still numb, a sharp pain in my side when I moved. Falling and climbing to my feet again and going on.

When I fell next time I grabbed a bar instead of stone to lever myself to my feet.

Bar?

I pulled and tore at the rocks over the half-buried cage until I uncovered his face. Still and pale. Dead? I had no time to stop and find out because the rocks around the cage were churning and beginning to move. I hurled lumps of stone aside until I uncovered the gate that I had closed such a very long time ago. By pure chance it was on top. If it had not been he would have gone on to certain death because I did not have the strength to turn it over.

In fact, I hadn't even the strength to pull him out once I had grabbed the gate open.

I had my hands under his shoulders, pulling. Nothing happened. He was too heavy, too tightly wedged. I exerted all my strength once again—and he still didn't move. I had to let go or we would both be in the rock crusher.

Then I felt him stir.

"Berkk, you miserable bastard!" I screamed into his ear. "Push with your feet. Try. Or you have had it. Push!"

In the end he did. I kept pulling as he pushed against the imprisoning bars—until he tumbled out of the cage and fell on top of me. After that we crawled, on all fours, because that was all we were able to do. Across the lacerating rock surface until we were free of it. Went on until we had stumbled over the last of the boulders. Collapsed onto the ground.

Under the reddish glow his blood looked black—and there was a lot of it on his pale, filthy face. His clothing was torn, his skin cut and abraded. But he was alive. We both were.

"Do I look as bad as you do—?" I asked, my voice grating and rough with dust, ending in a coughing fit.

"Worse," was all he managed to say.

I looked up at the pyramid of rock down which we had tumbled, as high as a mountain it seemed. By all rights we should have been dead.

But it was done. We were out.

"Let us not do that again," I said with some feeling.

"We won't have to. Because—we did it! We're away from the mine and we're never going back."

CHAPTER 20

I GENTLY TOUCHED MY RIBS and yelped. "Sore, maybe broken—but there is nothing we can do about it now. And you?"

Berkk had climbed slowly to his feet and was hobbling painfully. "The same, I guess. I hurt from all that banging about. I panicked, didn't I?"

"It can happen to anyone."

"It didn't happen to you. You got me into the cage and into the pit—and got yourself into it as well."

"Let's say that I have had more experience at this kind of thing—so don't let it bother you. Most important is what do we do next?"

"Whatever you say we should do. You saved my life and I owe you—"

"But you saved mine when you tripped the thug who was trying to brain me. So we are even. Right?"

"Right. But you still decide what we should do now. Maybe I made the rebar cages, but it was you who made the plan work. What's next?"

I looked around. "Find out where we are, and try to do it without being seen. I have had more than enough excitement for one day."

We walked beside the moving belt, trying to look ahead into the red-lit darkness. A distant rumbling grew louder as we went. We passed one of the glowing pits that provided the feeble illumination and I looked into it. It was filled with a liquid, maybe water, and the glow was coming from the bottom. I dropped in a piece of rock. It splashed nicely then slowly vanished from sight as it went under. Another mystery, but not one of any great importance at the moment.

"Lights ahead," Berkk said, and so there were. White for a change—and they were on our side of the rumbling, moving belt.

"Wrong side," I said. "I would prefer to be in the dark when investigating. Think you can climb over this thing?"

"Lead the way."

It was easy enough once we had clambered, slowly and painfully, up onto the belt, since it wasn't moving very fast. We slipped and stumbled over the broken stone, jumped painfully down on the other side. Walked alongside it as we came closer to the lights, the rumbling getting louder all the time. We bent over as we walked, hiding in the shadows. Trying not to stumble over the bits of rock that had fallen from the belt. Reached the end of the belt and looked out.

It was about what I had expected. Seen one rock crusher you have seen them all. The belt ended and the crushed rock fell from the end into a wide hopper. Below this a series of paired metal rollers, each set above the other, crushed the rock into ever-smaller pieces. Undoubtedly ending up as the fine dust that I had seen dumped onto the sorting tables. The rollers were set into a steel frame that vanished out of sight into an immense pit below. Spotlights were set into the pit walls to illuminate the scene. We bent over, then crawled the last bit and peered over the edge. Berkk pointed.

"Steps. Looks like they go all the way to the bottom."

I nodded agreement, leaning out so I could see. "Landings at various levels to service the machine. And what looks like a control area at the very bottom."

"See anyone?"

"No—but we are still going to be very careful. I'll take a look down the stairs—"

"No way! You move, I move. We're in this together."

He was correct, of course. There was no point in splitting up at this time.

"All right—but I go first. Stay behind and cover my back. Ready?"

"No," he admitted with a rueful grin. "And I doubt if I ever will be. But it's not going to get any better. So I guess that I'm as ready as I am ever going to be."

He was learning fast. I moved over against the wall and started down. When I reached the first landing I waved him after me, then stayed in the shadows of a great discarded and cracked roller. When he had joined me I pointed at the thick dust on the stairs. "Notice anything?" I shouted over the clattering roar of the rock crushers.

"Yes—the only footprints are ours."

"And the dust is centimeters thick. No one has been on these stairs in a very long time. But they could be waiting for us down below. Careful as we go."

The noise grew with each level we dropped, until it reached an almost brain-destroying volume. Still no one in sight—nor footsteps in the dust. I went faster now, driven on by the noise. Slower when I was just above the floor of the pit with the grouped instrumentation and controls. I waved Berkk to my side and pointed; he nodded agreement. There was no way that we could hear anything other than the eternal roar. But we could see where the dust had been disturbed, scuffed and covered with footprints in front of the controls. On the far side a jumbled trail of prints led beside a thick pipe that vanished into the wall.

Beside the pipe there was a sturdy metal door set into the same wall.

I pointed at the door and punched my fist into the air in a victorious gesture.

Now—out of the pit—before my brain was curdled. I let the cosh, still secured in place by its strap, slip into my hand. I crouched before the door and touched the big locking wheel that was set into it, then pointed to Berkk. He clutched it in both hands, exerted his strength. Muscles stood out in his neck with the strain.

Nothing happened. I pulled at his arm and when he looked around I made gestures of turning the wheel in the opposite direction, clockwise.

This worked fine. It turned and the door opened a fraction when I put my weight against it. Massive and heavy. I pushed it open enough to look through the crack into a small, metal-walled room. Empty as far as I could see—with another door set into the far wall. We pushed it wide and went in, closed and sealed it behind us. As we did the sound was cut to a distant rumbling.

"It's like an airlock," Berkk said. I could barely hear because of the ringing in my ears.

"More like a soundlock."

There was still a rumbling sound. From overhead. I looked up at the thick pipe that passed through the room; the rumbling was coming from it.

"Try the other door?" Berkk asked.

"In a moment—when the jackhammer in my head goes away."

The room was featureless. Nothing on the walls, just a light in the ceiling next to the pipe. And a track of dirty footprints leading from one door to the other. Ending in a floor mat. I kicked my boots clean on it.

"There must be something a little more civilized on the other side. Keeping their floor clean—"

I shut up as the wheel on the door in front of me began to turn.

"Behind the door!" I whispered as I plastered myself against the wall.

I could take care of one man all right. If there were more than one we were in trouble.

It opened wider. I crouched and raised my weapon. A metal foot and a metal leg appeared. I lowered the cosh as the robot stepped in. It ignored us completely as it turned and sealed the door through which it had entered. I leaned forward and read the identification plate on the back of its shining skull.

"It's a compbot-707. Wonderful! It's little more than a meter reader with legs. Have you ever used one?"

Berkk nodded happily. "I ran a string of fifteen of them once, in an assembly plant that I managed. After they have been programmed they can do only what's in their memory. The thing has no idea that we are even here."

We watched as it sealed the door, went over to the other door and opened it. We covered our ears as the sound blasted in, then died away as the door swung shut.

"Now let's see what's on the other side," I said as I spun the inner wheel and opened the door a crack. A hall with no one in sight. I opened it wide, stepped through.

"Going to leave me here?" He sounded worried.

"Not for long. But we have to find out what we're getting into. Let me take a quick look."

What I got into was a long, well-lit corridor with the rumbling pipe running the length of it, just below the ceiling. Doors opened off it, and there was another door at the far end—which might very well open at any time. I hurried to the first door I had seen, tried the handle, found it unlocked. Took a breath, readied the cosh—then opened it.

A storeroom, shelves and boxes—and perfect for our needs. I hurried back to Berkk.

"Let's get out of here. There's a storeroom we can get into."

With this last door closed behind me I slid down and sat on the floor. Berkk did the same.

"What do we do next?" he asked eagerly, as though I knew all the answers. I wished I did.

"Rest. And plan. No, no plan. We can't do anything until we find where in hell—or Heaven—we are." I shut up because I was getting light-headed. All the banging, crushing, crawling, bleeding, clotting had not done me any good. "You rest," I said, clambering painfully to my feet. "I'm going to check out the other doors and find out what I can. Be right back."

The first three rooms I looked into were spectacularly un-interesting. Cases of ball-bearing races, computer boards, miles of wire. Nothing that we could use, eat, or drink. But I hit the jackpot on the fourth, hurried back to get Berkk.

"All of the doors along the hallway open into storerooms—but I found one that is not only filled with bogey wheels but also has a medical emergency box. So not only can we clean up and get some dressings on—but some good person put a bottle of medicinal brandy in with the rest of the gear."

We drank the drinking medicine before we went on to antiseptics and bandages. Considering what we had been through we had gotten off lightly. Cleansed and purified—and half-sloshed—I thought of the future.

"Rest, sleep if you can," I said. "I'm going to take a reccy."

"What's that? Is it a pill?"

"No, you civilian, it's a military term left over from my army career. Short for reconnoiter. I'll try not to take any chances and will be back as soon as I can. One person can do this far better than two, so don't argue."

He didn't. "Good luck," he said.

"I don't believe in it. I make my own luck," I bragged. To lift his morale—or my own. I left.

The door at the end of the corridor opened into a very large open-plan room. The thick pipe carried on across to the center of the room where it made a bend and vanished down through the floor. I didn't like this room. I kept my eye to the crack for a long time. There were workbenches in there, with chairs before them. And chairs meant people. Instrument consoles glittered with lights and in the distance there was the sound of running motors. If it was empty for now—how long would it stay empty?

The waiting didn't help because nothing stirred, no one came. Muttering darkly I finally opened the door wide and slipped through. Slinked along between the workbenches, trying to look over my shoulder and in every direction at the same time. Through swinging doors and into an even bigger and brightly lit room. Still no one—though I found this hard to believe. I crept on, wondering how long my luck was going to hold out. I passed a door with a round window set into it, looked in carefully before going by. And swallowed.

A food and drink dispenser—it could be nothing else.

I was through it, the door closed behind me, and punching the button for drink. Caffeine-aide—exactly what I wanted, needed.

Paradisical . . . I drained two cups in a row before I slowed down. Triggered the controls that slipped a frozen catwich and a dogburger into the microwave while I sipped. I glanced out occasionally, but my heart wasn't in it. Food and drink first, more reccy later. I felt a slight twinge of sympathy for Berkk, but food washed it away. He was sleeping and resting and I would bring some of this back for him, or take him to it.

Stomach rounded, swishing inside as I walked, I decided to see what was around just one more bend before I returned.

Around the bend was something new. A stairwell leading down between rough concrete walls. And I remembered that the pipe with its contents of ground rock had gone down through the floor. Which meant its destination might be down here. Should I look? Why not? My stomach was full, caffeine was coursing through my blood—and I was very, very curious.

I went down the steps into a wide corridor that stretched away in both directions. There was a thick tubular thing hanging in the middle of it, running in both directions as well. It was made of polished metal and was much bigger than the ground-rock pipe we had been following. The corridor walls were even rougher, with rock shapes under the plastering. It had been drilled and dug out of the solid rock. Heavy electrical cables hung in festoons and electronic gear was mounted on the metal tube. I could make no sense of it. I walked along it a bit and realized that tunnel and pipe were both curved. A steady, long curve that remained the same. I walked on and the curve, the radius, never changed. If it stayed like this it would eventually form an immense circle and I would be back where I started. A circular tunnel with a circular pipe in the middle of it. It seemed familiar and—

There was the sound of footsteps coming towards me along the tunnel. Time to leave—but they stopped.

Leave, Jim, leave, while you are still in one piece!

Any sensible person would have beaten a hasty and silent retreat and saved curiosity for another day. I have always thought of myself as a sensible person.

Then why was I easing off my heavy working boots and stuffing them into my jacket? For what sane reason was I tip-toeing forward, trying to see around the curve.

I stopped, one foot raised, frozen.

My curiosity was satisfied in a rather large way.

There, just meters away, was Professor Justin Slakey peering through a window into the large tube's interior.

CHAPTER 21

I DREW BACK INSTANTLY. SURELY he could hear the bass drum of my heartbeat echoing loudly in that quiet corridor. Had he seen me? I waited one second, two—and there was no sound of pursuing footsteps.

I started back as silently as I had come—just as the following footsteps sounded behind me. All I could do was run. Trying to stay ahead of the plodding sound. If he went a bit faster, or if I went slower, he would be far enough around the curve in the tunnel to see me. Or if I made a sound. Or—there were too many ors.

There were the stairs ahead of me, where I had come down. Should I try to climb them? No, they went straight up and weren't curved like the tunnel. I would still be climbing them when he came to their base. Onward ever onward. I passed them. Solid concrete steps leading up out of the tunnel. With a dark recess under them.

I took the chance, jumped and pressed myself against the wall under the steps. Tried to slow down my breathing, which sounded in my ears like a porcuswine in heat. Slakey's footsteps came closer. Was he passing by the stairs? If he did he would discover me. And no matter how fast I attacked and rendered him unconscious, he would have seen me and every other Slakey would know at the same time that I was here.

That would be the end.

Slap, slap, the sound of his footsteps came closer. Sounded different, closer—then dying away. He *was* going up the stairs.

When the last clack-clack had dimmed and vanished I let myself slump down to sit against the wall. And put my shoes back on.

Jim, I said silently to myself, *I do hope you enjoyed your little reccy. You were that close to ending the whole thing.*

Then I waited, a good long time. I waited far longer than I thought necessary, then I waited some more. By the time I did move my bottom was numb from the hard floor. Creaking, I stealthily climbed the steps. I twisted my head about so much that I quickly got an even sorer neck. Back through the large lab and out the door. Unseen as far as I could tell. Down the corridor and into the storeroom.

Jumped back in fright at the horrible growling sound.

Relaxed and closed the door behind me as Berkk emitted another gargling snore. My toe lightly planted in his ribs brought him around.

"Snoring on duty is punishable by death," I said.

He nodded glum agreement. "Sorry. Meant to stay awake. Thought I could. Didn't. What did you find?"

"Food and drink for openers. That got your attention, didn't it? Look at you—up on your feet, nostrils flaring, snoring forgotten. After I lead you to it I'll tell you what else I found."

We didn't linger in the food hall. In and out and back as fast as we could in case Slakey had a touch of appetite.

"It could have ended in disaster just as easily," I said, licking a last crumb from my fingers. "Maybe it was that luck you wished me. If so—thanks."

"Don't mention it. We're alive, full of food and drink, safe for a moment—and we even know our way around a bit. And we are out of the rock works at last. A good beginning!"

"Indeed." I ticked the points off on my fingers. "It is a rocky road that we have taken—but we're still on the move. First, we got away from the rock-digging works along with a lot more rocks. Second, we find that our rock is being ground to dust in an underground rock-grinding mill." I touched another finger. "Third, after the rock is ground it is moved through a pipe to the place where we are now hiding. And we are still underground. The circular tunnel I found at the foot of the stairs has been dug, drilled and plastered with great effort. And fitted out with some pretty complex machines. For what reason I do not know. Can you think of anything it might be used for?"

"Not a clue. But what I do know is that we are still not out of the woods. Or the tunnels."

"Quite right. We can rest a bit, eat a bit—but that is not going to solve our problem. Sooner or later we are going to have to move on. It stands to reason that the ground-up rock is going someplace for some important reason. Slakey has gone to an awful lot of trouble and expense to get it this far. I'm willing to bet that it eventually ends up in that place with the tables and the women I told you about."

"Yes. Where you were just before you came through to the rock works."

I thought about that hard. "I went from the tables to the stairs that led up to the room that opens into the rock works. But you went from a different planet right to the room." He nodded agreement. "Which means that the interuniversal transmitter leads from that room. But—" My head was beginning to ache but I pressed on. "But I entered the table place by falling down a hole in Heaven . . ."

Sudden realization sizzled and burned in my brain and I leapt to my feet with the strength of it. "Think about it. We both went through the transmitter to the room that opens on the frozen planet where the opencast mine is. Then we dropped into the pit with the crushed rock. We undoubtedly went through another transmitter. To Heaven! Maybe we are underground on Heaven right now—and the entire complicated operation is completed here."

He had a glazed look and was not following me.

"Think!" I ordered. "If we are in Heaven—then we are at the heart of the Slakey operation. Everything begins here and ends here. Whatever he has been up to, whatever he is spending all those billions of credits on is right around us." I stabbed a finger upwards. "There, on the surface, is Heaven. And Professor Coypu of the Special Corps knows how to get there!"

"Great. But what good is that going to do us now?"

I slumped back to the floor, deeply depressed. "None, really. We're still in deep doodoo and still trying to find a way out."

He looked worried. "Are we? If what you figured out is correct then all we have to do is go on. Follow the ground rock to this place with the tables that you talked about. You came in there—so there might still be a way out. We just follow the rock dust."

"It's not that simple."

"Why not?"

Why not indeed? We couldn't go back—so we had to press on. It was the only chance we had.

"You're right—we'll go on in the same direction."

"Now?"

I thought about that for a bit. "Slakey is awake and wandering around. But he might not be alone. And there is always a chance someone will come into this storeroom. It's taking a chance whatever we do."

"Aren't you tired?"

I thought about it, then shook my head. "In fact I'm jumping with caffeine. Not in the least tired. So let's get moving."

We did. Scurrying like mice through the rooms ahead. More mysterious machinery—and a hopeful sign. Berkk pointed and I nodded agreement. A thick pipe had emerged from some complicated apparatus and was rumbling on nicely overhead. Through a large opening in the wall and into a room beyond. Not really a room, more of a cavern carved from solid rock. It was dimly lit by feeble lights, the concrete floor pitted and dusty. But the pipe was still there, no longer suspended from the ceiling but running along the floor now.

"It's still rumbling," Berkk said, putting his hand against it. "Vibrating. Something is surely going through it."

Which was fine. The only thing wrong was that the pipe went straight ahead and vanished into the roughly carved wall. A very solid-looking rock wall with no openings in it.

"No door," Berkk said.

"There *has* to be a door!"

"Why?" he asked with repulsively simple logic.

Why indeed? Just because we had been able to follow the pipe this far didn't mean it was always going to be easy.

"Think!" I said, thinking very hard. "That black rock was dug up with great labor. Dumped down here where, with even more labor, it was ground to dust. In those rooms or in the tunnel back there something was done to that dust, it was processed somehow, something added or subtracted or who knows what. Then the stuff keeps moving on to . . . where?"

"To the place you told me about, with the robot and the women and everything. There has to be some way of getting there, though it doesn't have be anywhere near the pipe."

"You're right, of course, good man. We look and we find. But which way first?"

"Left," he said with positive assurance. "When I was a Boy Sprout we always started to march—"

"With your left foot. So we go left."

We did. With no results whatsoever. The lights behind us grew dim and distant. We moved in almost complete blackness, feeling our way along the rough stone wall. Which resulted in nothing more than sore fingertips. We came to a corner, then an endless time later to another one. Then as dim lights appeared we saw that there, right ahead of us, was the pipe again. We had worked our way around three sides of the rock chamber to the place where we had come in.

"Maybe we should have gone right," Berkk said brightly. This did not deserve an answer.

Back to where the pipe ended. But we turned right this time and went on into the darkness, Berkk first, running abraded fingertips along the stone.

"Ouch!" he said.

"Why ouch?"

"Because I cracked my knuckles on what feels like a door frame."

We traced the outline with our hands and it not only felt like a door frame but it was one. With a very familiar wheel in the middle of it. It was not easy to turn, but between us we managed to get it moving a bit; metal squealed and grated inside.

"Long time . . . between openings," I grunted. "Keep it going."

With a final squawk of protest the locking bolt was free and the door swung away. We looked into a small room, feebly lit by green glowing plates on the wall. This was more than enough light for our darkness-adjusted eyes to see another door on the far wall. With a handle.

"And a combination lock!" Berkk said, reaching out.

"Stop!" I said, slapping his hand away. "Let me look at it before we try anything."

I blinked at the thing, trying to make out the details in the feeble light, moved my head from side to side.

"I can just about make out the numbers," I said. "It is an antique drum lock that was old when I was young. I know this lock."

"Can you open it?"

"Very possibly. Possibly not since there are no tumblers to drop that I could listen for. But—there is one long chance. To lock this lock it must be turned from the last number that is set in when you open it. Many people forget to do that."

I did not add that most people did not forget most of the time. The thought was too depressing. And we couldn't go back. I needed some luck again—a very lot was riding on this. My fingers were damp and I rubbed them on my shirt. Reached out and grabbed the handle and pulled.

The door didn't budge.

But the handle rattled a bit in my hand. Did it turn? I tried. And it did. The lock had not been locked after all.

I pulled the door open a bit and put my eye to the crack.

CHAPTER 22

"WHAT DO YOU SEE?" BERKK WHISPERED.

"Nothing. Dark."

And very quiet. I opened the door all the way and enough light filtered through from the glowing plates to reveal a rough floor littered with debris. A bent sign on the wall spelled out, in glowing letters:

PLEASE LEAVE THIS PLACE AS YOU FOUND IT

They must have found it pretty awful if was like this now. Broken lengths of plastic littered the floor, as well as empty, half-crushed containers. And it stank.

"Yukk," Berkk said. "Something is rotten in here."

"No, not in here. In this entire place, that's the smell I told you about, that came from the dust or sand. I'm back where I started. In Heaven."

"Doesn't smell like Heaven."

"That is because Heaven is up there on the surface. I was grabbed there by that robot with a built-in gravchute. We dropped into a pit and ended up here. Heaven is above."

"It usually is."

"On the planet's surface, you idiot. The planet is named Heaven."

"Great. But how do we get up there?"

"That is a very good question. For which, at this moment, I do not have an answer. So let us start by getting out of this place first. Is that a chink of light over there? Close the door partway—enough. Yes, stay here while I take a look."

I stumbled and kicked my way through the junk to a vertical crack of some kind with a reddish light shining through it. My fingers pulled at the edges, apparently the gap between two thin metal plates. I pressed my eyes close and looked out. A barren landscape with glowing red pits in the ground, some with bursts of flame rising from them. And that smell, blowing in stronger. I was back in the same place in the underworld where I had arrived.

"Berkk."

"Yes?"

"Feel around in the junk and see if you can find something thin to pry with. This wall, or whatever it is, is made of sheet metal plates—and not too well joined."

The first shard of hard plastic bent, then snapped. We tried again with a length of angled metal and managed to make a bigger opening. It was wide enough to get our fingers through, to pull and curse as the sharp edges cut into our flesh.

"Heave now, together," I said. And we did. Something screeched and broke free, leaving a gap big enough for us to push through.

Out of one prison and into another. I kept such defeatist thoughts to myself and looked around. Dark shapes.

"Buildings," I said. "I didn't see them when I was brought here that first time. Not that I had much of a chance to see anything while I was dragged along."

"Shall we take a look?"

"Any choice?"

There was no answer to that one. In the red-shot semidarkness it was hard to see very far. The landscape was open with no place to hide. But no one moved, there was nothing in sight.

"Let's go."

When were closer we could see that they were buildings, with dark openings cut into their sides. They looked like windows and doors without glass or covering. There were more of the glowing plates inside shedding some light; we approached cautiously. No sound, no one in sight. Looking through the empty rectangle of a window I could see rows of what could only be beds or bunks.

"The women," I whispered, pointing. "They can't work all the time—and some of the bunks are occupied."

"Like us digging rock, two shifts maybe, so work goes on right around the clock."

We skirted around the silent building—and there they were—stretching out of sight in red-lit darkness. The tables. The women bent over them. The sudden rustle of sound, accompanied by the foul odor, as another mass of the finely ground rock was released.

"I want to talk to them," I said. "They will certainly know more than we do about this place. They came here from somewhere—so if there is a way in there must be a way out."

I started up and Berkk held my arm. "Not alone. I'm coming with you."

We ran together to the nearest table, dropped down in its shadows by the legs of one of the workers. If she knew we were there she gave no sign.

"*Ni estas amikoj,*" I said. "*Parolas Esperanto?*"

At first she did not answer or respond. Just kept her arms swinging in slow motion over the moving surface of the table. Then she stopped but did not look down.

"Yes. Who are you—what are you doing here?"

"Friends. What can you tell us about this place?"

"There is nothing to tell. We work. Finding that which must be found. When we find enough, that *thing* knows about it. It always knows. Then it comes and takes what we have found and

then we can eat and sleep. Then we work again. That is all
there is."

As her voice died away her hands began their slow sweeping motions again.

"What *thing?*" I asked. "What makes you work?"

She lifted her arm, then turned and slowly pointed across
the table. "That thing, over there."

I raised my head up just high enough to look—dropped
down instantly and fearfully pulled Berkk after me into deeper
shadow.

"Her *thing* is my robot. The one I told you about, that
brought me here. It's the devil in this particular corner of hell."

"What do we do?" There was fear in his voice as well—for
good reason.

"I tell you what we don't do—we don't let it see us. We'll
be dead, or at the very best back with the rocks and our obnoxious keeper, Buboe."

We pressed as hard as we could against the dusty flank of
the table. Hoping that we were concealed by the shadows as the
robot appeared farther down the line of structures.

A woman was with it, head down, shuffling slowly along.
They walked towards the building we had so recently left.
Passed so close that the smears of rust were clearly visible on
the robot's flank. That single glowing eye. As they entered one
of the doorways I scrambled to my feet.

"Let's go—as far away from that robot as we can get!"

Berkk needed no urging, was in fact well ahead of me in
what was possibly a life-or-death race.

No heads turned in our direction as we ran by; the women's
arms kept sweeping, brushing.

"Something up ahead there, lights of some kind. Maybe
buildings," Berkk said.

I took a look behind us and put on a panic burst of speed,
enough to pass him.

"It's seen us. It's coming after us!"

When I dared to look again it was closer, running faster than
us, steel legs pumping like pistons. We couldn't win—

I turned my head back just in time to see one of the women leave her position at the table, just a silhouetted figure against the distant lights. She turned and was stepping out in front of me. I tried to go around her but she put her arms out to grab me. A sudden twist and I was thrown breathless to the ground.

An instant later Berkk fell on top of me. And the robot was almost there!

The woman arrived first. Throwing her body forward so that she landed on top of both of us, her face almost pressing against mine.

"It's about time you showed up," Angelina said.

CHAPTER 23

DARKNESS VANISHED AND I BLINKED against the sudden glare of bright lights. I could feel Berkk writhing under me—while directly before my eyes was the most beautiful sight in all of the known, and unknown, galaxy.

Angelina's black-smeared, smiling face. I lifted my head and kissed the tip of her nose.

"Errgle . . ." Berkk errgled, trying to wriggle out from under our weight. I moved a bit so he could get free, still clutching harder to Angelina's warm, firm body. We kissed enthusiastically and it was more of heaven than the Heaven we had just left would ever be.

"When you are through with that you might report what you found," Coypu said. I would recognize that voice anywhere. We separated reluctantly and stood up. Still holding hands.

Behind Coypu was a very familiar laboratory.

"We're in Special Corps Prime Base!" I said.

"Obviously. We moved the entire operation back here when you failed to return from Heaven. Slakey is very dangerous people. Soon after we got here there were a number of attempts to penetrate our defenses. They have all failed and the shields are stronger than ever."

"You would like a drink?" Angelina said, whistling over the robar. "Two double Venerian Vodka Coolers."

"After you, my darling. And another for my friend, Berkk, here."

He still sat on the floor, looking around and gaping. His fingers clutched the glass the robar gave him and we all glugged enthusiastically.

"Now, tell me, Professor," I said, holding out my glass for a refill. "What was Angelina doing in that terrible place—and how did she get us back?"

Before he could answer the door burst open and Bolivar— or was it James?—burst in followed by his brother. With Sybil a short pace behind.

"Dad!"

There were enthusiastic embraces all around, and some more drinks from the robar so we could toast our successful return. As we lowered our glasses Berkk dropped his. When he bent over to pick it up he just kept going, falling heavily to the floor, unconscious. I grabbed his wrist—almost no pulse at all.

"Medic!" I shouted as I rolled him onto his back and opened his mouth to make sure that his air passages were clear. But as I did this I was pushed not-too-gently aside by the medbot that had dropped out of the ceiling. It put a manipulator into Berkk's mouth to secure his tongue. At the same time it pressed an analyzer against his skin, took a blood sample, extruded a pillow under his head, did a fast body scan, covered him with a blanket and had already radioed for a doctor who burst through the door scant instants later.

"Stand clear," he ordered as the medbot slid an expanding metal web under Berkk's body, popped wheels out of the ends and carefully drove off with him. "The surgeon is standing by," the doctor said. "There appears to be a small blood clot on the patient's brain, undoubtedly caused by a blow to the skull. Prognosis good." He hurried after the medbot while Sybil hurried after him.

"I'll see what happens and report back," she said. She left with Bolivar and James right behind her. The three were inseparable now. Which might lead to problems that I did not wish to consider at this moment.

This put a bit of a damper on the party and we sipped glumly at our drinks. Before we finished them—modern medicine sure works fast—Coypu's phone rang and he grabbed it up. Listened, nodded, then smiled.

"Thank you, Sybil," he said and hung up. "Operation successful, out of danger, no permanent brain damage. He'll stay in narcsleep until the treatment is finished."

We cheered at that. "Thank you, Professor," I said. "With this last emergency out of the way we can now relax and listen. While you tell us how my Angelina managed to drag me out of the hell in Heaven and how she got there in the first place. After which we will try to figure out what all the strange happenings that have been going on really mean. Professor."

"We will take the explanation one step a time, if you don't mind. To go back to the beginning. When you did not return after a good deal of time had passed I activated your undetectable interuniversal activator and the boot returned. Without you. Since you were not wearing the boot I reached the inescapable conclusion that my machine had been detected. Therefore I had to improve its undetectability. I did this rather quickly because I was feeling very, very rushed."

"I held a gun to the back of his head with my finger trembling on the trigger," Angelina said, smiling sweetly. "I was going after you and intended to bring you back—with a better machine than the duff one he had supplied you with."

"It was an early model," Coypu muttered defensively. "I improved the design greatly then constructed three devices of varying degrees of undetectability."

"I carried the first hidden in the lining of my purse," Angelina said. "The second was under the skin on my arm, here." She rubbed at the long white scar, easily visible under the dusty smears, and scowled. "I will have to get this unsightly thing removed."

"That is not the only thing that is going to be removed," I grated through tight-clamped teeth. "I'm going to kill that particular Slakey for that botched bit of surgery."

"Not if I get there first, darling. He of course very quickly found the one in my purse, and then he detected this one, with great difficulty I must say. He was so pleased with himself that he never considered that there might be a third."

"Where is it?" I asked.

"Where Slakey obviously could not find it," Coypu said, happily rattling his fingers on his foreteeth. "I knew that there was no way to detect the pseudo-electrons, so it must have been the pseudo-electron paths in the solid state circuitry that he found. So I impressed my neural network on Angelina's neural network where it would be concealed by her neural activity."

"You mean that you built your machine right into her nervous system?"

"Exactly so. Since my pseudo electrons move at pseudo speed, there would be no interference with the electrical function of her synapses. The circuitry ended directly in her brain."

"So when I thought *go,* we all went," she said, throwing her empty glass towards the robar, which plucked it out of the air with a flip of a tentacle. "Now I am going to wash off this mud and stench and I suggest, Jim diGriz, that you do the same."

"I will—after I ask you a single question . . ."

"It can wait." Then she was gone. I whistled up another drink.

"Tell me all that happened," Coypu said.

"You let her go after Slakey alone!" I accused. "With all the massed strength of the Corps to hand."

"And a gun to my head. Do you think that there was any way to stop her?"

"No—but you could at least have tried."

"I did. What happened?"

I slumped in a chair, sipped my drink, and told him the entire repulsive story. My descent into Purgatory from Heaven and the women at the sorting tables there. Then being tossed through Slakey's machine to the living hell of the mining world.

He popped his eyes a bit when I told him about our escape in the rebar cages. Narrowed his eyes into pensive slits when he heard about the laboratory and the mysterious circular tunnel.

"And that was that. My dearest Angelina was there and whisked us back here and you know the rest."

"Well, well, well!" Coypu said when I had finished, jumping to his feet with excitement and pacing back and forth.

"Now we know what he is doing and how he is doing it—we just don't know what he is doing it for."

"Perhaps you know, Professor, but some of us are still in the dark."

"It's all so obvious." He stopped pacing and raised a didactic finger. "Heaven is the seat of all of his activities, we can be sure of that now. It matters not in the slightest where the mineral is mined. Because it was brought to Heaven after you and the male slaves extracted it from the ground. Dropped through an interuniversal field to end up in Heaven where it is ground finely and bombarded in a cyclotron—"

"A what?"

"A cyclotron, that is the machine that you saw in the tunnel. Your description was quite apt, even if in your ignorance you did not know what you were looking at. It is an ancient and rather clumsy bit of research apparatus that is not used much anymore. It is basically a very large, circular tube that has all the air inside evacuated. Then ions are pumped in and whirled around and around through the tube, held in orbit away from the tube walls by electromagnets. After building up tremendous speeds the ions smash into a metallic target."

"Why?"

"My good friend, how did you manage to obtain an education without studying basic science in school? Any first-year student would remember the simple fact that if you bombard platinum with neon ions you obtain element a hundred and four, called unnilquadium. It follows, obviously, that if you hit lead isotopes with a beam of chromium you will obtain unnilsextium."

"What is that?"

"A transuranic element. In the Stone Age of physics there were believed to be only ninety-eight elements, the heaviest of which was uranium. As new ones were discovered they were named, we think, after household gods. Curium after the god of medicine who cures disease, that sort of thing. Anyway, after the discovery of mendelevium, nobelium and such, the elements were numbered in an ancient and lost language. One hundred and four is unnilquadium, one hundred and five unnilquintium and so forth. Slakey has created a new element, much further up the atomic number table I am sure. It is obviously generated in very small quantities and comes out of the cyclotron still mixed with the original ore. Machines cannot detect it or they would have been used for this onerous task. But obviously women, and not men, can find it. Angelina will tell us more about that . . ."

"About what?" she asked. Making a glorious entrance in a green space jumper that went beautifully with her now red-gold hair.

"What were you and the other women looking for in the grit?" I asked.

"I have no idea."

"But exactly what were you doing?"

"An interesting phenomenon. All the bits of sand and gravel looked exactly alike. But some of the grains, when you touched them they felt—slow? No, that's not right, perhaps the other grains felt faster. It's almost impossible to describe. But once felt never forgotten."

"Entropy," Coypu said firmly. "That's Slakey's special field of research. I am certain now that he is producing particles with different entropy."

"Why?"

"That is what we will have to find out."

"How?" I asked. Puzzled, bothered and bewildered.

"You will find a way, you always do," Angelina said, patting me on the arm. Her smile turned to a frown when she looked at her filthy fingertips. "Go burn those clothes," she ordered. "Then wash until your skin glows, then wash some more."

I went willingly, well aware now of the stench, itch and scratch of my battered body. In the guest suite a burst of flame in the bathroom burner incinerated my clothing. I punched for antiseptics as well as soap in the bath, sank with a sigh under the warm water with a weary *whew*. . . .

Woke up drowning as my nose slipped beneath the surface. Hawked and spat out water; I must have fallen asleep. My body was giving me a message that I was happy to receive. Dried and dusted I went on all fours into the bedroom, crawled dizzily into bed and knew nothing more.

Angelina and I were having a relaxed drink before dinner. The twins and Sybil were off somewhere, while the professor was busy in his laboratory. We had a few moments alone.

"Any particular way you would like me to kill Slakey in Heaven?" I asked.

"Messy and painful. Though he wasn't really that awful to me. But he was an irritating fat old git. Cackling with joy when the surgicalbot cut out the implant. Painless really, just messy. He couldn't have cared less after that. I was just another woman for his slave labor at the tables. That terrible one-eyed robot grabbed me—now *that* is one piece of rusty iron I intend to dispatch personally—and took me off to the sorting place. One of the other women let me touch a grain she had found and that was that. Unlike those other poor creatures I knew that I could leave at any time, so it wasn't too awful. I also knew that you would be making a breakout from somewhere somehow as soon as you could, so I didn't mind waiting. I worked along with the others until I saw you and your friend running away from the robot. That was when I decided that it would be better if we all came back here."

Better! Not a word of complaint about what she had gone through to rescue me. My angel, my Angelina! Words could not express my gratitude, but some fervid kisses did get the message across. We separated when Coypu arrived. I ordered him his favorite Crocktail while Angelina went out to do whatever women do when their hair is mussed.

"A question, if you please, Professor."

"What?" He sipped and smacked his lips happily.

"How are you doing with that little difficulty you had—about not being able to send machines through between the universes? You will recall that when we went to Hell the only weapons that worked were salamis."

"I do recall it—and that is why I instantly tackled the problem. It is solved. An energy cage protects any object you wish from the effects of transition. You have an idea?"

"I certainly do. You will remember that my son James hypnotized that old devil Slakey in Hell."

"Unhappily, unsuccessfully. He was too insane to be questioned easily. And there wasn't enough time to do more."

"What if you had him or any other of the Slakeys here?"

"No problem at all then. We have highly skilled psychologists who work with computerized probes that can track thought processes down through all the levels of the brain. Mental blocks can be removed, traumas healed, memories accessed. But we don't have him here or any of the others. And the one in Hell. We know that he has been there too long. He will die if he is moved out."

"I know—and I'm not suggesting that. Now run your mind back to the adventurous past. You must recall the time war when the Special Corps was almost destroyed?"

"*Was* destroyed!" He shivered and sipped. "You restored us to reality when you won the war. Shan't forget that."

"Anything to help a friend. But what I am interested in now is the time fixator. The machine you built when reality was getting weaker and people were popping out of existence. You told me that as long as a person remembered who he was he was safe from the effects of the time attack. So you put together the machine that records the memories of an individual and feeds them back every three milliseconds."

"Of course I remember the time fixator—since I invented it. We have plenty in stock now. Why?"

"Patience. Then you will also remember that I took *your* memories with me. Then, when I had to move back through time again, I let your memories take over my body to build a time helix, the time-traveling machine that is also your invention."

His eyes opened wide as his speedy thoughts leaped to the conclusion that I was slowly building towards. He smiled broadly, finished his drink, jumped to his feet, rushed over and seized my hand and pumped it enthusiastically.

"Brilliantly done! An idea that is as good, almost, as one I might have thought up. We take the time fixator to Hell—"

"Plug Slakey into it and take a recording. Then leave him there in the flesh—but bring back all of his memories!"

Angelina had returned and heard this last. "If you are off on one more interuniversal trip you are not going alone this time."

Said without anger but with an unshakeable firmness. I opened my mouth to protest. Closed it and nodded.

"Of course. We're going back to Hell. Wear your lightest clothes."

"But no salamis this time."

"Quite right. That was an emergency measure—that succeeded I must remind you—that won't be needed now. We'll take the marines again, but well-armored and armed this time. To defend us while we make a memory recording of the Slakey in red."

"No troops," she said. "They would only get in the way. It will be just you and I in a fast armored scout tank. A lightning attack, find the old devil. Then I fight off anyone who gets in the way while you plug his brain into the memory fixator. After that it will be home in time for lunch. Tomorrow?"

"Why not? They want me in the hospital today. Some therapy for my bruises and cuts, and a broken rib or two that they are going to put right. Tomorrow morning will be fine."

It was. The body scan showed that two of my ribs were cracked. But microwindow surgery soon took care of them. The incision was so small that all that was needed was a local anesthetic. Since I am always very interested when someone fiddles around with my insides, I insisted upon having a hologram monitor, just like the surgeon's, so I could watch what was happening in glorious color 3D. The flexible needle snaked in through my skin and on into the bone of the rib itself. Once in place nanotechnology devices poured out of the tip of the needle, a submicroscopic crowd of molecular machines that grabbed the broken bone ends with their manipulators, then held tight onto each other. Micromotors whirred and the broken ends were neatly pulled together. Wonderful. The little machines would remain in place as new bone grew over them. I went right from the operating table to the laboratory where the interuniversal transporter and Angelina were waiting.

"I'm ready whenever you are," she said. She certainly was. Tastefully garbed in a black uniform, all metal studs and grenade clips, black boots—and a heavy weapon holstered on each hip.

"Very fetching," I said, slipping on the backpack that held the time fixator. "How was the test drive in your steel steed?"

"Very nice indeed," she said, patting the armor plate on the scout tank. "Fast, tough, with impressive fire power. More than enough weaponry to cover you in Hell. How was the bone operation?"

"Fast and efficient and I'm all mended and raring to go. Shall we?"

"In a moment. Before we leave I want to impress on Professor Coypu a few important facts. Like the fact that we are not setting up housekeeping in Hell and want to be returned here soonest."

"Exactly."

Coypu strolled over from his control console looking decidedly miffed. "There will be no problems with the operation of the interuniversal activator this time, I can assure you of that."

"That's what you told me when you sent me to Heaven and I almost died with my boots off."

"Improvements have been made since then. Your vehicle has one activator built into the hull while you once again have one in your bootheel. And if worse comes to worse just clutch Angelina tightly—"

"Always a pleasant thought!"

"—and she will bring you both back."

"I feel relieved," I said, feeling relieved as I climbed into the scout tank and slammed the hatch. Angelina revved the engines and I gave Coypu the thumbs-up. His image scowled back at me from the communicator screen.

"You can turn the engine off," he said. "We have a small problem."

"How small?"

"Well . . . perhaps I should say big. I can't seem to find Hell."

"What do you mean you can't find it?"

"Just that. It appears to be gone."

CHAPTER 24

ANGELINA CUT THE POWER, I opened the hatch, and, quivering gently from *actio interruptus,* we slammed over to interrogate Professor Coypu who was laboring anxiously away at the controls.

"Why did you say *not there . . . ?*" Angelina asked angrily.

"I said that because it isn't. Where the hell has Hell gone?"

"It is a little difficult to lose an entire universe?"

"I didn't exactly lose it. It's just not where it should be."

"Sounds the same as losing it," I said.

He gave me a surly scowl before turning back to his button pushing and switch throwing. Apparently with no good results. "I cannot access Hell with the former setting. I have checked it a number of times. There appears to be no universe at all there."

"Destroyed?" Angelina asked.

"Since that takes a great number of billions of years I doubt it very much."

"Is Heaven still there?" I asked.

"Of course." He made some rapid adjustments and pressed a button. Widened his eyes and gasped. Groped behind him for his chair and dropped into it. "Not possible," he muttered to himself.

"Are you all right, Professor?" Angelina asked, but he didn't hear her. His fingers were flashing across the keyboard now and the screen was filled with rapidly flowing mathematical equations.

"Leave him to it," I said. "If anyone can find out what happened it's him. We're just in the way now."

We went to the lounge area and I snapped my fingers for the barbot. Angelina scowled.

"Little early to hit the booze, isn't it?"

"No booze, just a simple glass of beer to slake my thirst. Join me?"

"Not at this time of day."

I sipped and thought. "We have to go back to the very beginning of events. Forget the other universes for the moment. When this entire thing started, when you disappeared from Lussuoso, I had Bolivar and James do a thorough sweep of all the planets, to see if there were any other operations run by a Slakey under a different cover. We didn't find another Temple of Eternal Truth, but we did uncover the same kind of operation under a different name. We went to Vulkann and located the fake church. Went in there—and you know what happened after that."

"From Glass to Hell to Heaven and back here. Where we are stuck since the good professor can't find any of them any more."

"We don't have to wait for him." I grabbed for the phone. "The search we instigated may have uncovered other Slakey operations on other planets. Let's see what the boys found out."

I heard the splash of water and shrieks of joy in the background when Bolivar, or James, answered the phone.

"Can I interrupt your jollities?" I asked.

"Just a day at the beach, Dad. What's up?"

"I'll tell you when you get here. But first, do you remember if there were any other Slakey operations uncovered by the original search, when we were on Lussuoso?"

"We dropped everything and got out of there so fast—I just don't know. But I do know that the computer was still running the search program when we left. We'll get onto it. See you there as soon as we have the records."

Professor Coypu was still hammering out equations, Angelina had a cup of tea, and I was thinking of another beer when the boys arrived.

"News?" I asked.

"Good!" they said in unison.

I flipped through the printouts, then passed them to Angelina.

"Very good indeed," I said. "A few remote possibles, a couple of maybe probables."

"And one dead certain," Angelina said. "The Sorority of the Bleating Lamb. A women-only congregation, and rich women at that."

"Did you note the name of the planet where this operation is now taking place?"

"I certainly did—Cliaand of all places. You boys are too young to remember the planet, in fact you were in your baby carriage at the time. There were certain difficulties on Cliaand, but your father and I sorted them out. We'll tell you about it when we have the time. The important thing is that now it is a museum world."

"A museum of what?"

"Warfare, militarism, fascism, jingoism and all that sort of old nonsense. It was a very poor planet when we saw it last, but that must have changed by now. Tourist money, no doubt. Shall we go see?"

A heartfelt groan caught our attention. Professor Coypu was in the pits of despair. "No good," he groaned again. "No reason to it. Nothing makes sense. Gone. Heaven and Hell. All gone."

He looked so glum that Angelina went over and patted his arm.

"There, there, it is going to be all right. While you were sweating away at your equations—we have located what we are sure is another Slakey religious operation. We must now plan, very carefully, how this matter should be handled. I don't think we can afford to make any more mistakes."

There was a serious nodding of heads on all sides.

"Can we use the TI, temporal inhibitor again?" I asked.

"I don't see why not," Coypu said, coming up for air, his depression forgotten at the thought of action. "You told me that it did not work in the Glass universe. Did you leave it there?"

"Threw it into the ocean—it was just a worthless lump of metal. And I remember! Slakey said something like whatever my weapon was, it wouldn't work. So he does not know that we used the TI when we went to that church to grab his machine."

"In that case there is no reason why we cannot use the TI along with the time fixator."

"We'll do it! Hit hard without warning, during one of the services when we know that Slakey will be there. Freeze them all in time with the TI, walk in and put the TF on Slakey's head and make a copy of everything there. Can that be done, Professor?"

"Of course. Both machines operate on basically the same principle. They can be connected by an interlock switch. It will turn off the TI just as it turns on the TF, and will reverse the process a millisecond later."

I was rubbing my hands together in happy anticipation. "Freeze them solid, stroll in and pump his memories dry, walk out—and when we are well clear turn off the TI back in church. The Slakey service and operation will then go on as usual since he will have no idea that we have copied his mind. But we will need a bigger machine, something that will stop them and keep them frozen in a time stasis, everyone in the building. With a much bigger neutralization field than last time, which only protected a few operators. We will have to open doors to get inside the building."

For Professor Coypu all things scientific were like unto child's play. "I envisage no problems. There will be a large TI that will produce a field exactly the shape and size of the building you wish to enter. Time will stop and no one will be able to move in or out. Except you. Your TII, temporal inhibitor inhibitor, will cover you alone."

"Not alone," Angelina said. "Not ever again. It makes good sense to have aid and backup. Shall we do it?"

We were looking forward to a small family-sized operation, but Inskipp, who had spies and electronic snoopers everywhere, complained as soon as he heard about how the operation was planned. I obeyed his royal command and appeared at his office.

"Sincerely, do we really need more than four people?" I asked.

"Sincerely, the number of operators involved in this operation is not the point. It's your nepotism at work that bothers me. This is a Special Corps operation and it is going to be run by Special Corps rules. Not by familial felicity."

"How can there be rules for use of a temporal inhibitor to be used to get a time fixator into a church? Show me where it says that in the rules!"

"When I say *rules* I mean *my* rules. You are going to take another special agent with you so I will know just what is going on."

"Who?"

"Sybil. I am sending her ahead to survey the target."

"Agreed. Then all systems are go?"

"Go." He pointed at the door and I was gone.

The machines were manufactured and tested, but it was almost a week before our interplanetary travel in a warpdrive cruiser was completed. We left the military at the orbital station and went planetside in a shuttle along with a number of cruise ship passengers. Like them we were holiday makers in holiday clothes, with nothing in our luggage except a few souvenirs; our weapons and equipment were going down in a diplomatic pouch.

"For old times' sake I have booked us all into the most luxurious hotel in town—the Zlato-Zlato."

"Why is that name familiar?" Angelina asked. "Isn't that the same hotel where we stayed, where that horrible gray man tried to kill you?"

"The same—and you saved my life."

"Memories," she said, smiling warmly. "Memories. . . ."

When we reached the hotel the manager himself was there to greet us. Tall and handsome, a touch of gray at the temples, bowing and smiling.

"Welcome to Cliaand, General and Mrs. James diGriz and sons. Doubly welcome on your return visit."

"Is that you, Ostrov? Still here?"

"Of course, General. I own the hotel now."

"Any assassins booked in?"

"Not this time. May I show you to your suite?"

There was a fine sitting room, glass-walled on one side with a spectacular view of the surrounding countryside. But James and Bolivar cried aloud with pleasure at a spectacular view of their own.

"Sybil!" they said while she smiled warm greetings.

"Target survey completed?" I asked, hating to intrude business into all this pleasure.

"All here," she said, handing me a briefcase. "There will be a solemn assembly of the Sorority of the Bleating Lamb tomorrow morning at eleven."

"We shall be there—if our equipment arrives on time."

"Already arrived. The large trunk over there with the skull and crossbones patterns on it."

Angelina had a lovely time passing out the weapons while I unpacked the time fixator, which very cunningly had a casing constructed to resemble a Cliaand burglar alarm. It would stick to the outside wall of the assembly hall of the Sorority of the Bleating Lamb where it would attract no notice. Nor could it be dislodged once activated since it would be frozen in time along with the building. I popped out the holoscreen and fed in the building's dimensions and shape from Sybil's complete and efficient report.

"Done," I said happily. I clipped the metal case of the TII, the temporal inhibitor inhibitor, to my belt and actuated it. Nothing happened until I pressed the red button on the case that turned on the TI. Silence fell. But nothing else did. My family and Sybil were frozen, immobile in time. I turned it off; sound and movement returned. All the machines were in working order, all systems go.

There was celebration this night, dining and drinking and dancing, but early to bed. Next morning, a few minutes after eleven, my merry band was strolling down Glupost Avenue, admiring the scenery—but admiring Angelina even more where she stood on the corner waving to us. The wire from her earphone led to the musicman that she was wearing, which was really an eavesdropper amplifier.

"That stained-glass window up there," she said, pointing unobtrusively, "is in their assembly hall. Slakey's vile voice is vibrating the glass and I can hear him far too clearly. He is in the middle of some porcuswine-wash pontificating."

"Time," I said, and we joined arms and strolled happily across the street, dodging the pedcabs and goatmobiles. The rest of us went on while Bolivar stepped into the alleyway beside the building and pressed his beach bag against the wall. The beach bag cover stripped away and a handsome burglar alarm hung in its place. No one on the street had noticed. He rejoined us as we approached the front door.

"This is it, guys," I said. "Showtime."

I turned on the TII, then the TI. Nothing happened. Nothing happened that anyone could see that is. But the building and its contents were frozen now in time. Would remain that way— for an hour or a year—until I turned the machine off. The people inside would feel nothing, know nothing. Though they might be puzzled by the fact that their watches all seemed to be reading the same wrong time.

"James, the door if you please."

The field of my TII interacted with the field of the TI and released the front door from time stasis. James pulled it open, closed it behind us, and we marched into the building. Once the door was closed not even an atom bomb would be able to open it. Such power I possessed!

"The big double doors ahead," Sybil said.

"The ones with the blue baa-baas on them?" She nodded.

"Despicable taste," Angelina said and her arm holster whipped her gun out and back in microseconds. She was looking for trouble and I hoped she didn't find it.

The boys each took a handle—and pulled when I nodded. There, directly ahead of us and staring at us was Slakey.

Reflex whipped out six guns, Angelina had one in each hand, which were slowly replaced.

Like his frozen audience, Slakey was pinned into an instant of time. Mouth open in full smarmy flight, fixed beads of perspiration on his brow. Not a pretty sight.

We walked around his audience and up the steps to his pulpit. "Are you ready my love?" I asked Angelina.

"Never readier."

She reached out and placed the contact disk of the temporal inhibitor against the side of his head, just above his ear. She nodded and I touched the button.

Nothing that we could observe happened. But for that brief millisecond the TII field had been turned off and the machine had sucked a copy of Slakey's memory, his intelligence, his every thought into its electronic recesses.

"The readout reads full!" Angelina said.

"Slakey, you devil from Heaven and Hell," I exulted. "I have you now!"

CHAPTER 25

I WORRIED AT A FINGERNAIL with my incisors, waiting for something to go wrong. Slakey had been one step ahead of us every time so far—and not one of our operations against him had ever succeeded to any measurable degree. We had avoided disaster only through heroic efforts and last-minute leaps. It did not seem possible that on this occasion everything had worked according to plan. I had both hands around the TF; I kept it with me at all times. Now it sat on my lap as the shuttle eased into Special Corps Prime Base. I looked at the needle, as I had hundreds, thousands of times before, and it was up against the red post that read *full*.

Full of Professor Justin Slakey? It had better be.

It was an expectant crowd that assembled in the laboratory. Even Berkk was there, fully recovered from the brain operation and now enjoying some much deserved R and R. The talking died away and a hushed silence prevailed when I presented, almost ceremoniously, the TF to an expectant Professor Coypu.

"Is he in there?" I asked.

"I don't see why not." He tapped the dial. "Reads full. We'll see. But of course there remains the major problem. How do we get Slakey out of this TF? I can't feed him into another machine—there would still be no way to access him. I need a human host. You will remember what that is like, Jim, when you used my brain and memories to build a time machine."

"I let you take over my own gray matter. It was not nice. And you left me a note saying it was the hardest thing you ever did, to switch the TF off after you had built the temporal helix. To literally commit suicide."

"Exactly. We need a volunteer to be plugged into this TF so that a madman can control his brain and body. And Slakey will not want to leave once he is there. Not too tempting a prospect. So—with those facts in mind, who will volunteer?"

This got a very impressive silent silence as everyone present thought hard about it. I realized that I had better volunteer again, better me than my wife or sons. But as I opened my mouth Berkk spoke up.

"Professor, I think you have your man. I owe you people an awful lot, owe Jim who got me out of the rock works, owe Angelina who got us out of that hell in Heaven. I was dying down there with the others. I owe my life to you both and I don't want to see you or your sons, or Sybil, letting this nutcase near their gray matter. Just one question, Professor Coypu. Are you sure you can get him out—and get me back in when it is all over?"

Coypu nodded furiously. "Can be done, no doubt, just blast him out with a neural charge if I have to."

"Wonderful—what will happen to the *me* in there if you do that?"

"Interesting thought. A neural blast cleans everything out and sets the synapses back to neutral. But—not to worry. We'll make a recording of you in a different TF. This technique works quite well, as Jim will tell you. So whatever happens with Slakey, in the end we will get yourself back inside yourself."

"All right." He rose to his feet slowly, his face very pale under the dark scars. "Do it quickly before I have a chance to change my mind."

Quickly really was very quick with Coypu. He must have been holding a psycho blaster in his lap because there was a loud humming and Berkk folded. Angelina and I were there to catch him before he hit the floor.

A padded operating table rolled out of the massed machinery and we placed him gently on it. Coypu got to work. He took an empty TF from the shelf and plugged it into the back of Berkk's head. Worked the controls and nodded happily. "There. This very brave young man can now go back on the shelf. If Slakey causes trouble I will then zap him out of the neurons and get Berkk back with this. Now—to work."

He seized up the Slakey TF and placed it onto the workbench, then slipped a multiganged plug into the TF's socket. He ran an electronic check of the contents before reeling out the contact and connecting it to Berkk's head.

"Wait," I said. He stopped. "How about securing Berkk's body in place so he doesn't hurt himself—or us."

"I will have him securely under electronic control—"

"Slakey has *never* been under control in the past. So let us be sure and take no chances now."

Coypu threw a few switches and padded clamps hummed out from below the table. I locked them securely into place on ankles and wrists. Found a large belt and secured that around his waist and nodded to Coypu. He put the final connection into place, then threw some more switches as he swung a microphone down in front of his mouth.

"You are asleep. Very much asleep. But you can hear me. Hear my words. You will not wake up. But you will hear me. Can you hear me?"

The speaker rustled a bit and there was a sound like a sigh. Then the words, almost inaudible:

"I can hear you."

"That's very good." He turned up the amplification a bit. "Now, tell me—who are you?"

I don't know why they are called pregnant silences, perhaps because they are pregnant with possibilities. This one had all kinds of possibilities. The loudspeaker rustled again.

"My name is . . . Justin Slakey . . ."

Who can blame us for shouting with joy. We had done it!

Not quite. Berkk, or his body, was writhing and fighting against the bonds. He bit his lips until they bled. Then his eyes opened.

"What are you doing to me? Are you trying to kill me? I'll kill you first . . ."

The writhing stopped and he dropped back heavily as Coypu let him have it with his handy psycho blaster.

It was not going to be easy. Even with James helping, a far more skilled hypnotist than Coypu, it was impossible to exercise any control over Slakey. Just about the time they would hypnotize one Slakey another would take over. And all the subsequent thrashing about wasn't doing Berkk's body much good, what with fighting against the restraints, chewing on his lips and so forth.

"Time for some professional help," Coypu said. "Dr. Mastigophora is on his way. He is the leading clinical psychosemanticist in the Corps."

"Super-shrink?" I asked.

"Absolutely."

Dr. Mastigophora was lean to the point of emaciation, all sinew and leather, carrying an instrument case and sporting a great growth of gray hair. "I assume that is the patient?" he said, pointing a long and knobby finger.

"It is," Coypu said. Mastigophora glared around at his audience.

"Everyone out of here," he ordered as he opened his instrument case. "With the single exception of Professor Coypu."

"There is a physical problem with the patient," I explained. "We don't want him to hurt the body, which is only on loan."

"Up to your mind-swapping tricks again, hey Coypu? One of these days you will go too far—" He looked at me and scowled. "I said out and I mean out. All of you."

As he said this he sprang forward and seized my wrist and applied a very good armlock. Of course I let him do it since I don't beat up on doctors. He was strong and good enough—I hoped—to handle Berkk's body in an emergency. I left with the others as soon as he let go.

A number of hours passed and we were beginning to yawn and head for bed when the communicator buzzed. Angelina and I were wanted in the lab.

Coypu and Mastigophora were slouched deep in their chairs trying to outmatch each other in looking depressed.

"Impossible," Mastigophora moaned. "No control, can't erect blocks, can't access, terrible. It's the multiple personality thing, you see. My colleague has explained that Professor Slakey has in some unspecified manner multiplied his body, or bodies. His brain or brains or personality is in constant communication or something like that. It sounds like absolute porcuswine-wash. But I have seen it in action. I can do nothing."

"Nothing," Coypu echoed hollowly.

"Nothing?" I shouted. "There has to be something!"

"Nothing . . ." they intoned together.

"There is something," Angelina said, ever the practical one. "Forget Slakey and get back to looking into the guts of your interuniversal machine. Surely there has to be some way to get it working again."

Coypu shook his head looking, if possible, even gloomier. "While Dr. Mastigophora was brain-draining I tackled the problem again. I even stopped all the other projects that were running in the Special Corps Prime Base Central Computer. In case you didn't know it, the SCPBCC is the largest, fastest and most powerful computer ever built in the entire history of mankind." He turned on the visiscreen and pointed. "Do you see that satellite out there? Almost a third the size of this entire station. That's not a satellite—that's the computer. I had it working flat out on this problem and this problem alone. I used the equivalent of about one billion years of computer time."

"And?"

"It has tackled this question from every point of view in every way. And the conclusion was the same every time. It is impossible to alter the access frequencies in the interuniversal commutator."

"But it happened?" I said.

"Obviously."

"Nothing is obvious to me!" I was very tired and my temper was shredding and all this gloom and doom was beginning to be very irritating. I jumped to my feet, walked over to the shiny steel control console, looked at its blinking lights and tracing graphs. And kicked it. I hurt my toe but at least I had the pleasure of seeing one of the needles on a meter jump a bit. I started to bring my foot back for another kick. And froze.

Stood there on one leg for long seconds while my brain raced around in circles.

"He has just had an idea," Angelina said, her voice seemingly coming from a great distance. "Whenever he freezes up like that it means he has thought of something, had an inspiration of some kind. In a moment he will tell us—"

"I'll tell you now!" I shouted, jumping about to face them and neatly clicking my heels in the air as I did. "Your computer is absolutely right, Professor, and you should have more respect for its conclusions. Those universes will always be in the same place. As soon as we realize that, why the answer becomes obvious. We must look for the real reason why you cannot access those universes. Do you know what that is?"

I had them now, professorial jaws gaping, heads shaking, Angelina nodding proudly, waiting for my explanation.

"Sabotage," I said, and pointed at the control console. "Someone has changed the settings on the controls."

"But I set them myself," Coypu said. "And I have checked the original calculations and conclusions over and over again."

"Then they must have been changed too."

"Impossible!"

"That's the right word for it. When all the possibilities have been tried—then it is time to look to the impossible."

"My first notes, I think that I still have them," he said, stumbling across the room and tearing open a drawer. It fell to the floor and spilled out pens, paper clips, bits of paper, cigar butts and empty soup cans, all the things we leave in desk drawers. He scrabbled among the debris and pulled out a crumpled piece of paper, smoothed it and held it up.

"Here. My own writing, my first calculations, the beginnings of determining the locations and settings. This could not be changed." He stamped over to the controls, flickered his fingers across the console keys, pointed a victorious finger at the equation on the screen. "There you see—the same as this."

He looked at the paper, then at the screen, then back to the paper until it looked like he was watching an invisible Ping-Pong match.

"Different . . ." he said hoarsely. I must admit that my smile was a bit smug and I did enjoy it when Angelina gave me a loving hug and a kiss.

"My husband the genius," she whispered.

While Coypu hammered away at the computer, Dr. Mastigophora went to look at his patient.

"How is he?" I asked.

"Unconscious. We had to use the psycho blaster on him, paralyze his entire body as well as the brain. Nothing else seems to work."

"There it is! Hell!" Coypu shouted and we turned to look at his screen which showed a loathsome red landscape under a redder and even more loathsome sun.

"Hell," he said. "And Heaven. They are all there still. It was the calculations, the primary equations. Changed, just slightly, just enough to make the later calculations vary farther and farther from the cor ect figures. But—how did it happen? Who has done this?"

"I told you—a saboteur. There is a spy in our midst." I said, very firmly.

"Impossible! There are no spies in the Special Corps. Certainly none here in Prime Base. Impossible."

"Very possible. I have been thinking about it in great detail and, unhappy as I am to say this, I can identify the spy."

I had them now. Even Angelina was leaning forward, waiting for further revelation. I smiled serenely, buffed my fingers on my shirt, turned and pointed.

"There's your spy."

They all turned to look.

"The spy is none other than my good companion from the rock mine—Berkk."

CHAPTER **26**

"How can you say that, Jim!" Angelina said. "He saved your life."

"He did—and I saved his."

"He was a prisoner like you. He wouldn't spy for Slakey."

"He was. And he did."

Coypu got into the disbelieving act. "Impossible. You told me, he's a simple mechanic. It would take a mathematician of incredible skill to alter those equations so subtly that I would never notice the changes."

I raised my hands to silence the growing protest.

"Dear friends—why don't we put this to the empirical test. Let's ask him."

In a matter of seconds the professor had pumped a massive electronic charge into Berkk's brain and drained it out of his heel. Leaving the brain empty of all intelligence. The captive Slakey was now just random fizzling electrons, which was fine; there were certainly enough other manifestations of him around. Then Coypu seized up the other fully charged TF that was full of Berkk and plugged it back to his body. A switch was thrown and, hopefully, Berkk was back home again. Dr. Mastigophora filled a hypodermic with psycho blaster antidote and shot it into Berkk's arm. He stirred and moaned and his eyes fluttered open.

"Why am I strapped down?"

I recognized his voice. Slakey was gone and Berkk was home again.

"Free him if you please, Professor." The clamps jumped open and I went to remove the restraining belt.

"Ouch," Berkk said, touching his bruised lips. "It was Slakey, wasn't it? He did this to me." He sat up and groaned. "Was it worth it? Did you get what you needed?"

"Not quite," I said. "But before we go into that—I would like to ask you one simple question."

"What's that?"

"Why did you sabotage Professor Coypu's interuniversal transporter?"

"Why . . . why do you think I would do a thing like that?"

"You tell me, Berkk."

He looked around at us, not smiling, with a very trapped-animal look. This suddenly changed. He looked up blankly; and a horrified expression transformed his face. "No!" he shouted hoarsely. "Don't do that—you can't . . ."

Then he dropped his face into his hands and wept unashamedly. No one spoke, not knowing what was happening. Finally he looked up, dragged his sleeve across his wet eyes.

"Gone," he said. "Back to the rock quarrying. Back to that hell in Heaven."

"Would you be kind enough to explain?" I asked.

"Me, I, you know. Me twice. He, I mean me, is back in the quarry. Grabbed by that foul one-eyed robot."

Sudden realization struck. "Did Slakey duplicate you the way he duplicates himself?"

"Yes."

"Then all is clear," I said smugly.

"Not to a lot of us, diGriz," Angelina said, all patience gone. "Spell it out so we peasants can understand. And quickly."

"Sorry, my love. But the explanation is a simple one. When Slakey had me thrown into the rock works he must have been worried about my presence in Heaven, and even more concerned about what Coypu or the Special Corps would do next. So he enlisted Berkk here to watch me. Doubled him and must have done horrible things to one of him to make the other be his spy."

"Chains," Berkk moaned. "Torture. Electric shock. I had to do what he told me because I felt everything that he was doing to the other me. Chained to the wall in Slakey's lab."

"And of course because you knew everything that you and I were doing, the other you also knew everything that we were doing and reported it to Slakey?"

"All the time. Slakey had me build those rebar cages so we could escape. He knew just what we were doing at the very moment we were doing it."

"But escaping in those cages was very dangerous!"

"What did he care? If we died it wouldn't have bothered him in the slightest. But once we had landed on the rock pile safely, he cleared out the cyclotron building so we could get through it. When we reached the unnildecnovum sorting tables he sent the robot after us to see what would happen, if we had any way of escaping. We did."

"You spying rat," Angelina said, and I saw her fingers arching into claws. "A viper in our bosom. We save your life and all you can do is sabotage the professor's machine."

"I had no choice," Ron moaned. "The me with Slakey told him everything. Slakey was ready to kill that me at any time if I didn't do what he ordered. When I woke up after the operation you had all gone away. I came here and this laboratory was empty—the professor was sleeping. That was Slakey's perfect chance to do the sabotage. I did exactly what he told me to do. Changed the equations and the settings and everything."

"Did he also order you to volunteer to have his brain pumped into your head?"

"That was my idea, I really meant I was volunteering—he also ordered me to do it, knowing you would get nothing out of it. And it would add to my credibility. I had no choice . . ."

"Forget it," I said. "It's all in the past and we can get through to the other universes again since the professor has undone your damage. Your spying days for Slakey are over, so now you can spy for us. You could very well be the key to putting paid to all the Slakeys. Help us and maybe we will be able to save the other you."

"Could you really?"

"We can but try. Now—the first question. What is going on with all the rock mining and crushing and sorting? We still have no idea of what Slakey's operation is all about. You used the word 'unnildecnovum.' What is it?"

"I have no idea. But since the other me was with Slakey all of the time I could see and hear everything that he did. He used the word in reference to the sorting tables, just once."

"It must be the substance we were looking for," Angelina said. "But what is it used for?"

"I don't know. But I do know it is the most important thing for Slakey. Nothing else really matters. And I think I know where it goes. Slakey kept me chained to the machine, the one like the professor's there, so I could tell him everything that was happening. But I could also see everything that he was doing. There were sometimes up to three of him present at one time. They didn't talk because, after all, they were all the same person. But one time he had that robot on the screen and he said something like 'Take the unnildecnovum there.' That was all."

"That's enough," Professor Coypu said, throwing some switches and pointing at the screen. Blue skies and floating white clouds. "Heaven. That's where it is all happening. He could have his mine on any one of a thousand planets, but what he mines ends up in Heaven for processing—"

"Just a moment if you please, Professor," I said. "What was that remark about any one of a thousand planets?"

"The substance he is mining. Very common."

"You know what it is?"

"Of course. Your clothing and Angelina's were coated with it. It is called coal. A crystalline form of carbon. It can be found on a great number of planets. He has it mined and ground to a fine powder. It is then bombarded in the cyclotron where a certain small proportion is changed to unnildecnovum, which is then sorted out by the women. Its very name reveals its identity. Unnildecnovum, one hundred and nineteen in the periodic table. A new element with unknown qualities. Entropy is involved, that is all we can be sure of. The women can detect that, so they can sort the unnildecnovum from the coal dust. This is then collected by that shoddy robot and taken—some place for some reason."

"Find the place—and we find the reason," I said triumphantly. "It *has* to be in Heaven, that is one thing we can be sure of."

"I'll take care of that," Inskipp said as he marched in. He had undoubtedly been monitoring everything that was happening in the lab and had picked the right moment to take over. "The Space Marines are on their way here. Gunships, tanks, flame throwers, field guns . . ."

"No way, José," I said with a great deal of feeling. "You can't hijack my operation at this late date. Nor do we need all the troops and armaments. We keep this small. Remember—we have only one man to fight. Even if he has a number of manifestations. Him—and his rickety robot which Angelina has promised to take care of in a suitably destructive manner. We have put together a good fighting team and we all go in together. If Professor Coypu can give us defenses against Slakey's weapons."

"Already done," Coypu said with unseemly self-satisfaction. "I have analyzed the atmosphere of Heaven. I know that he uses energy weapons and has an hypnotic gas, in addition to the addictive gases already present in the atmosphere."

He pressed a button and what appeared to be a transparent space suit popped out on the end of an extending arm. He pointed out its attributes.

"It is made of transparent seringera. A substance that is almost indestructible, unpierceable, a barrier to force fields and impervious to gases. Under the outer surface there is a nanomolecular structure that responds in a microsecond to a sudden impact such as a bullet. These molecules lock together and become stronger than the strongest steel, stopping the projectile before it has penetrated less than a millimeter. This small powerpack on the back, here, recycles and reconstitutes the gases and water in your breath so the suit may be sealed and worn for up to one hundred hours. It also powers a built-in gravchute that can be used for levitating if needs be. I will demonstrate."

He tore off his shoes, stripped off shirt and sarong, to reveal the fact that he wore purple undershorts with little mauve robots embroidered on them, trimmed with gold. He seized the transparent suit and wriggled into it, pulled the bubble helmet down to seal it. His voice rasped from the external speaker.

"There is no blade sharp enough to cut it." He opened a box of equipment and seized up a knife, plunged it into his chest. It bounced off. As did the other weapons he attacked himself with. Powering up the gravchute, he bounced off the ceiling, still firing his deadly devices. Soon the air was filled with noxious gases, whizzing missiles that threatened the rest of us, if not him. Coughing and gasping, we fled the chamber and did not return until the demonstration was over and the aircon turned up high.

"Wonderful, Professor," I said dabbing my eyes with the corner of my handkerchief. "We pull on your fancy suits and go to Heaven. When I say *we* I of course mean me and my family, along with Berkk and Sybil. The professor monitors our movements and our leader, Inskipp, stands ready to send any reinforcements that we might need. Any questions?"

"Sounds just insane enough to succeed," Angelina said. "How soon do we get our playsuits, Professor?"

"They'll be ready by morning."

"Fine." She smiled at us all. "We can have a little party tonight to celebrate our coming victory, the rout of Slakey, and the reunification of Berkk with himself. All right?"

A chorus of agreement was her answer. The robar hurried over to open the cocktail hour, and even Inskipp condescended this once to sipping a small dry sherry.

"I am very interested in this unnildecnovum," he said licking a trace of wine from his lips. "This madman has organized numerous religions to raise money to imprison slaves to mine coal to convert it to unnildecnovum—why? It must have some very unusual properties or why should he go to all this effort? I am very curious about what can be done with it. Or what it does to other things, or whatever. And I am going to find out. Go forth, Jim, and succeed. And bring me back a sample and an explanation."

"Good as done," I said and raised my glass.

We all drank to that.

CHAPTER 27

WE ALL WORE SWIMMING OUTFITS under the transparent suits. Angelina and Sybil looked quite fetching. I quickly averted my eyes from one, blew a kiss to the other.

"Equipment check," I said, drawing my gun and holding it up. "One paralysis pistol, fully charged. A container of sleep-gas grenades, another of smoke. Combat knife with silver toothpick. Manacles for securing prisoners, truth drug injector for making them talk."

"Plus a diamond-blade power saw for cutting up a certain robot," Angelina said, holding up the lethal looking object.

"All in order, all accounted for. Just one thing more." I picked up a backpack that had a medical red cross on a white background printed on it. "For emergencies. Are you on the circuit, all-powerful Inskipp?"

"I am," his voice rattled in my ear. "I have countless deadly standbys standing by in case you need help."

"Wonderful! Professor Coypu, if you please—unlock the door."

He threw the switch and the red light above the steel door, studded with boltheads and massive rivets, turned to green. I grabbed the handle and turned it, threw the door wide and we strode into Heaven.

"What's with the clouds?" I asked, pushing my finger into one floating by; it tinkled merrily.

"*A life-form indigenous to this planet,*" Coypu's voice said in my ear. "*It has crystalline guts, which explains the tinkling sound, and it floats because it generates methane. Be careful with sparks because they could blow up.*"

Not only could, but did. In a blast of flame that washed over me. I blinked at the glare but felt nothing. Apparently Slakey had us under observation and had opened fire. Other clouds were now floating our way, but were shot down before they could get close. They blew up nicely. When the last cloud of smoke had drifted away I pointed across the neatly cut greensward.

"There, that's the way we go. Valhalla is a con and just for show and Paradise is still being rebuilt. Nor do we wish to visit the rubbish dump. The bit of Heaven I found Slakey in is off in that direction. All we have to do is follow the yellow brick road."

Angelina looked around as we walked. "This would be a very pleasant planet if it weren't for Slakey."

"We are here to do something about that."

"We will. Do I hear music?"

"Are those birds up ahead?" Sybil asked.

"Not quite," I said, recognizing the fluttering creatures. "I looked them up in a volume called *Everything You Wanted to Know About Religion But Were Afraid to Ask*. They are legendary creatures called cherubim or cherubs. Asexual apparently, and great harp players, not to mention choristers."

The flying cloud came closer, plucked strings tinkling and falsettos singing. Another swarm appeared, singing lustily despite the fact they had no lungs, being just heads with wings sprouting from behind their ears. This was pretty strange and I was beginning to have certain suspicions.

"Are these creatures native to this planet?" Angelina asked.

"I have no idea—but I would dearly love to find out."

They flew lower, circling and chorusing high-pitchedly just above our heads. I bent my knees—and sprang. Grabbing one by the leg before it could float away. It kept on singing, blue eyes staring upwards. I squeezed it, touched the wings, tried to lift the ribbons around its loins. So that was it. I twisted with both hands and tore its head off.

"Jim—you monster!" Angelina cried.

"Not really." I pulled the head away and wires came out of its neck. It kept on singing and fluttering its butterfly wings. I released it and it floated away still singing from its dangling head.

"Null-G robots filled with recorded music. Slakey must have built them to add verisimilitude to the landscape for conning his suckers."

The road curved through a glen filled with flowering shrubs. As we approached something burst out of the bushes and galloped towards us.

"That's mine!" Angelina cried out happily as she ran towards it. A stained and scratched robot with one good eye. I hurried after her, not to spoil her fun but to stand by in case of accidents.

There were none. It was all done quite deliberately. When it swung its mighty hand, tipped with razor-sharp fingers, at her she swung her power saw up even faster. The hand clanked down on the road leaving the robot with a metal stump. Two stumps an instant later.

It tried to kick her. There was another clang and it tried to hop away on its remaining leg. Then, limbless, it rolled along the ground.

"You are not nice to people," she said, saw ready. "You are just insensate metal so you do not feel what I am doing to you. You do only as you are instructed. It is your master who is next."

The head rolled over close to my feet. I looked down and smiled as the light in its single eye faded and died.

"One down," I said as I kicked it aside. "Now we follow this road to its master's lair. And please stay alert, gang. Slakey knows that we are coming and will throw everything at us that he can."

Sudden memory flashed and I jumped. Shouting.

"Off the road!"

A little too late. The slurping sounded and the road rolled out from under our feet disclosing the chasm beneath.

"Gravchutes!" I ordered, turning mine on. Our descent into the pit stopped just before we hit the jagged stalagmites and sharp blades that projected up from the pit floor below. We zoomed up and out to safety and our advance continued. Beside the road.

"There it is," I said, pointing to the white temple on the hill ahead. "That's where I met a fat old Slakey playing God in this unheavenly Heaven. I wonder if he'll be there now?"

We were about to find out, approaching the marble steps with caution. They were not moving this time, no celestial escalator for us. We strode up resolutely until we could see the throne. And Slakey sitting on it. Scowling ferociously.

"You are not welcome here," he said, shaking his head. His fat jowls jiggled and the golden halo bounced with the movement.

"Don't be inhospitable, Professor," I said. "Answer a few questions and we'll be on our way."

"This is my answer," he snarled as he reached back and seized his halo—and hurled it at me. It exploded as it struck my suit, knocking me down with the impact. I climbed back to my feet and saw Slakey, throne and all, vanish into the floor.

As he went down—so did the ceiling. The supporting pillars must have been pistons as well. Before we could escape out of the way the entire thing, stone ceiling, roof and lintels and all, crushed us like beetles.

Or it would have crushed us like beetles if we hadn't been wearing our battle suits. As the weight of stone struck the nanomolecules in the fabric locked and the suits became as rigid as steel.

Steel coffins. "Can anyone move?" I shouted. My only answer was grunts and groans. Was this the end? Crushed under a power-operated temple in Heaven. Waiting for our air to run out. One hundred hours—and then asphyxiation.

"No . . . way!" I muttered angrily. My hands were at my sides. All the pressure was on my chest which stayed as hard as nanosteel. But there was no weight on my hand and I could wiggle my fingers. Move them, feeling along my belt in the darkness. Plucking out a percussion grenade by feel. Pushing it into the rubble of broken stone, as far out as I could reach. Taking as deep a breath as I could. Triggering it.

Flame and a great explosion of sound. Smoke and dust of course—that settled and blew away to disclose a crater in the stone. With sunlight filtering in.

A few more grenades did the job. I stumbled to my feet, staggering as another explosion rocked the ruin of the temple, and Angelina emerged from the cloud of smoke. We embraced, then blasted free the others.

"Could we please not do that again," Sybil said, more than a little shaken by the experience.

"An act of desperation on his part," I told her. "Trying to pick us off before we closed in on them. It didn't work—and now we take the fight to them."

"How?" Angelina asked, ever practical.

"This way," I said, leading them back down the steps. "That first pit we fell into in the road was just that. A pitfall pit for killing people. But this pit leads to the underworld where his entire operation is taking place."

As I said that, I flipped another grenade towards the place on the road where I and the robot had dropped through. It blew up nicely and opened a hole into the deep chasm below.

"I'll lead since I've been this way before."

We powered up our gravchutes and leaped into the jagged opening. Floated down slowly instead of dropping as I had the first time. The jagged stone walls moved past at a leisurely pace, lit by the ruddy glow from below. Then the bleak, black landscape with its sporadic gouts of flame came into view. The table-like structures were still there, barely revealed by the ruddy light. But there was a difference—the women were gone.

We soon discovered why. They were all grouped together before the buildings. My troops landed and spread out, weapons ready.

"Don't shoot!" Angelina called out. "Those women, they're the victims, the workers here."

As we warily came closer we could hear a low moaning, and the familiar coughing. It was pretty obvious why. They were tied together, ten or twenty in a bunch, bound with ropes.

"Safety is here!" I called out. "We've come to free you."

"Oh no you're not," Slakey said in chorus. Behind each group of women was a Slakey with a gun. They all spoke at the same time because of course they were all the same person.

"Leave or we kill them," he/they chorused as each of them raised his gun and aimed it at the captive victims.

It was stalemate.

"You can't get away with this," I said, playing for time, wondering what I could do to save them.

"Yes I can," the massed voices said. "I will count to three. If you have not gone by then, one in every group will die. You will have killed them. Then another and another. One . . . two . . ."

"Stop," I called out. "We're going."

But we didn't—the women did. The coughing and moaning was replaced by silence and a whooshing sound as they popped out of existence. I had a moment of dreadful fear that they were gone, dead—until I saw the shocked expression on every Slakey's face.

Professor Coypu—of course! He had been watching and had snatched them out of Heaven to the safety of Prime Base.

I raised my gun and shot the nearest Slakey, ran towards his inert body. Everyone else was shooting now and a blast of fire rocked me back. I stumbled, ran on, grabbed for the Slakey I had shot.

Grabbed empty air as he vanished. The firing was dying down, stopped, as the Slakeys disappeared one by one. Angelina reholstered her gun and came over to me, patted my arm. "I saw that you killed one. Congratulations."

"Premature. I used my paralysis pistol since I wanted to talk to him."

"What next?"

"A very good question. There is no point in going to the coal mines right now because that's just the place that supplies the raw ingredient. The same goes for the cyclotron chamber because we know that the unnildecnovum is made there, but brought here for separation from the coal dust."

"Then we find where it is taken."

"Of course—and it can't be far." I turned to Berkk. "You heard Slakey order the now extinct robot to bring it somewhere?"

"That's right."

I turned and pointed past the rows of empty tables. "That way, it has to be that way. The opposite direction from the cyclotron. Let's go look."

We went. Warily. Knowing that we were getting close to the end of our quest and that Slakey would not like this in any way. He didn't.

"Take cover!" I shouted as I dived. I had only a quick glimpse of the weapon as it floated into position in front of us, a large field gun of some kind.

It fired and the shell exploded close by. The ground rose and slammed into me; chunks of shrapnel and shattered rock rained down. This was not good at all—even Coypu's battle suits could not protect a body from a direct hit. It fired again—then vanished.

"*Got it,*" Coypu's voice spoke in my radio earpiece. "*A remote controlled siege gun. I dropped it into a volcano in Hell from a great height. Are there any more?*"

"Not that I can see. But—thanks for the quick action."

We advanced, past the spot where the gun had appeared, and on towards a solid metal fortress-like structure. I didn't like the look of it—liked it even less when ports flipped open and rapid-firing weapons appeared. Firing rapidly.

"Professor Coypu!" I shouted as slugs struck all around us, and into us, knocking us down and rolling us over.

The professor rose to the occasion. An armored gun carrier appeared between us and the building, firing even as it thudded to the ground. The weapon traversed and the weapon positions were obliterated one by one. With the defense silenced the gun traversed once more and blew away the front entrance to the building. A hatch opened as I passed the machine and Captain Grissle of the Space Marines poked his head out.

"I'll cover you when you go in. Just shout and point."

"Right—and thanks." I pumped my right fist in the air, then pointed forward. "Charge!"

We did. Right up to the front of the building, beside the gaping hole where the door used to be.

"Grissle—can you hear me?"

"Loud and clear."

"Put a couple of rounds in there before we go in."

"No problem."

A couple proved to be more than a hundred; he must have had plenty of ammo. Flame and smoke exploded inside the building. Sounding farther and farther away as the interior was demolished. The firing stopped. Then a last large-caliber shell whistled by—the resultant explosion was so distant it sounded like a mere crump.

"Holed through to the other side."

"Cease fire then—we're going in."

Whatever defenses and traps that would have been awaiting us were gone now. Flame and destruction had blasted any obstruction aside. We felt our way through the debris in the darkness. Which began to lift as the smoke cleared. Light poured in from a ragged opening in the wall ahead. Weapons at the ready, we crept forward, looked out.

"Now isn't that nice?" Angelina said. "It looks like we have finally reached the end of the trail."

CHAPTER 28

WE WERE LOOKING OUT ON the pleasant valley of Heaven. Blue sky above, green grass below. A gentle breeze stirred the leaves on the ornamental trees and brought sweet perfumes to our noses. Set into the valley floor were white marquees, small buildings with tiled roofs half concealed by flower-filled gardens. Paths twined through the landscape, past fountains and statuary. All of this surrounded the most unusual object I had seen in my unusual life. A matte-black sphere at least ten meters high. Smooth and unmarked in any way; a giant eight ball without the eight, a Brobdingnagian bowling ball without finger holes. We stood and gaped.

"Can't you feel it," Angelina said, holding out her hand towards the enigmatic object. "That sensation, indescribable—but that's what we looked for in the coal dust."

As soon as she said this I became distantly aware of what she meant, knew why the sensation could not be described. A weight that was no weight, an experience unfelt, a movement that stayed still. Women could detect small quantities—but there was enough in the sphere before us for mere men to feel.

"Unnildecnovum," I said. "That's where it all has been going, that's what Slakey has been doing with it. A few particles of unnildecnovum at a time to make that thing. It must have taken an awful lot of years."

"Why is he doing it?" Angelina asked.

"I don't know—but I think that we are going to find out very soon. Look."

A round, fat figure that could only be the Slakey from the temple waddled out of one of the tents and made his way to a conference table surrounded by chairs, dropped into the largest chair. He sat staring at the ground for long seconds before looking up. He looked angrily in our direction—then made a single wave of his hand to signal us forward.

"It's a trap," Angelina said.

"Possibly—but I think not. This is his grail, whatever it is, that he has been working so energetically to build, fighting so hard to defend. The battle is over. So let's go down and see what he has to say."

Warily, spread out with our weapons ready, we walked down the valley. It was peaceful and serene and undoubtedly very dangerous. I felt better when I approached Slakey, closer and closer. I was too near to him now for the other Slakeys to use heavy weapons. I sat down in the chair nearest to him, swung my backpack off so that it rested on my lap. Leaned back comfortably and smiled. Slakey scowled.

"Draw up some chairs, guys, and listen," I said, "this is going to be interesting."

"How I wish I could kill you, diGriz. That was my primary mistake. If I had killed you the first time I saw you none of this would have happened."

"We all make mistakes, Slakey. You have made a lot of them. It's the end now and you know it."

His face blazed with suppressed fury. I could hear his teeth grating together. It was very nice to look at and my smile broadened.

"I knew that we would get you in the end," I said, "So I made certain precautions. This is for you."

I took the backpack off my lap and set it on the table between us. This was totally unexpected; he looked at it with bewilderment, at the square white cross on the red background.

"Are you mad? First aid . . . medicine?"

"Sorry," I said. "This will make it much clearer." I leaned over and peeled off the cross.

Underneath was a glaring red radiation symbol. And a notice spelled out in red letters:

TEN-MEGATON ATOMIC BOMB

HANDLE WITH CARE

KEEP AWAY FROM CHILDREN

"Just a small precaution. I armed it when I put it down. It has nothing to do with me now, although it is tempting to look at the switch. You see, Professor Coypu has another ignition switch and is watching us closely at the present time. Keep that in mind at all times."

"You can't—"

"Oh, but I did. I am very serious about this. Just one more thing before we draw this matter to its close. Professor Coypu, now is the time."

I had arranged it all with him, beaten down his reluctance and convinced him that it was the only course possible. Slakey had to be stopped and this was the only way that it could be done. I smiled with relief when Angelina and the twins, Sybil and Berkk, all vanished.

"Safe back in Main Station." I looked up and waved. "Sorry, Angelina, but I had to do this my way. If you were here I would not have had the guts to go through with it. Now I can. If something should go wrong—and I don't think it will—remember . . . that I have always loved you."

I jumped to my feet and patted the bomb. "Enough emotion. I shall put love aside for the moment and get involved in some solid hatred. And, oh, how I hate you you multibodied monster. And I have you at last. There is no escape. It's just you and I now, Slakey. End of the line."

"I want to make an arrangement with you, diGriz—"

"No deals. Just unconditional surrender. And don't make

me angry or I might lose my temper and just press the button and settle you once and for all."

"But wait until you hear my offer. It is an irresistible one. You see—I am going to offer you eternal life. Wouldn't you like that?"

He was right. It *was* a very attractive offer. But this nutcake was a fruitcake and I couldn't believe anything that he said.

"Tell me about it, Professor Slakey. Convince me and perhaps I will consider it."

"Entropy," he said sinking automatically into professorial didactic lecture mode. "That is my field of expertise, as you know. But you do not know how far I have advanced my knowledge, or to what lengths my research has gone. In the beginning was the theory. I did a mathematical analysis of the transuranic elements. I found that as the atomic numbers became higher the rate of entropy slowed. By very little, but the reaction was there. When I extended the equations they revealed that the maximum reverse entropy would be at element one hundred and nineteen. And the equation was correct! When the cyclotron produced the first speck of unnildecnovum I could feel it. And the more concentrated the mass the greater the effect." He hauled himself to his feet. "Come, I will show you."

"Mind if I bring this?" I asked, pointing at the bomb. He hissed with anger.

"Eternity is about to be revealed to you—and still you jest . . ." He got his temper under control at last, turned and walked towards the black sphere of unnildecnovum. Someone moved out of sight in one of the white buildings that we passed and I knew that the other Slakeys were present and watching. Closer and closer to the featureless sphere we walked until we stood next to it, with the bulge of blackness blocking out the sky above.

"Touch it," Slakey whispered. Leaning out and pressing his hand flat against it. I hesitated, then did the same.

Indescribable but incredibly exciting. This was a sensation I could learn to live with.

"Follow me," he said, walking around the sphere, running

his hand along it as he went. I followed, doing the same. There was a short flight of white steps ahead, the top resting against the sphere. He touched a button beside the steps and a great plug of unnildecnovum swung out above us, leaving an opening in the sphere's exterior. We climbed the steps and went inside.

The sphere was hollow and the wall was at least a meter thick. And the indescribable sensation was even more indescribable. Slakey pointed at the row of black coffin-like structures in the center of the sphere. We approached them and looked into the first. A thin Slakey was lying inside, eyes closed, scarcely breathing. His right arm lay across his chest and I recognized him now. His hand was missing.

Not quite. I leaned over and looked and saw that a tiny pink hand was growing out of the stump.

"Life everlasting!" Slakey shouted. Drops of spittle flew. "I rest here and rejuvenate. If I am wounded, my body repairs itself. And I grow younger here. Surrounded by the unnildecnovum, entropy is reversed. Instead of getting older, tireder, senescent—I grow younger, energeticer, youthfuler. And the more unnildecnovum I add to the sphere the faster reverse entropy moves. So you see what I am offering you? Eternity. Join me and live forever! One of these entropy shells could be yours."

That is the kind of offer that is very hard to refuse. Who could possibly say no to the offer of immortality?

I could for one. Not because I wanted to but because I had to. If I joined him I would be no better than him. I must admit I quavered. But I thought of Angelina waiting for me and summoned up all the strength that I could. It was impossible to move. Almost impossible. I turned, very slowly I must admit, and walked—even more slowly—towards the light of day.

This was not for me, not alone. But it was oh so tempting! Maybe I could do it if I took Angelina with me. But then we would of course have to bring the boys too. And naturally Professor Coypu would like the idea—as would our boss Inskipp. It would get to be mighty crowded inside the sphere.

If it was hard to walk away, it was even incredibly harder

to get out of the thing. I don't know how long I stood in the exit. I couldn't force myself to step forward and leave. It took every iota of willpower I possessed to just shift my weight, to lean forward, off balance. I fell, automatically did a shoulder roll down the stairs and out onto the grass. I lay unmoving for quite a time. Finally sighed and climbed to my feet. Slakey was standing at the entrance above.

"I must say that you make a very good offer, Professor."

"I do. And you will of course accept."

"Let's go sit by the bomb and discuss it."

I didn't really care about the bomb; I just wanted to be as far away from the lure of eternity as I could get.

"Let's talk offers," I said patting the bomb. He nodded stiffly. "I am saying no to your offer. Thanks a lot but no thanks."

"Inconceivable!" he spluttered.

"For you—but not for me. Thousands must have died because of you and your obsessive desire to hold onto your single miserable life. If I could snuff it out at this moment I would. In all of its multiple aspects. I wish I had the guts to trigger this bomb—but I value my own life too much. I have a lot to live for—and I look forward to living a long and happy and rejuvenated life. Now we come to you."

I leaned over the bomb and pointed a judicial finger in his face. "Here is what you will do. You will mine no more coal. The miners will be restored to their loved ones. The two Berkks will be reunited. Buboe will be turned over to the shrinks. The cyclotron will cycle no more. The women of the tables will work no more. They will get a good wash and return to their homes and their loved ones as well. This operation is closed down."

"I won't be—"

"Oh yes you will. The reconstruction of Paradise will stop and the building crews will be paid off. The mead will be swilled no more in Valhalla. You have no choice. You will also close down all your religious operations on every one of the planets and all of your personas will return here. When you are assembled in all your strength you will remain here. Forever."

"You cannot do that!" he screamed.

"It has just been done."

"How can I trust you?"

"You have no other choice."

"You will set off the bomb."

"Only if you force us to. You see that is our mutual guarantee. We can never be sure that one of you is still not out there, ready to start this whole monstrous process again. The bomb is our guarantee that you won't do that. And we can't detonate it if we think that one of you *is* still out there. It is a paradox, a problem with no solution. A beginning with no end—like your reverse entropy. So you sit and think about it, talk to yourself about it. Remember that this is the last, first and only offer that you are going to get."

I rose wearily and stretched.

"Get me out of here, Professor Coypu. It has been a very very long day."

CHAPTER 29

"THERE MUST BE FIFTY SLAKEYS at least," Angelina said, curling her lips in disgust. "All of them equally repulsive. Press the button, Professor, and set off the bomb. We will all sleep better at night."

The three of us sat staring into the permanent screen set up to monitor Slakey. Coypu looked very unhappy as he shook his head no.

"Too risky. All he needs is one of him out there on one of the thousands of planets in the millions of universes to get the whole process moving again."

"We'll monitor, watch, be on our guard . . ."

"I wish we could set off the bomb," I said with deep sorrow. "His death could never make up for the death and destruction he has caused—but it would sure help. But the professor is right. He may be mad but he's not stupid. If he did this all again he would not use the fake-religion ploy. He would do it in a more undetectable manner. Find another planet with a decent climate and resources of coal and set up another operation there. He would proceed slowly and carefully and untraceably—after all, he has all eternity to do it in. Ahh—there they go!"

A flicker of motion beside the unnildecnovum sphere showed where the Space Marines were springing into action. They had practiced the operation countless times in order to speed it up and perfect it. They got the time down to three seconds and that was all it took now. Two large marines slammed the heavy hydrogen bomb against the sphere, where it stuck. Captain Grissle hit the activating switch and then they all vanished as quickly as they had appeared. A viewscreen beside the professor lit up and Berkk's image appeared.

"In the green, Professor. Monitoring apparatus engaged and auto switch operating."

"Thank you, very good."

"Over and out."

His image twinkled and vanished and Coypu sighed with relief. "A good technician, Berkk. I'm glad he decided to accept a position with the Corps. Both of him. He helped me design the auto switch so that it is completely fail-safe."

"Am I missing something?" Angelina asked.

"Last night. I couldn't sleep and you were doing fine. I came here and found a very red-eyed Professor Coypu staring at the screen, worrying at the same worry that was worrying me. A what-if."

"Which what-if?"

"What if a Slakey is still out there somewhere. What if he builds a big enough interuniversal transporter to grab and transport that unnildecnovum sphere to another universe? The Slakeys would get away and start the whole deadly cycle over again. Between us we worked out a solution. We got a hydrogen bomb from stock, fixed it up with a molebind, a molecular binder that makes it part of the sphere."

"And," Coypu said, "it contains a detector. If the sphere does go somewhere it gets there as a mushroom cloud. If that thing goes away the bomb goes off."

"But if he doesn't try to move the sphere, why then he is still very much alive in his multiple bodies?" Angelina asked with irresistible female logic. "What do we do to get rid of this possibly eternal threat?"

The professor and I sighed a duet of sighs.

"We have experts working on other possibilities," I said. "We have prepared our dilemma as an abstract problem that will be presented on all of the tests given in every philosophy department in every university in the galaxy. Someone, somewhere, may come up with the answer. Meanwhile—all we can do is watch."

"Forever? Some legacy for our grandchildren. And theirs until the nth generation."

It was all too depressing to think of and I changed the subject.

"At least we have done something for Slakey's victims. The women from Purgatory, the ones who didn't need hospitalization that is, have all gone to the planets of their choice. With lifetime pensions—mostly paid for by the seizure of Slakey's various properties. The same thing has been done for the miners—with the exception of one. Buboe is on the way to a hospital for the criminally insane, to see if he might be cured."

"What about those poor creatures in Hell?" Angelina asked. "Can't anything be done for them?"

"A lot. Since they can't leave Hell we will have to do the best we can for them there. Interstellar charities have already put up temporary—and air-conditioned—buildings for them. Volunteers are giving them medical treatment, meals, outdoor barbecues, booze, counseling, that sort of thing. Since they can never leave Hell, permanent provision must be made for them. They should be self-supporting soon."

Angelina's eyebrows rose at that. "Self-supporting—in Hell?"

"There is no accounting for taste," I said. "A firm named Holidays in Hell has already been formed and the first tourists are happily on their way. They photograph the natives—for a fee. Grill steaks on the lava, shudder when the gravity waves grab them. Generally have a frightening but safe time."

"Outrageous! I hope that old red devil Slakey shoots and eats them."

"Alas, that is not possible now. Before we got there the locals grew tired of being shot at and, well, sort of had him for dinner."

"Wonderful! They can cook up all the rest of the Slakeys as far as I'm concerned. That would be a good solution. Which reminds me. A question or two, Professor, something that has been bothering me for a long time. Why so many Slakeys—and how did he do it?"

As usual, Coypu had all the answers. "The answer to your first question is obvious. Who else could he trust? He wanted to keep eternal life for himself. So he went into partnership with himselves to set up the operation. As to how he duplicated himself, I discovered that by accident. You will remember that we obtained the frequency settings from one of their machines for many other universes. That is how I found you on Glass and brought you back. When I have had the time I have been investigating some of the other universes. Some of them are rather nasty. To keep under budget and not lose too many machines I constructed an armor-plated recorder that I sent through to measure temperature, gravity density, air pressure and contents, the usual things. I was greatly surprised when it returned from Gemelli, which I named this universe for obvious reasons, with a replica of itself. A little bit of research showed me that all of the radiation frequencies are doubled there. So matter from our universe is doubled as well when it returns here. Interesting phenomenon. So every time Slakey needed reinforcements he popped in and out of Gemelli. You know that you are the second person to ask me that question today."

"Who was the other?"

"Me." Sybil said, walking in through the door and smiling happily. "Mr. and Mrs. diGriz—I would very much like to call you Mom and Dad. I can conceal it no longer. I am madly in love with your son and wish to marry him."

"Which one?" Angelina asked.

"Both of them," Sybil said walking in through the door again. The same words were spoken by both Sybils at the same time.

I looked from one to the other and for the first time in my life was at a loss for words. Angelina wasn't.

"You have duplicated yourself. You are now two Sybils."

"Of course. I had no choice," she said with impeccable female logic. "I was in love with your sons, and love can always find a way."

"Have you broken the good news to them yet?"

"Not yet," the Sybils said in unison. "But I know they love me, women can tell, just as much as I love them. But they are both too noble, honest, brave and irreverent to ask for my hand because it would mean the other one losing out. That problem has now been solved."

"Indeed it has," Angelina said firmly, with the instant decision women make in matters of the heart. "And what do you say, Jim?"

"I say it is up to the boys to decide."

She nodded agreement.

"They should be here soon," the doubled voice said. "I sent a message before I came."

James and Bolivar came in at that moment and did the best double act of double-takes I had ever seen in my life. Before they could speak each Sybil stepped forward and seized a twin and kissed him with passion. The response, I could tell, was equally passionate.

"I love you," Sybil breathed. "From the bottom of my heart, with all the depth of my being. Do you love me?"

That, as you might very well realize, was that. Angelina and I, smiling happily, joined hands and turned our backs on the embracing couples, sat and began to discuss their wedding plans.

It would be the grandest social occasion the Special Corps Prime Base had ever seen.

I snapped my fingers at the robar, which produced a chilled bottle of sparkling wine, opened it dexterously with its two right hands, poured and passed us brimming glasses. We clinked and drank.

"A toast," I said, "Can you think of one?"

"Of course. To the future newlyweds. And may their lives be filled with happiness."

"Like ours," I said.

"Of course."

We kissed and drank the toast. Over Angelina's shoulder I could see the screen with the image of that monstrous black sphere.

I turned my back on it, not wanting to spoil this memorable day. Still, I couldn't stop thinking about it. Neither could Angelina.

"Do we have enough money in the bank to buy a cyclotron?" she asked.

I nodded. "We could even afford a coal mine as well. Why do you ask?"

"I was just thinking. What a wonderful and unusual wedding present we could give the newlyweds . . ."

A DEVILISHLY GOOD PIECE OF ADVICE

JIM DIGRIZ HAS A SWOLLEN ego these days, ever since he discovered that his annals have been published in a great number of countries and languages. In addition to the American and English editions his adventures have been read in all of the Western European countries, as well as in Japan and China. Since glasnost he has penetrated Russia, Poland, and Estonia. A total of fifteen countries. And very soon now we will see the first publication of *Rustimuna Ŝtalrato Naskiĝas*. That's *The Rat Is Born* in Esperanto.

Esperanto? There's that word again. We know that Jim speaks it like a native. As does almost everyone else he meets. But does it exist in the present?

It certainly does. It is a growing, living language with millions of speakers right around the world. It is easy to learn and fun to use—and a lot more practical than Klingon. There are many books, magazines, and even newspapers published in Esperanto.

So be the first on your block to enjoy the excitement and fun. Put your name and address on a postcard and send it to this address:

Esperanto
PO Box 1129
El Cerrito, CA 94530

Tell them the Rat sent you. You will never regret it!

—Harry Harrison

DEC 20 1996   SF

WITHDRAWN